CHANT

Stella Drexler

An imprint of Diogenes Club Press

Worldly, Whimsical, and Weird Books

www.diogenesclubpress.com

Dallas, TX

DC Dreams, an imprint of Diogenes Club Press
8619 Reva St. Dallas, TX 74227
www.diogenesclubpress.com

The characters and events in this book are fictional. Any similarity to real persons, living or dead, is coincidental and not intended by the author.

ISBN: 9781622010080
Library of Congress Control Number: 2017955894

CHAPTER 1

Night fell upon Spectra City. The city emptied as quickly as though a blaring alarm had resounded through the streets. Doors slammed. Shutters drew down over windows. Bolts slid into their locks with abrupt, metallic clicks. The silence that followed was charged and ominous. "Anyone out there tonight," said the tall, thin publican of the Phantasm Bar as he peered out the dark, tinted glass into the dreary alley outside, "is looking for a fight."

Tamsin's gaze shifted to Cedric. He did not meet her eyes. He hunched over his glass. He took a sip of the warm, watered-down gin and tonic as if to steel his nerves.

A chilling, ear-splitting scream rent the electric stillness outside.

The publican flinched. He covered his head and ducked behind the bar. The patrons of the Phantasm looked around with bleary, hunted eyes. Tamsin vaulted off her stool at the bar. Her body vibrated with excitement.

"It's happening again," Cedric said. He rose swiftly from his seat. The expression on his sharp, handsome features was so cold and so severe, Tamsin took a step back before she remembered that he was on her side.

"Finally!" Tamsin exclaimed. She started for the door. Cedric overtook her with longer strides. He threw open the battered wooden door and stepped out into the alley with chilling resignation. "Cedric, wait--"

He ignored her. "It's going to happen. This time we're ready."

The scene on the thoroughfare outside the Phantasm was gruesome.

Half a dozen creatures in long, black hooded overcoats tore through the alley. They were not men. Men did not move quite that way, as though they were gliding inches above the ground. Their faces were shadowed by their hoods, but when the flickering streetlights momentarily illuminated them, the skin underneath was mottled grey, withered and lined as though they were crumbling to bits as they moved.

Their lips did not move to form words, but a low, monotonous drone issued in chorus from their cavernous maws. It seemed to come from somewhere low in their bellies. The air around them was pungent with a strange, metallic bitterness. An acrid taste coated Cedric's and Tamsin's throats as though they had swallowed battery acid. The wraiths left a blaze of fire in their wake. It

3

ignited the detritus littering the streets, stealing across the alley and up the sides of the dark, stained and deteriorating buildings looming in hushed terror around them.

Tamsin caught her breath. She was motionless was dread. "They're real."

Beside her, Cedric's body pulsated like a live wire. "Yes. You knew they were."

"I didn't want to believe it. Is anyone else here yet?"

"No."

His reply was lost in the wraith's strange, macabre din. A young woman stumbled on wobbling legs from the False Haven Tavern next door. The wraiths moved as one towards her. She did not move away. She goggled at them. She did not seem to even realize her danger until the wraith at the head of the uncanny procession seized her by the throat.

It lifted her effortlessly off the ground. She kicked feebly. She clawed desperately at the misshapen hand clutching her throat. It held her in an unyielding grip. Her eyes bulged. The wraiths hummed as one with no sense or emotion. Tamsin started towards them. "Stop!" she shouted. They did not seem to hear her cry. They did not turn toward her. The wraith did not release the girl. The others were eerily still. They peered up at the struggling girl with identical ghastly faces.

Beside Tamsin, the air around Cedric changed. She spun to look at him.

His lips moved rapidly. The words he spoke were a soft, incomprehensible stream of passionate, urgent gibberish. His stunning blue eyes rolled back to reveal glowing, milky whites. Tamsin did not bother to speak to him. He would not have heard her. He had slipped into a trance.

The wraiths' low whine intensified. The leader dropped the hapless, frantically thrashing girl. She tumbled to the ground. She clutched her throat. She gasped desperately for breath. The air around the wraiths shimmered. In a flash of brilliant, violent light, the leader exploded in a puff of fetid grey smoke. The eerie, terrible sound swelled into a sonorous roar as the others turned toward Cedric.

Tamsin raced forward. She seized the trembling girl's arm to tug her urgently to her feet. "Come on! Get up. Get up! Get inside."

The girl did not move. She stared at Tamsin with a shocked and terrified expression. "You're chanters."

4

"Get inside!" Tamsin barked. "Now! Now!"

"I saw him. He's chanting."

"For god's sake, get up and go inside."

"You aren't supposed to chant."

Tamsin glared at the stupefied girl. She shoved her roughly towards the False Haven. "We saved your ass, didn't we? Go. Go!"

The young girl's eyes slid to the wraiths. She spun on her heel and lurched towards the sanctuary of the tavern. Tamsin did not spare a glance to ensure she was safely indoors. The creatures turned. Their heads swiveled from side to side like dogs scenting their prey in the air.

Brilliant, white light burst from Cedric's eyes. His eerie, resonant chant crackled around him in a strange, shimmering haze of static. Tamsin's heart leapt. "No! Cedric!"

He was as impervious to her words as to the looming wraiths. They swarmed him. They caught him up in their arms. His tall, vibrating form disappeared between them. Tamsin could not reach him. She took a deep breath. The surge of rage and panic inside her rushed to her belly. It gathered into a tight, vibrating ball of energy. She opened her mouth. She raised her hands. She willed the trance to overtake her body. She called the chant to her lips.

Cedric's shout broke the spell abruptly. Tamsin staggered slightly as the pressure of the unreleased energy flooded the length of her body. "Tam, go! Run! Get away from them!"

"Cedric!" She could not see him among the wraiths as they moved toward the darkness beyond the flickering streetlights and garish neon of the tavern signs.

"Don't chant! Just go! X can find me!"

"Cedric!"

"Please, Tam! Go." But his voice faded. The wraiths slipped into the darkness and shadows as though they had never been there at all.

Tamsin cursed. She spun on her heel and ran the other way.

* * *

A red light blinked steadily on the tiny black box in Cedric pocket. He opened his eyes slowly. The ground upon which he lay was soft, plush cream carpet. His fingers clawed reflexively at it. "Ah," a low, smooth voice murmured above his head. "I believe he's waking up."

Cedric turned his head slightly to roll his eyes towards the voice. He sighed deeply. The man was tall and lean. His dark hair was combed neatly back from his sculpted, angular features He was watching Cedric steadily through cold, ice blue eyes, as though he were nothing more than an interesting specimen. His suit was expensive Italian wool. He had dressed for the occasion.

Cedric had expected to recognize his abductor. He did. It was Nico Creed.

The room in which Cedric lay face down upon the ground was an opulent, richly furnished study. There were chairs scattered about the room as though Nico expected company. Rather than a desk in the center of the room, there was a large, polished oak table covered in strange instruments: metal rods, scattered geodes and crystals of multiple colors, dog-eared books and small, glass discs filled with strange, glowing liquids.

Inside his pocket, the tiny black box bleeped once, quietly.

Nico Creed scowled and lurched toward Cedric. "What is that?" he growled. "What's that noise? Tully! Search him."

Cedric hadn't noticed the tall, thin man dressed like a footman or butler in a neat black jacket until the man stepped forward into his view. Tully turned Cedric over as though he were nothing more than a small child's toy. Cedric did not resist. His limbs felt strange. He struggled to think clearly. His mind was sluggish and slow. He tried to roll away from Tully. He didn't get far. The tall man seemed completely unaffected by his struggles. His hands quested impersonally over Cedric's body.

"It's a black box, sir," Tully announced. He held up the small object he'd discovered in Cedric's jacket pocket.

"Let me see it." Nico snatched it from Tully's hand. He knelt beside Cedric. He held the black box in front of his eyes. "What is this?"

Cedric didn't reply. He held Nico's glacier pool eyes steadily.

"Tell me what this is!"

"It appears to be some sort of tracking device, sir," Tully said evenly.

Nico rose to his feet. His sculpted face was as immovable and cold as marble, but his blue eyes burned with an infernal flame. "Is this some sort of trap?" He spun and slammed the black box abruptly on the oak table. It shattered in a shower of plastic splinters and chips. "Who are you working for? Is it Chant?"

6

Cedric stared silently back at Nico. Nico raised his hands to his sides. His lips moved rapidly. The words they formed were strange, intense and incomprehensible. His blue eyes rolled up into his head so they glowed brightly white. The air crackled around him.

On the floor, Cedric writhed in sudden, awful pain. He snapped his mouth shut against a scream and tasted blood as he bit his tongue. His limbs flailed helplessly. He didn't scream. He didn't make a sound. When it was over, he lay once more upon the ground. He gasped for breath. He looked back up at Nico.

Nico looked smug. He lifted his eyebrows expectantly.

"They could already be on their way," Cedric said in a low voice.

Nico glanced at Tully. He strode to the window. He threw it open. Cold, wet rain pelted into the room and upon the rich Oriental rugs. Nico waved his arm wildly behind him. "Go. Check the front of the house."

Tully was gone in an instant. Nico didn't speak to Cedric. He paced the room for several long moments. He checked the window as though he expected sirens or soldiers to emerge from the darkness outside and climb the walls. He avoided Cedric as if he were a dangerous, unpredictable creature.

Nothing happened.

The door opened once more. Tully strode into the room and bowed smartly. "Nothing, sir."

"Are you sure?"

"Yes, sir. I'm sure. There is nothing."

Nico's eyes gleamed triumphantly. He spun towards Cedric with a laugh. It was low, cold and humorless. "No one seems to be coming. I suppose not even Chant is stupid enough to come here."

Energy gathered around Nico once again. The strange, unintelligible murmur was soft and lilting. There was no pain. Cedric's eyes drooped. He fell instantly into darkness. "Keep this one," Nico said, spinning away from Cedric dismissively. "He may have useful information. Bring me another."

Tully inclined his head. He disappeared through a crack in the wall.

Nico paced swiftly from one side of the room to the other. He stepped over Cedric's prone figure. He glared out the window. Rain dripped down the thick panes of glass. A canopy of trees blotted out the sky above. A few bleary lights burned in the distance beyond. None of them were red or blue or flashing.

Tully reappeared, moving slowly and laboriously backwards. He was not a man accustomed to heavy lifting. His breath came in ragged huffs. Nico sighed impatiently. "Just leave him there," Nico snapped.

Tully dropped the young man's ankles. They flopped limply against the ground. The young man was thin and dirty. The jeans and tee shirt he wore were slightly tattered. They were the same clothes he'd worn the night the wraiths had taken him. His mouth lolled slackly. Even as Nico bent over him, he did not open his eyes.

Nico waved his hand behind his back. Tully caught up the glittering silver wand on the worktable and placed it in his master's hand. Nico exhaled deeply, as though the feel of the smooth, cool metal soothed his impatience. He stood and ran his hands along the wand in exaltation. It was a foot in length, an inch in diameter and featureless silver metal from end to end. A dull, uncut crystal was roughly mounted upon each tip.

Nico knelt back down before the young man. He seized his collar and lifted him so they were eye to eye. He balanced the wand between them. He pressed the jagged orange stone of one end of the wand against the young man's forehead. He leaned toward him. He rested his own forehead against the smooth, dark grey stone on his end. He inhaled deeply.

A strange, breathy murmur issued from his lips. His eyes flashed brilliant white. Tully faded quietly from the room. He closed the door behind him with an inaudible click. Energy surged through the young man. His body jerked, as though electricity coursed violently through him. The wand heated and burned against Nico's fingers as the energy traveled along the shining shaft, crackling with a sound like static. Nico ignored it.

His body tensed as the young man's energy rushed into him. It gathered in the pit of his stomach until it felt as though he must surely explode with the intensity of it. He threw his head back. He gasped. The wand dropped meekly on the floor between the men. Nico tossed the young man aside as though he were nothing more than a child's forgotten toy.

Nico spun away from the deflated figure. The young man's skin hung loosely from his bones as though he had been hollowed from the inside out. He breathed still, but his breath was low and rattling. He didn't move. Nico ignored him. He rushed from the room. His breath was shallow and harsh. His body felt charged and powerful.

He took the stairs toward his bedroom three at a time with long, agitated strides. He did not pause when he reached the large, lavish chamber but darted to the wide, elegantly carved French doors on the farthest wall. He threw them open. They banged violently against the walls on either side. A large, ornately engraved mirror crashed to the ground and shattered.

Nico ignored it. He stepped out onto the stone balcony. Rain fell in powerful, furious sheets, spattering his expensive suit and plastering his fashionably gelled hair to his forehead. He raised his hands. He turned his face up to receive the thick, shining drops upon his hot, tingling cheeks. Then he opened his eyes and glared across the tops of the trees in the courtyard below him.

A light burned across the lawn. The Mobley house was so close to Creed Manor, situated almost directly behind it, that Nico could see the occupants moving around the fourth floor library. Lochlan Mobley stood beside the window. His outline was tall and broad and still powerful for his advancing age. He held a glass in one hand. He might have been laughing, for his strong, square jaw was tilted slightly up. His shoulders moved in a slow, sweeping tremor.

Colin Mobley moved in front of the window beside his father. He was the image of a younger Lochlan, as tall and as strong. His dark hair fell roguishly across his forehead. He poured his father more of the amber liquid from a bottle in his hand. His young, handsome face was lit with a smile. Nico smiled, as though in return, but his smile was as cold as ice and as sharp as a rapier.

Inside his belly, energy pulsed and burned like hate. Words tumbled from him in a wild, feral scream. He threw out his hands in front of him. Across the courtyard, the window shattered in the Mobley's library. Colin dove out of view. Lochlan spun towards Nico. His lined, handsome face was austere and twisted with rage.

Lochlan's lips moved feverishly. The whites of his eyes shone brightly across the lawn, but Nico was blind to his enemy's retaliation. His body jerked as Lochlan's chant struck him. He hardly noticed. Power flowed out of him in a steady, violent stream. The trees beneath them ignited as the energy passed over them. The fires went out as quickly as they were lit. They were no match for the fierce, relentless rain.

All around Nico, planters and chairs exploded, showering him in shards of ceramic and carved stone. Across the way, shingles and shudders tore from the Mobley Mansion, tumbling to the gardens below. Colin stood beside Lochlan. He raised his hands to his sides. Like his father, his eyes rolled back, and his lips moved reflexively.

Nico trembled. In a startling instant, the energy drained from his body. The combined force of the Mobley's assault struck him fully in the chest, knocking him to his knees. He gasped, pressing his hand to his side. The rain mixed with his blood and ran in pink rivulets across the stone balcony. He grasped the frame of the French doors desperately, dragging himself inside the dry, brilliantly lit bedchamber. He slammed the doors quickly behind him.

For a long moment, he lay helpless on the floor. "Tully!"

His voice was weak. He struggled frantically against the pain and darkness. His eyes drooped. He slipped away.

CHAPTER 2

Lex pounded on his brother's bedroom door. There was no response from within. He pressed his ear to the door. Inside, he could hear the French doors rattling, as though Nico had failed to latch them properly. The wind outside howled faintly. "Nico! Open the door!"

He sighed and tried the knob. It wasn't locked. Nico never locked his door. No one had ever dared to enter uninvited before. When Lex found him, he was sprawled in front of the French doors in a small pool of blood. Rain leaked in through the cracked doors and spattered his motionless face. Lex sighed.

"Damnit, Nico."

Lex knelt beside his brother. He turned him over carefully and tore open his stained white shirt. The wound wasn't as bad as Lex expected. It was a long, thin gash along his side. Blood still leaked half-heartedly from the wound. Lex lifted his head. His eyes rolled back. He pressed a hand against his brother's side. He fell effortlessly into a trance. The rhythmic chanting was barely audible. He blinked once and sat back on his haunches, scowling.

Nico sat up, running his hand across the unmarked flesh where the wound had been. He glanced at Lex. "Thanks, big brother." There was a cold, ironic edge to his voice.

Lex's eyes narrowed to slits. "What were you doing?"

Nico tossed his head. Flecks of rain showered Lex, who wiped them away impatiently. "The Mobleys attacked me. I had to fight them off."

"They attacked you?" Lex sounded skeptical.

"Yes."

Lex sighed and rose abruptly to his feet. "I think it's time we all stopped attacking each other."

Nico's eyes glittered coldly. "The Mobleys killed our father. Is that not enough reason for you to fight? Don't you want revenge?"

"Revenge?" Lex considered, wiping a hand across his brow. "No. Justice? Yes."

Nico shot to his feet. "This is justice!"

"It is not justice. None of this is justice."

"The feud has been going on since long before our father was born."

"Yes," Lex agreed, meeting his glare rigidly. "And I see no reason for us to continue it. It's nothing to do with us. I have no real quarrel against the Mobleys. I barely know them. We've only been fighting them our entire lives because we grew up with it. That doesn't make it right."

"You dishonor our father's memory with talk like this," Nico told him in a low, furious voice.

Lex sighed deeply. "Yes. Perhaps you're right, Nico. Dad would probably turn over in his grave if he heard me speak like that."

"You cannot fight who you are, Lex." Nico's tone was slightly mocking now. His mouth turned up in a cold smirk. "You're one of us. A Creed and a chanter. Don't start pretending you're something you aren't. It doesn't suit you."

"And what am I pretending to be, do you think?" Lex sounded weary.

"A decent man. A man with pity and scruples and morals. We both know that isn't you, is it?"

Lex lifted his chin angrily. "What do you know about me?"

"I know everything about you, Lex, and I know you're no better than me. Lochlan and Colin killed our father, and they killed your slut, Diana."

His brother was in front of him so quickly, Nico had barely seen him move. "Don't talk about her that way!" he snarled.

Nico glared into his eyes. "She was one of them. You intended to betray your family for one of them!"

"I intended to be free! The Mobleys didn't kill her. It was all of this. The fighting, the feud!"

"Don't pretend you don't want revenge as badly as I do. You just want it your own way."

Lex took a step back, away from Nico. "You're right about that," he said in a low, toneless voice. "I do want revenge my own way."

He did not look back at Nico as he stormed from the room, slamming the door behind him. Nico did not follow or call to him. Lex hadn't expected him to. His quick, angry strides brought him to the second floor. The wide, oak double doors of the Creed library were ajar. It was handsomely furnished in rich leather wing backed chairs, scarlet cushioned armchairs and a large, polished mahogany library table. Elegant, rare and expensive fine art decorated the walls in the spaces between the ceiling-high rows of equally rare and expensive books.

A handsome oak mini bar lined the north wall beneath the wide, panoramic stained glass window. Lex filled a tumbler with scotch from the mini bar and tossed it back without tasting it. It burned his throat.

"It's a little early for that, don't you think? I'm sure you want to make a good showing tonight. It would hardly do for a Creed to compromise himself at such an important function."

Lex had not heard her enter the room. Simone Stowe moved as silently as a slinking cat, despite the tall, spiked jeweled heels upon her feet. She was a tall, effortlessly beautiful and willowy-slim woman. Her long, blonde hair tumbled in waves around delicate shoulders. Her dress was short, tight, black and extremely expensive. She leaned against the library table, crossing her long, shapely tanned legs in front of her as though to display them to their greatest advantage. Her lips, painted a deep, dark scarlet, were twisted in an ironic smile.

"It's never too early for Nico," Lex replied wryly. He poured himself another drink. Before he raised it to his lips, Simone strode forward and took it gently from his fingers.

She lifted her eyebrows and raised the glass to her own crimson lips. "Did you two have another row? I do wish you two would try to get along."

Lex smirked. "Do you? I was under the impression you enjoy the tension."

Simone laughed. "Now, you are very unkind, Lex." Her eyes drifted toward the opened doors. She seemed not to see them at all. "Is he very upset?"

Lex's expression was not calculated to give her hope. Her chest lifted again in a delicate sigh. "Maybe you can calm him down."

Her eyes slid away doubtfully. She swallowed the scotch as though it might steel her nerves and strode past Lex to pour herself another drink. "I do wish you two wouldn't fight so much," she repeated in a hushed, serious voice. "You're brothers."

She handed him back his glass. He sipped it reflectively. He sighed. "It's been like this since Dad died." He turned away from her, staring at the stained glass window as if he could see beyond the delicate patchwork of color. The sky outside was grey, and rain streaked across the glass, running in streams along the cracks. "He just can't let go. He keeps fighting. The feud has already killed our father. Isn't that enough? And for what? Does he really mean to kill the entire

Mobley family? Does he think that will end it, and we can all live in peace?"

Simone sighed. He felt her pause beside him. Her perfume was musky and intoxicating. "I don't know if Nico knows what peace is like."

"I think he likes it. The fighting. It gives him a purpose."

She glanced sharply at him. Her turquoise blue eyes glittered angrily. "You think he lives for fighting and murder? You think that is his only reason? What am I, then? What is the rest of it?"

"I didn't mean it like that, Simone."

She sighed deeply. "I know. It's just..."

Lex glanced at her, but she did not voice the suspicions or nagging doubts in her mind. Simone could do better than Nico. Neither one of them said it. He leaned his forehead against the window, peering out. He could barely make out the Mobley house, blurry and distorted by the rippling glass. The stained glass hadn't always been there. Years ago, he'd been able to see straight through, into the glowing rooms across the gardens that surrounded both mansions and offered little privacy or protection from the other.

She'd been there, all those years ago. He had watched her moving around the rooms across the courtyard. Sometimes she'd looked back. He couldn't see her now, even if she had still been there. Disgust roiled in his belly.

"Maybe he's right," Lex muttered. "Maybe I do want revenge."

Simone paused at the door and turned back to him. "Perhaps you should spend less time fighting him and more time helping him, then. He wants what you want."

He turned away from the window when she'd gone. He paced to the mini bar again. He poured himself another drink. He stared at the pale liquid moodily for several long moments. He tossed the contents of the glass abruptly into the small, stainless steel sink. He regretted it almost immediately. He poured himself another.

"I'm glad to see I'm not the only one starting early today." Peyton Creed said behind him in a sardonic voice.

Lex sighed and spun towards his mother. He'd been expecting her to sneak up on him. She was a tall woman, still slender in her advancing age. She was dressed to the nines in a long, green silk gown that swirled around her ankles. Pearls glowed at her throat and on her earlobes. Her long, dark auburn hair was swept into an elaborate twist, displaying her long, ivory neck and sparkling ornaments.

She was still very beautiful. She knew it.

She held a tumbler of amber liquid in her perfectly manicured hand. She lifted it as if in salute. "I heard voices. Is Simone here?"

"Yes."

"What are you doing, Alexander?" Her voice was sharp. Her eyes narrowed shrewdly as they had when he's been a child and she'd suspected him of wrong-doing.

Lex pushed his hands through his blonde hair so it stuck up from his head. Peyton frowned. She stepped toward him and smoothed it almost reflexively. "Nothing," Lex replied, batting her hand gently away.

Peyton turned away from him, swallowing her drink as though it were nothing more than water. "Something more constructive, I hope, than your brother."

Lex didn't reply. He strode to the window and peered broodingly out.

Peyton paused beside him. Her breath smelled strongly of whiskey. Her perfume was powerful, flowery and sweet. It was a scent he remembered so well, it might have been emblazoned on his brain. "Those damn Mobleys," she hissed resentfully. "They were all your father thought of, too. When Caleb was alive, all he did was fight. You and Nicholas are more like him every day." She turned to him. There was no sentiment in her watery blue eyes. "You will die like him, too. In the war."

Lex met her gaze. She wobbled slightly on her high heels. He didn't reach out a hand to steady her.

"The war will never end," she told him, glaring at him as though he'd started the whole thing. "Not until they are all dead. Or we are."

He sighed, turning away from her. "I know."

* * *

Nico slumped sullenly in a wing-backed arm chair when Lex pushed open the door to his bedchamber. Nico's eyes followed his brother indifferently as he paused to peer guardedly at him from the center of the room. Nico curled his lip insolently. "What do you want?" There was no rancor in Nico's voice. He sounded weary.

"Where is Simone?"

"Gone."

"Smart girl. At least she isn't a complete pushover." Lex strode forward and kicked his brother's foot. "You need to get ready for the gala. You're suit's a damn mess. Dad would roll over in his grave if you showed up at his fete looking like that." Nico didn't smile. Lex sighed. "The Mobleys will be there, Nico. Do you think you can behave?"

Nico scoffed. He looked away disdainfully. "Of course. Unlike some, I would not disparage our father's memory."

Lex's expression was cold. "I need you to be cool tonight, Nico. No attacks."

"I'm not going to attack anyone! I'm not an idiot. I know how to behave in public, Mobleys or no Mobleys."

"Good. Change clothes. Mother will kill you if we're late and blame me for it." Lex spun and strode towards the door. He paused. "Simone is still coming, isn't she?"

Nico snorted. "Yes. Of course she's coming. She wouldn't let a lover's quarrel spoil a chance to wear an expensive dress and brush elbows with Spectra City's elite. I'm picking her up on the way." He lifted an eyebrow, straightening in his chair. "I don't suppose you have a date?"

Lex scowled. He did not respond to this.

Nico smirked. "No, I didn't think so." He rose so abruptly, Lex tensed as though preparing for an attack. "I'm getting ready. Go."

Lex spun on his heel. He slammed the door on his way out.

CHAPTER 3

The Caleb Creed Memorial Wing of the Spectra City Museum of Fine Art glittered under hundreds of small, silvery globes hung from the three story cathedral ceiling. Fine, rare art hung strategically on the walls, carefully lit to display their beauty to its greatest advantage. The security ropes had been removed to allow the revelers to eye the famous paintings and sculptures at their pleasure. The museum staff hovered invisibly nearby.

The white marble floors were so polished, they shone, reflecting distorted, multi-colored images of Spectra City's social and political elite. The guests were as elegant and fine as the art decorating the enormous, three-story hall. Jewels sparkled on their necks, throats and fingers. They milled around the gallery in tuxedos and ball gowns, sipping champagne and tittering half-heartedly at each other's jokes.

High above the gilded revelers, a steady, rhythmic rain pelted the skylights. No one noticed. A soft, unobtrusive orchestra played a waltz. Some of the guests were already spinning around the glossy floor in stiff, dispassionate pairs. Grace Creed looked around her, smiling in satisfaction. She raised her flute of champagne to her lips. All the right people were there.

Grace slipped her arm through her brother's. She batted her eyelashes. "Aren't you going to compliment your baby sister on her spectacular accomplishment this evening, Nico? Have I not honored our father's memory in style and elegance with my little gala?"

Nico smiled charmingly at the guests around them. He patted his sister's hand. "Why don't you ask Lex? He was always his favorite. He never seemed to find the time to tell me what sort of party would do him the most justice."

Grace cuffed him playfully on the arm. "Don't be ridiculous, Nico. Dad loved you. He thought you hung the moon."

"Yeah, right. Ah. And here's Lex now to tell us what he thinks." He stepped away from Grace. He bowed ironically to Lex.

"Great party, Grace. You've done very well." Lex said, leaning forward to kiss his sister's bronzed cheek.

She tossed her carefully coiffed auburn hair. She lifted her eyebrows archly. "You hate it. You always hate my parties."

"No. No, I don't hate it. It's really very nice"

Grace snorted doubtfully. "I don't know why I even try. I suppose if I'm not working for the family business, my own business is of no interest to either of you."

"Grace, don't be petulant. No one said anything of the sort."

"Planning parties isn't exactly a business," Nico muttered snidely. "It's more of a failure to grow up."

Grace opened her mouth to retort angrily. Lex sighed and held up his hand. "Not tonight, you two, all right? Don't listen to Nico, Grace. You've done a great job. Dad would have been really honored."

She glared at Nico once more. She seemed to forget her ire almost at once. Her lips twisted into a sly smile. "Have you two seen the Mobleys yet?"

Nico's eyes narrowed to icy slits. "Yes. They've been talking to the mayor."

Lex stiffened slightly. "Leave it alone, Nico."

His brother glanced at him sharply. "I'm not going to do anything. I'm not a child. I don't need you to keep me on a leash."

"Leave him alone, big brother," Grace scolded gently. "He knows how to handle himself in public."

"I didn't say he didn't," Lex replied tersely.

"Spectra has been unaware of the feud for decades, Lex. I don't think tonight will blow the lid off it," Nico said. His head swiveled, as though he'd spotted more interesting conversation. His face transformed so suddenly, it was as though he were an entirely different man than the one who'd been arguing with his siblings seconds before. He smiled pleasantly. "Ah, there's Mayor Rainey over there. I should go say hello. He's been expecting a phone call from me all week. I owe him a little face time."

Lex didn't try to stop him. He stepped back so Nico could pass without barreling into him. He did anyway. Their shoulders collided painfully. Nico smirked. Lex resisted the urge to rub his shoulder. He exhaled deeply as though to calm himself. Grace giggled.

Mayor Robert Rainey exclaimed jovially when Nico approached his small group, clapping the young man on the back as though he were a long lost son. "Nicholas! What have you been up to, my boy? I've been waiting to hear from you all week."

Nico smiled. "I'm a busy man, Mayor.

"Of course, of course. You know Colin and Lochlan, of course," Rainey gestured towards the two men beside him. They had the same thick, dark hair and even, squared features. They wore matching black tuxedos and inclined their heads stiffly.

Nico's smile widened slightly. "Yes. How are you both?"

Lex spun away without bothering to listen to their forced replies. It was always the same, anyway. Nico loved to provoke the Mobleys. One of these days, he would go too far. Lex kissed Grace on the cheek and spun toward the bar along the far end of the room.

A tall, slender, stunning woman with a sleek, shining black bob glided purposefully into his path. She wore a dazzling, floor-length peacock blue ball gown. Her throat, arms and fingers sparkled with huge, dramatic diamonds. She lifted one elegantly arched eyebrow at him and smirked. "Alexander."

Lex smiled. "Hello, Carlie."

Assistant District Attorney Carlie Tabb stepped forward to take his arm. "I see Nico is making the Mobleys squirm," she said. Her full, scarlet lips turned up in a devious smile.

"He's trying, anyway."

Carlie laughed. "Were you on your way to the bar?"

Lex glanced toward it longingly. "Yes."

"Well, isn't that convenient? Me, too. Would you care to escort me?"

"How have you been, Carlie?"

She smiled radiantly. "Oh, you know me. Catching the bad guys, buying Fendi bags, living the dream."

He laughed. "Nothing's changed, I see."

The cropped-hair, burly young man tending the bar moved toward them immediately as they reached it. Carlie smirked. "No, not much. It's still good to be on the arm of a Creed. I had to wait fifteen minutes before he served me, and then he ogled my breasts the entire time."

Lex smirked. "I suspect you did encourage him somewhat." She shrugged, but her lips twitched.

"You do know me well." She smiled, lifting the flute of champagne to her lips.

"So. You? Has anything changed with you?"

He lifted his eyebrows. He did not respond. He knew where this was going.

"Are you seeing anyone?"

"Not at the moment. You?"

She lifted her shoulders delicately. She swept a gaze across the room. "Here and there." She smiled mischievously. "You didn't bring a date, then? I'm not surprised, of course. "

"You know me, Carlie."

"Yes. I do. Very well. You are as unreachable as an uncharted island."

"People do reach uncharted islands, occasionally."

"Yes. And are usually dashed against the rocks and never seen again."

Lex rolled his eyes. "It's not so dramatic as all that."

She raised her eyebrows wryly. "No? You aren't the one waiting around for you." When he sighed, she laughed, leaning against his shoulder. "Perhaps tonight isn't the right moment for such conversations. It is a party, after all. You little sister has done a remarkable job putting the whole thing together."

Lex snorted. "Do you really think so?"

"Oh, god, it's so boring," she said earnestly. "But I suppose it's everything it's meant to be."

"It is that. Everything it's meant to be."

"You seem unusually maudlin this evening. Is there anything I can do?"

"No."

She was not to be deterred. "Well, then, shall we have a dance?"

He smiled. "Of course. As you like."

Lex was a good dancer. Carlie was much better. She moved gracefully, following his steps effortlessly. Carlie was the sort of woman who made her partner look good. She was exactly the sort of woman of whom his mother would approve. She smiled radiantly at him. She twined her fingers into the pale hair on the nape of his neck. "I've missed you, Lex."

His smile was reserved. "I missed you too, Carlie."

"Did you really?" She sounded unconvinced.

"Of course."

"Hm." She was silent a long moment. When she spoke again, her tone was light. "Have you heard the rumors going around Spectra lately?"

"What rumors?"

She rolled her eyes. "The rumors about the creatures stalking the streets at night, terrorizing and kidnapping people."

He blinked. His dark, blue eyes focused on her as though he were seeing her for the first time. "What? What creatures?"

"No one knows what they are. We had a few reports from the PD, but no one seems to have any information about it. They are chalking it up to mass hysteria."

Lex frowned. "That seems a bit unlikely, doesn't it?"

"Does it? Perhaps. Perhaps not. It could be the work of chanters."

His face went blank. "I thought the city had officially ruled against acknowledging they exist."

"Oh, you know how it is, Lex. Just because we don't officially recognize it doesn't mean it doesn't still happen now and again." She lifted a sly eyebrow. "I don't suppose you know anything about it?"

"What? Why would I know anything about it?"

She shrugged. "Well, I don't know. I just thought...maybe you'd heard something."

"Well, I haven't. It's nothing to do with me or my family. The city's scum is not our concern." His gaze slid away from her, as though searching for someone. Nico still stood with the Mayor. The two men were talking animatedly, laughing like old chums.

Carlie pursed her lips and narrowed her eyes at him.

He turned back to her and caught her expression. "What is it, Carlie?" he asked wearily. "Why are you looking at me like that?"

She sighed. "I hate to spoil your sister's dreadfully dull party, but Nico is under investigation by the SCPD again."

Lex exhaled deeply. His eyes rolled up toward the ceiling as if he were calling upon a higher power. "What is it this time?"

"Money laundering or some such nonsense."

Lex raised his eyebrows. His gaze sought his brother again. He was smiling and shaking hands with Thomas McGuire, one of Creed Corporation's wealthy and powerful stockholders. "Will he be formally charged this time?"

Carlie smiled. "Come on. No. I made it disappear, as always."

His gaze snapped back to her sharply. "How?"

She shrugged. "I have my ways." Her expression became suddenly stern. "I am as keen as anyone on your family's contributions to Spectra City's economy, Lex, but I do wish your brother would have a bit more discretion."

Lex frowned. "If not for Nico, you would not be wearing that designer dress or buying any more Fendi bags."

She rolled her eyes. "I know, I know. And I am grateful. But I can't keep backlogging these investigations. Someone's bound to notice eventually. Just make sure he keeps his head down, okay?"

"Who's going to notice?" Lex growled. "D.A. Rutherford is our man."

"Yes, well, there are people higher up than Ryan who aren't bought so easily. And they aren't so keen on seeing the Creeds happy and out of prison." Lex's eyes narrowed to slits. She raised her eyebrows. "Can't keep a leash on your little, brother, huh, Lex?"

For a moment, his sculpted features hardened into a cold, dangerous mask. His brilliant blue eyes glinted in icy fury. The air seemed to crackle around him, as though charged with electricity. "Just do your job," he told her through clenched teeth. "Let me worry about my family."

Carlie quelled. "Okay. Okay," she said in an injured tone. "Sorry. I didn't mean to hit a nerve."

"You haven't." His jaw set rigidly.

"Okay." Her eyes slid away uneasily. When she looked back at him, the arctic expression had gone entirely as though it had never been there at all. She eyed him warily. "You should know there's a new ADA in the office. He might become a problem."

"A problem?" His tone was easy and unconcerned.

"He seems interested in you and Nico. Particularly Nico."

"Interested how?"

"He's just asking a lot of questions. He seems to suspect someone is burying cases."

"Someone is."

She ignored him. "He's not stupid. Far from it. I'm not sure Ryan and I can keep him quiet for much longer."

"What's his name?"

"Balthazar Barbosa."

Lex raised his eyebrows, but he nodded. "You needn't worry about him. He won't become an issue."

For a moment, she watched him as one would a dangerous, capricious animal. Then she smiled. It was as though the tense moment between them had never been. She batted her eyebrows flirtatiously. Her eyes sparkled. "You haven't called me in a while, Lex. Why is that?"

He smiled noncommittally. "I am a very busy man, Carlie."

"Sure you are. You were never too busy in the past." She lifted an eyebrow. "Are you sure you aren't seeing someone else?"

"I told you I'm not."

"Well, maybe we could get together again some time. Relive old times?"

"Yeah. Sure. I'll call you." He spoke without conviction.

She noticed. She sighed. "Sure you will."

When the song ended on a long, wavering note, Lex released Carlie abruptly. With a short, compulsory nod, he spun away from her. He didn't get far. Peyton stepped away from the state senator with whom she'd been dancing. She caught her son's arm. Her smile was wide and brilliantly white. It didn't reach her blue eyes.

"I saw you dancing with Carlie Tabb," she purred.

"Yes, Mother," he replied ambiguously.

"She is a lovely girl. Just the sort our family likes. Beautiful, cunning, powerful...easily persuaded."

Lex frowned. His eyes slid away evasively under his mother's expectant stare. "Don't look at me like that, Mom."

"Can't a mother desire a suitable mate for her son?"

"Just leave it alone."

Peyton sighed. "Fine." She watched Carlie glide across the dance floor toward the bar to lick her wounds. "Your father would have liked her. He would have approved of her."

Lex lifted his chin. "I'm not entirely sure that's a good thing."

Peyton wasn't listening to him. "Ah. Here is Mr. Cole for the dedication." She turned to straighten his black bowtie. "Don't let the cameras see you like that, Alexander. We must always present a good face for the papers." She fluttered her fingers over his cheek. There was no tenderness in her touch. "Don't let your father down."

He sighed, but he offered his arm to her as the museum curator stepped up to a podium stationed in front of the orchestra. The curator cleared his throat gently. "Good evening, everyone," he said in a slightly uneasy voice. "Thank you for joining us this evening for the grand opening of the Caleb Creed Memorial Wing."

The guests clapped politely. Peyton led Lex up to the podium as though he were nothing more than a show pony. He did not resist. He met Nico's gaze as they reached the podium at the same time. Nico smiled ironically and dropped an arm around their sister's shoulders.

"Caleb Creed was a beloved friend and a pillar of our esteemed community," the curator droned. He was reading stiffly from a series of index cards. He probably hadn't liked Caleb any more than anyone else. The old man had been a ruthless, bloody-minded bastard. It did not matter. He'd had enough money to buy all the love and esteem a man of such an aloof and dispassionate nature could possibly want. "His good works and selfless deeds..."

Lex wasn't listening. No one was really listening. They had all heard it before, many times. Caleb's "good works" and "selfless deeds" generally involved the bequeathing of a shameless pile of money. He'd known how to buy a reputation. Lex smiled and shook the curator's hand. Flashbulbs went off in his eyes. Peyton clutched his arm.

"Smile for the cameras, Lex."

He wrapped an arm around his mother. He smiled and he waved to the cameras.

CHAPTER 4

The air was thick and pungent with smoke. Soft, moody jazz music drowned the murmuring voices of the people around her, sitting in couples or small groups. Cerys Knight was drinking alone. A television mounted above the bar was tuned to the local news. Cerys read the running commentary at the bottom of the screen. The Spectra City Museum of Fine Art dedicates the new Masters' Wing to the late Caleb Creed...

Cerys raised her eyebrows. A handsome family of four gathered before the podium, posing with fixed smiles for the camera. Caleb is survived by his wife, Peyton, two sons, Alexander and Nicholas and daughter Grace. Since his father's death, Alexander has taken up the reigns as the new CEO of Creed Corporation, and he continues his father's charity work in his honor...

She turned to the bartender. She tilted her chin towards the screen. "Who are they?"

The bartender frowned and glanced cursorily at the television. When he turned back to her, he looked slightly surprised. "Those are the Creeds."

She held out her glass for another beer. "I've heard rumors about them. I heard they're chanters."

He slid her beer across the bar and scowled reproachfully at her. "Those are just rumors."

"Yeah? There sure are a lot of them."

"Yeah, well, you'd be a lot better off if you didn't ask about things like that. People who ask things like that about the Creeds tend to disappear."

Cerys sipped her drink reflectively. "He's just afraid of them," a voice said scornfully. "Everyone's afraid of them."

Cerys glanced toward it. A short, slim girl with long, curly blonde hair sat a few barstools away. Her delicate, elfish features were twisted into a hateful glare. She wasn't looking at Cerys. She stared up at the screen. "But not you?" Cerys asked.

The blonde woman's lips curled. She looked at Cerys. "I'm not afraid of monsters. I haven't been since I was a little girl."

"You think they're monsters? Is it true, then, that they're chanters?"

The bartender glared at the blonde woman. She lifted her chin defiantly. "It's never been proven, but they must be."

"Why?"

"No one gets that sort of power without having something up their sleeve."

"Keep that sort of talk out of my bar," the publican growled.

The blonde woman rose abruptly from her stool. "Fine. I'll just take my business elsewhere."

"You do that."

"Wait—" But the blonde woman had already slammed the door. Cerys frowned at the barkeeper.

He turned his scowl on her. "And you can, too, if you want to keep asking dangerous questions."

She sighed. "How about a less dangerous one?" When he lifted an eyebrow, she drew a small, creased photograph from her jacket pocket. "I'm looking for someone. My brother. He came to Spectra about six months ago. I haven't heard from him in a while. You ever seen him?"

The barkeeper took the photograph. He glanced down at it for a long moment. His eyes slid towards the door. "No. I've never seen him." He handed the photograph back quickly, as if it might burn him if he held it too long.

Cerys frowned. "You sure?"

"We get a lot of lost souls wandering in here. I don't remember them all."

She narrowed her eyes at him. He moved away from her to take an order across the bar. Cerys sighed. It was not the first time she'd received that response. It wouldn't be the last. If anyone in Spectra City had ever heard of Cedric Knight, they weren't talking about it. And if they were talking about the Creeds, they were sure to deny it.

What they were talking about were the creatures.

She motioned the bartender for another drink. He hesitated.

"I heard some people have disappeared," she said. "They've been taken in the streets."

He glared as though she'd tricked him. "You ask a lot of very sensitive questions."

"Is it true?"

"I don't know anything about that."

"You don't seem to know a lot about much, do you?" She slapped a bill on the bar. She stood and strode out of the bar, into the cold, wet night.

She glanced up and down the dark, quiet street. There was no sign of the blonde woman. There was no sign of anyone. It wasn't safe to be out on the streets at night in Spectra City.

* * *

The tall, monolithic buildings towered over the lonely, breathless streets of Spectra City like dark sentinels. Cerys pressed her forehead against the cool glass of the panoramic window in her penthouse suite. Rain spattered the glass, blurring the splashes of color and glowing neon lights below. It looked ominous. It was as though the city was suspended in restless anticipation. It was waiting for something to happen.

She knew it would be bad, whatever it was.

Perhaps it already had. She sighed. She wished Cedric had never gone. She wished he'd never come here, to Spectra City.

She turned from the window abruptly. Her suite was large and lavish. The sitting room was furnished elegantly in rich wood and gold brocade with accents of blue on the windows and throw pillows she'd scattered carelessly around the room. It hadn't really mattered where she'd stayed. She paid little attention to the beauty and opulence of the room. The vaulted ceilings and hanging chandeliers were of no interest. It had been important to maintain appearances.

A large, white dry erase board stood in front of the television set on the far wall of the room. Cerys picked up a red marker, nibbling pensively at the end. She sat down on the plush gold sofa. She opened a thin file on the coffee table before her. Cedric's handwriting jumped out at her from the first page in the stack.

Little Sister,

Do you miss me yet? I arrived in Spectra City last week. I've taken a job with Mobley Enterprises, one of the larger corporations in town. They seemed almost as desperate to have a good tech guy as I was to find work. I won't bore you talking about my work writing code and programming networks. You never like to hear about that. I suppose the life of a techie is not half as interesting as one of a photographer who jet-sets all over the world at her leisure.

Who would have guessed I would be the one having the adventure?

It rains all the time, but that isn't much different than San Francisco, is it? It's different here. People are scared. Something is going on in the city, but no one talks about it. It's as though a dark cloud hangs perpetually over everyone. But no one leaves, and no one admits anything is wrong.

I've heard rumors on the streets about the chanters. People whisper about them in bars and in the dark alleys at night, but no one speaks out loud about them if they can help it. I don't know if it's them they fear or something else. You have to be careful what questions you ask around here and of whom you ask them. You never know what sort of reception you'll get. Looking for chanters can be dangerous. Some people would as soon turn you in as one of them.

They don't acknowledge that chanters exist here, but that doesn't stop them fighting each other in the streets. Some people think they're heroes. Other people think they're monsters. Perhaps they're both. Good and bad, one side or the other.

Cerys tossed the letter aside. It didn't help her. She reached for another.

Cerys,

It has taken a while, but if you keep your ear to the ground long enough, you're sure to learn something. They call themselves Chant. If you say the word, most people turn away shiftily, but sometimes there is something in someone's eyes. I met a man in a bar who's seen them. I don't know how reliable he was after several rounds of drinks, but he said they help people. They city doesn't acknowledge chanter attacks, but they doesn't mean they don't happen. These people, Chant, they fight them.

This is what I've been waiting for, Cerys.

He doesn't know how you find them. He says they find you. If there is an organization of chanters fighting in the streets, though, I'll find them. People like that don't stay hidden forever. I'm not ready to reveal my powers to draw them to me, but if I have to, I will.

Cerys rose to her feet. She scrawled the word *CHANT* on the board. It wasn't much.

The next letter was short, as though Cedric had penned it in a great hurry.

I met a girl named Tamsin in a pub. I know she's part of Chant. She didn't say it, but when I mentioned the name, there was something different in her eyes. I'm not sure how to make her trust me enough, but she might be my only way in.

She wrote *Tamsin*. It was better. It might not be much, but it had been enough for Cedric.

It's real, Cerys. I'm writing from Chant headquarters. There have been attacks in the streets. Some chanters are going missing. When I met Tamsin again at the pub, she didn't want to talk to me. I followed her, though, and I showed her what I can do. I don't know if she was impressed or if she just wanted to get me off the streets, but it worked well enough.

She brought me to a mansion on the edge of the city. It was dark, surrounded by skeletal, overgrown trees, and looked as though no one had inhabited it for several years. For a moment, I was afraid Tamsin intended to murder me and leave my body there. No one would ever have found it.

It wasn't uninhabited as it looked from the street. Inside, it was five stories high and furnished like a museum. There were people there, other chanters, I'm sure. They didn't speak to me, but they looked at Tamsin as if she'd done something she shouldn't have.

Their leader is called Jar. It isn't his real name, but it's safer not to write it down. It's safer not to say it at all. If the police force acknowledged us, he'd be the most wanted man in the city. Some of us don't mind if our names are used, but others are important around the city. If they were discovered, it would mean disaster.

Cerys, it's incredible. Inside the headquarters is a secret lab where we can watch everything that goes on in the city. Once he got over my unexpected arrival, Jar was happy to have another person on the team who can use computers. There's another one. We call him X. He isn't a chanter, but he's so good with systems, he's like one. He's found a way to pinpoint chanter attacks. He can monitor the energy levels of the city. When something changes, the map turns red. Sometimes it's just a power surge, but other times, it's chanters.

Jar is the real thing, Cer. A real superhero. He's obsessed with the Creeds. He chases the chanter signals, but it's like he's disappointed every time it isn't one of them. It's never one of them, but all he can talk about is taking them down.

The Creeds run the city, you see, Cerys. They're rich and powerful and greedy. Jar is convinced they're more than that. He thinks they're chanters and they're using dark magic to their own ends. No one gets that powerful without being a chanter. That's what Tamsin always says.

Whether they're chanters or not, they're dangerous. Their corporation is heaped in shady deals and probably organized crime. No one speaks against them. They have all the city's top brass in their back pockets, and no one dares do anything about it. Spectra is corrupt all around, Cerys. Zar is determined to take it apart brick by brick. I'm with him. We're all with him. If anyone can take them down, it's him.

Cerys sighed deeply. She wrote Zar--who are you really? on the board. None of Cedric's letters told her. They described battles with other chanters. They detailed the suspected crimes the Creeds had committed. They didn't explain Cedric's disappearance. The next looked more promising.

Creatures are attacking people in the streets at night. There are police reports, but no one seems to believe them. No one who's seen them up close has lived to tell about it, but the drunks and vagrants who've survived the attacks have seen men in cloaks moving through the streets. They leave fire in their wake, and they take people away. They don't look human. Some of us have gone to fight them, but no one ever comes back.

No one knows what they are or why they're taking chanters away. Zar, of course, believes the Creeds are behind it. He always suspects the Creeds are behind it. It's as though there are no other villains in the city or on the streets, though we prove there are everyday when we go against them. He's a good leader, and his intentions are good. He does a lot to help protect the city. I suppose a little obsession is pretty much what makes a good superhero, right?

We're doing everything we can to stop the attacks. They just don't make sense, and no one knows where they're coming from. They must be creatures of magic. No human disappears when they're struck with magic, do they? Cerys, these creatures are dangerous. No one knows when they might strike again or who will disappear when they do.

Cerys' stomach roiled. She noted the date on the board. It was three months ago. It didn't coincide with any of the newspaper clippings about the Creeds in the file. They weren't helpful anyway; the Spectra City Daily had taken the same line as the rest of the city in regard to the Creeds. By all appearances, they were a family of humanitarians and extremely savvy businessmen. The Daily didn't mention the attacks at all. No one mentioned the attacks but Cedric.

Cerys,

Members of Chant have gone missing. No one who has gone against the creatures has come back. We think they're targeting us. Though the papers and the police seem to think it's nothing more than the ravings of some drunks, there are people missing. It's as though Spectra has forgotten any of them ever existed, but Zar is sure. They are all chanters. It's us they want, not the innocents in the streets.

Someone wants us for something.

"Did they take you, too, Cedric?" Cerys whispered.

She sighed. She fingered the glossy press pass on the coffee table beside the open file. It was time to get ready for the party.

CHAPTER 5

The winding drive leading to Creed Manor was lit with bright, twinkling lights. The trees around it were so thick, only the top of the house was outlined against the gloomy sky above them. The drive opened abruptly into a wide, circular pavilion. Cerys caught her breath, peering anxiously out the window as they slowly approached the house. Her driver steered the plain black sedan behind a row of limousines, which idled patiently, waiting for the handsomely dressed doorman in front of the enormous stone mansion to escort the passengers to the front door.

Creed Manor was a white stone mansion surrounded by a wall of rose bushes. Balconies wrapped around every floor, railed with thick, wrought iron. They overflowed with flowers in planters and twined on vines up the wall. Vibrant green ivy wrapped around the tall, stone pillars. Small, hanging lanterns hung from each balcony, softly illuminating the floor below, swaying slightly in the gentle breeze. The white stone sparkled as though it were encrusted with tiny gems.

It wasn't raining. It was as though even the weather did not dare displease the Creeds.

The balconies were already bursting with guests in elegant cocktail dresses and designer suits, who sipped champagne and talked animatedly. When her car reached the head of the queue, the doorman stepped forward to open Cerys' door. He offered his hand to assist her out of the car. He was a young man, dressed in a crisp white suit. He smiled at her. "Good evening, miss. Do you have an invitation?" Cerys held up the press pass around her neck and shouldered her camera bag. The footman inclined his head. "Very good. This way, if you please."

She followed him inside the manor. Chandeliers hung from the high, vaulted ceilings, glittering brilliantly in the soft lights. Beyond the vestibule, a large sitting room was furnished with a stiff, expensive looking ivory settee and matching arm chairs. Art hung on the walls. It looked like a museum. No one was inside. It didn't look as though anyone ever went inside.

Cerys wondered that there wasn't a small, red velvet rope separating it from the vestibule and the rest of the house. She realized why moments later as she joined the general throng moving towards the ballroom. The entire house looked that way, as if their interior designer had intended the house to be a gallery, rather than a home in which a family might live comfortably. Every decoration was strategically placed. Children didn't play in this house. Animals didn't roam free. It was unlikely anyone ever had a cheerful conversation.

There were cheerful conversations in the ballroom, which twinkled with silver and gold streamers and crystal chandeliers hanging from the vaulted ceiling. The walls were textured ivory. There were few decorations along the walls. The room itself was huge and breathtaking, like the ballroom of a medieval monarch. Pillars gilded with gold filigree rose up around the room. They were not wrapped with streamers, for they needed no ornamentation. The floors were hard wood polished to a reflective shine.

A spirited band played upon a raised platform at the head of the room. A full bar completely lined the east wall. Cerys started toward it hastily. Most of the conversations in the ballroom centered mirthfully on Peyton Creed's birthday. She turned fifty today. The guest of honor and mistress of the spectacular manor was in rare form this evening. Surrounded by her three children, Peyton greeted her guests with a radiant smile. Her long, burnished red hair fell around her face in unbound waves. She was slender and regal in a stunning, scarlet red gown that glittered with sequins.

Had Cerys not known that her two sons were in their mid-thirties, Cerys might have believed the woman was turning fifty. The Creeds were a stunning family. The two eldest siblings, Alexander and Nicholas were tall and lean in perfectly cut black suits. Their features were so strikingly similar that Cerys might have thought they were twins but for the difference of two years in age. Nico had dark hair combed back from his strong, chiseled features. Lex wore his blonde hair roguishly across his forehead. They both smiled charmingly around them. Neither of their smiles reached their brilliant blue eyes.

Grace Creed was the image of her beautiful mother. She wore her hair in a short, sleek bob, which she tossed haughtily as the procession of guests approached them. She was younger than her brothers by several years. Her reputation was not as good. Her dress was short. She batted her eyelashes at the more prominent members of Spectra City's social elite as they approached her. Everyone knew Grace Creed was in the market for a husband.

The guests eyed Cerys with varying degrees of interest as she wove through the crowd towards the bar. Spectra City was a very large city, but in these circles, everyone knew everyone else. She had dressed to the nines in a black satin cocktail dress and glowing pearls. She still stood out among the glitzy party guests like a mutt among the pure bred. She wasn't concerned about keeping a low profile. She lifted her chin with dignity.

She snapped photographs of the laughing guests and the couples twirling on the dance floor. She knew many of them by sight and by reputation. She knew few of them personally. She did know Libby Gore, a reporter at the Spectra City Daily. They'd been given the same assignment.

Libby raised her glass to Cerys as she approached her at the bar. Libby was dressed in a short, hot pink ruffled dress as though she intended to stand out among the more conservative crowd. Her short black hair was slicked back from her face. She smiled impishly. "Swanky, huh?"

Cerys smiled and snatched a flute of champagne from a passing waiter's tray. "Yeah. Some party."

"I bet you see a lot of parties like this in San Francisco."

Cerys snorted. "Not quite like this." The champagne was tart. Bubbles popped in her mouth.

"Well, it's not given me a lot of content for a story yet, but here's hoping one of the more prominent city officials will have too much champagne and accuse his wife of cheating on him with the maid." Libby held up her glass in a solemn toast.

Cerys laughed and turned her camera towards the crowd. She zoomed her high-powered lens toward the Creeds. They were laughing together. By all appearances, the striking family was quite close. She didn't trust appearances. Their eyes were all cold and watchful and shrewd. She snapped a photograph. Would it capture the tension between them?

A tall, dark-haired man approached them. His smile was fixed. He might have practiced it in a mirror until he'd gotten it right and never let it lapse for fear he might forget how to do it again. His suit was expensive and well-made. He was good-looking in an ordinary way, the way used car salesmen were. He was good-looking because it suited his purposes.

"Ah, hello, Libby," he greeted cheerfully.

Libby did not move from her lounging position against the end of the bar. She lifted her glass. "Hello, Greg." She glanced at Cerys. She tilted her head towards the man. "Cerys, this is Gregory Holton. He works for the mayor's office."

Gregory Holton raised carefully plucked eyebrows. His smile didn't falter. "That's not much of an introduction, Libby." He offered his hand to Cerys. "I'm Mayor Rainey's press adviser. But I don't believe we've met."

"This is Cerys Knight. She's from San Francisco," Libby put in lazily. "She's a photographer. She's been freelancing at the Daily."

"Is that so?" Greg's tone was pleasant. "And what was brought you to our stormy little inlet?"

"It's not so much different than San Francisco," Cerys replied. Her gaze drifted over his shoulder towards the Creeds. "Aside from one or two things."

"I see you're interested in the Creeds."

Cerys shook her head. "No, I'm not interested in them."

Greg laughed. "Don't worry, dear. Most women are. The rest of us merely scrounge for table scraps."

"I have heard some conflicting details about them."

"Ah, yes, I'm sure you have. I assure you, they are merely rumors."

Libby rolled her eyes. "That's the official line from the Mayor's office, anyway," she said wryly.

Greg's smile chilled. "You would do well to remember it, Libby." He inclined his head graciously to them both. "Well. I see Robert beckoning me. I suppose he needs advice about which champagne will look best on the cover of the Daily." He winked at Cerys. "Ms. Knight, do be a dear and snap a few photos of the old man, will you?"

She laughed. "Of course."

When he was gone, Libby scoffed. "Politicians. You can't live with 'em, can't get an official statement from the mayor without them." Her next remark drew Cerys' eyes away from the Creeds and back to her. "You do seem a little interested in the Creeds." She smirked. "That Lex, huh? He is gorgeous. Well, and so is Nico, when you get down to it. I have to say, I do prefer blondes, though."

"It isn't about that," Cerys said coolly. "It's not what you're thinking."

"Yeah, right. There's nothing wrong with a girl having a little ambition outside her career, is there?"

"What do you know about them, anyway?"

Libby shrugged. "The usual line. Not much else. They don't really talk to reporters."

Cerys watched Lex Creed break away from his family. As he did, something changed in the set of his jaw and the chill in his eyes. He relaxed almost imperceptibly. He paused beside a tall, slender woman with a sleek, shining black bob. She smiled radiantly at him and touched his arm. She leaned close to whisper in his ear. His expression never changed.

"Who is that with Lex?" Cerys asked, nodding towards them.

"Oh, that's Carlie Tabb. She's an ADA." Libby lifted a sardonic eyebrow. "Word has it she's in the Creed's back pocket."

"I thought the Creeds weren't up to anything. What do they need an ADA in their pocket for?"

Libby chuckled. "The real question is, what do they need an ADA for when they have the D.A.?"

"So there is more to them than meets the eye."

"Oh, you can count on that. I've been itching to learn the truth about them for years, but it's a lost cause. You might as well give it up now, if it's in your head."

Cerys ignored her. Carlie lifted a graceful arm to point towards a man standing stiffly on the edge of the dance floor. He was tall and well-built. His shoulders were broad. The lines of his suit emphasized thick, lean muscle. He had dark, shortly-cropped black hair. His eyes were dark and almond shaped. They moved around the room alertly. There was so much life in them, so much vitality, that Cerys thought he stood out among the perfectly molded others like a flash of light in darkness. She didn't know him. He was surrounded by several older men. Cerys recognized D.A. Rutherford among them.

Lex glanced at him with cold, narrow eyes. Something about his expression chilled Cerys to the bone. He looked dangerous. "Who is that man?" Cerys demanded quickly, nodding towards the dark-haired man standing with the D.A.

"Who? Him? Oh. That's the new ADA. Barbosa is his name." Her pale pink lips turned up in a sly smile. "I heard he's after Nico."

Cerys turned back to her sharply. "For what?"

"Whatever will stick to him, I expect."

"Why?"

"Fame, fortune, revenge, just trying to make a name for himself in Spectra, I guess. Who knows? He's not the first rookie ADA to go after him, and he won't be the last. He won't make anything stick, anyway."

"Why won't he?"

Libby laughed. "You really haven't been in Spectra long. You have a lot to learn about it. I thought everyone had the measure of the Creeds."

Cerys shrugged. She looked at Libby expectantly.

"Well, everyone talks. There are a lot of rumors about them. There have been since before Lex and Nico were even born."

"Yeah, I've heard a few of those. So you think they're true?"

Libby lifted a shoulder casually. "It's not my place to say. I spin the press the way the editor sees fit."

"You don't want to know?"

"I suspect it's not worth my job or my life to try to find out. It's safer to do what you're told and keep your head down. It's the best way to stay out of trouble. If Barbosa knew what was good for him, he would do the same."

Cerys considered a moment. She snatched two flutes of champagne. She handed one to Libby. "What do you know about Chant?"

Libby looked completely astonished, as though Cerys had spoken a dirty and shocking word in mixed company. "Where did you hear that name?" Her voice sounded strained.

"Word on the streets. You hear a lot when you listen."

"There is no such thing as Chant," Libby spat.

"How do you know?"

"What do you mean, how do I know? I just know. Don't ask questions about that."

"Something else it's safer not knowing about? There seems to be a lot of that in Spectra City."

Libby glanced away. "I, uh...I think I see an old friend over by the band. I'd better go say hello. Can't stand here chatting all night, or I'll never get my story. Don't forget to take some shots of the other guests, huh? Not just the Creeds."

"Sure. See you at the office on Monday."

Libby was already weaving through the crowd, as though hurrying to be as far from her as quickly as possible. Cerys didn't mind. Lex was moving away from Carlie Tabb, towards the new Assistant District Attorney Barbosa. She dropped her camera around her neck and strode forward.

She was close enough to overhear them when Lex reached Barbosa.

He offered his hand to the dark-haired man. "I don't believe we've met. I'm Alexander Creed."

Barbosa smiled in the practiced way of a politician. It seemed to be the common expression in Spectra City. He shook Lex's hand vigorously. He seemed pleased to be meeting him. "Balthazar Barbosa, Assistant District Attorney."

"Yes. I heard you've just joined the office. Are you enjoying your post?"

"At times. Sometimes it can be disheartening."

"Indeed? How so?"

"Sometimes the bad guys get away."

Lex laughed. "Yes, sometimes they do. It is the way of the justice system, I suppose. Are you from Spectra?"

"Yes. I was born and raised here. I left for a few years to attend Harvard Law."

"And now you've returned."

"So I have."

"I don't believe I've heard of your family."

"No. Perhaps you would not have. My parents died when I was young. I was raised by a foster family."

"Were you? I'm sorry. That's very sad." Lex's blue eyes slid away pensively. "My father recently passed away."

"I am sorry to hear that."

"Thank you. I suspect I would not have been the same man, had he not been around when I was a child."

Barbosa inclined his head. Cerys wasn't interested in ADA Barbosa. She was interested in Lex. When he broke away from the ADA, she followed him. He paused to greet his guests cheerfully, as though they were old friends. He seemed to have a lot of old friends. He thanked them graciously for honoring his mother. "I wish my father was around to see this," he told Mayor Robert Rainey, a tall, paunchy gentleman with steel grey hair, who smiled and nodded sympathetically. "He always loved a good party."

"Yes, I remember Caleb was the life of every party."

Neither one of them seemed to be telling the truth.

Nico cleared his throat over a microphone upon the stage in front of the band. "If I could have your attention, everyone." His voice was like warm honey.

Lex nodded to Mayor Rainey and hurried to join his family in front of the stage.

Cerys followed him.

"I would like to thank you all for coming to honor my mother," Nico continued, smiling a brilliant white smile that caused his blue eyes to crinkle endearingly at the corners. "It is not everyday a woman turns fifty for the tenth time."

The party laughed appreciatively. Peyton glared at her son.

"You don't look a day older than when I was two years old, Mother."

Peyton laughed. She kissed her youngest son on the cheek. "Thank you, Nicholas."

He raised his glass. "To Peyton."

Cerys raised her glass with the others. Peyton smiled imperiously around at them. "Thank you all for coming," she purred.

Cerys stepped forward, holding up her camera. "Will you pose for a photo for the Spectra City Daily?"

Nico smiled at her. The smile chilled her to the bone. He motioned to his brother and sister. "Lex, Grace, come on up here."

Grace hardly needed prompting. She smoothed her gleaming hair and wrapped an arm around her mother, smiling brilliantly. Lex hesitated. Peyton held her hand out to him with a steely expression. He joined his brother. He turned towards Cerys and smiled. There was something different in his eyes than in his brother's.

She snapped the photograph.

Before she could fade into the crowd, Lex leapt off the stage and advanced upon her. She resisted the urge to rear backward. "Thank you for the photograph," she said evenly.

He smiled. "I haven't seen you before. Are you new to Spectra City?"

"Yes. I only just arrived. Cerys Knight." She offered her hand to him.

He gripped it firmly. "Alexander Creed."

"I know who you are. My brother, Cedric, came to Spectra about six months ago. It's all he could talk about."

Cedric's name did not seem to mean anything to him. Lex's eyes didn't change. He smiled pleasantly.

"I'm doing some freelance work for the Daily."

"I see. Well. Welcome. I hope you enjoy the rest of the party."

She smiled. "I am certain I will."

He inclined his head. He spun away from her. She turned to aim her camera into the crowd. Lex Creed seemed nice. He hardly seemed at all like an evil chanter kidnapping Chant members off the streets with hideous corporeal manifestations of power. Whatever was going on behind the closed doors of this opulent, modern palace, the Creeds hid it well.

* * *

Cerys tacked up photographs on her board. She captioned each one in small, careful letters, as though they might reveal Cedric's whereabouts. They didn't, not yet.

Lex Creed: CEO Creed Corporation. Seems nice.

Nico Creed: VP Creed Corporation. Under investigation by ADA Barbosa. Alleged crimes: Unknown.

Grace Creed: Event planner. Celebutante. Party girl.

Peyton Creed: Widow. Socialite. Alcoholic.

There was more than that, though. These were only their basic elements. She didn't notate that Nico was charming and good-natured. Lex was sincere and kind. Grace was fun-loving and spirited and likeable. Peyton was elegant and regal.

Cerys sighed deeply. Could they really be all those things and everything Cedric and Chant thought they were?

CHAPTER 6

Nico slouched moodily in a leather wing backed chair in the library of Creed Manor. He balanced a glass of wine on his knee. He barely glanced up when his brother entered the room. "I think the party was a success," he said off-handedly. "Mother seemed to enjoy it."

Lex did not smile. "Yes, it went very well."

"I saw you talking to the new photographer for the Daily." Nico lifted his eyes to his brother. "What do you think of her?"

Lex frowned. "Her photographs are very good."

"Yes. She made us all look very good." Nico twirled his wine glass between two long, slender fingers. He stared at the scarlet liquid as though it held the secrets of the world within.

"It isn't her I'm worried about."

Nico raised his eyebrows. He didn't glance up at his brother. "Oh?"

"Did you happen to meet the new ADA?"

"No. Who is he?"

"Balthazar Barbosa. He's a hotshot. Just in from Harvard law. That's not really important, Nico. Carlie tells me he seems especially interested in us. In you in particular."

Nico raised his eyebrows innocently. "Me? What did I do?"

Lex scowled. "Carlie can't keep burying your mistakes, Nico. If you aren't going to play by the rules, you are eventually going to face the consequences."

"And when have you ever played by the rules?"

"I don't call unnecessary attention to myself!"

Nico smirked. "What is the point of having power if you aren't going to use it?"

"Your vanity is going to get all of us tossed in prison."

"Don't be so dramatic, Lex."

Lex sighed. "Just try to stay out of Barbosa's way, won't you?"

"Of course. That is, if he stays out of mine."

"Nico…"

"We run this city, Lex. Not some upstart ADA with a misguided vendetta."

"You should give him a little more credit. Carlie thinks he's smart. He knows what he's doing, and he isn't going to be that easy to shove off."

"He won't be a problem. I'll make sure of that."

"What are you going to do, Nico?"

"Nothing with which you need to concern yourself. I'm sure we can convince him to see our way of things."

"I wouldn't be so sure."

Nico swallowed the scarlet contents of his glass. He smiled with ruby red lips. "Everyone has a price, Lex. I'm sure I can find his."

* * *

The Spectra City District Attorney's office was noisy and bustling. Balthazar Barbosa tucked a case file hurriedly into a sleek, black leather briefcase beside his chair. When he sat up, Nico Creed stood silently in front of him. Barbosa paused. His expression did not change. He lifted his eyebrows expectantly.

Nico looked completely relaxed. He offered his hand across Barbosa's desk. "Ah. ADA Barbosa. I don't believe we've formally met. Nico Creed. I'm just on my way to meet Ryan for lunch."

Barbosa shook Nico's hand. Nico's grip was firm. His eyes were cold. "Balthazar Barbosa."

Nico smiled. "My brother says you seem like a very reasonable man," he said amiably.

"Did he?" Barbosa asked evenly. "I am not sure you will find me to be especially so."

"No? Being unreasonable can be very dangerous in Spectra City."

"So I hear." Barbosa smiled. "I find that, despite the dangers, I'm willing to risk hanging on to my principles."

Nico laughed. "A principled man in the DA's office is very rare."

"So I've noticed."

"Perhaps you will become more reasonable as you become more aware of how things work around here."

"I am afraid I'm very stubborn. I am not sure I will."

Nico lifted an eyebrow. "Perhaps you would join me for lunch one of these days, Mr. Barbosa."

The ADA's smile did not waver. "I don't think so, Mr. Creed. I am a very busy man. And I am late for court." He offered his hand to Nico.

Nico stared at it coldly. Barbosa shrugged and strode swiftly away.

D.A. Rutherford rounded a corner and clapped Nico jovially on the shoulder. "Ah. Nico. What are you doing in the cube farm? I have reservations at the Specter."

Nico did not smile. He continued to watch after Barbosa with narrowed eyes. "Yes. I have something I'd like to discuss with you, Ryan."

The D.A. raised his eyebrows. "Not a problem, I hope?"

Nico's eyes glinted coldly. "No. Not a problem. Not yet, anyway."

* * *

Carlie Tabb nearly dropped her case file as she spun and found Lex standing silently behind her. She gasped and pressed her hand to her heart. "Lex!"

He smirked. He held two paper cups of steaming coffee in his hands. He held one out to her. "Plain latte. Two sugars."

Carlie lifted an elegant black eyebrow. "To what do I owe this unexpected visit this morning?"

"Do you think you can get me copies of the police reports on those creature attacks?"

She blinked. "I thought that didn't have anything to do with you or your family." Her sly look faded when she met his ominous eyes. "What do you want them for?"

"I'm just curious."

"Have you heard something else about them?"

"No. I'm just interested."

"Why?"

Lex rolled his eyes. "Why are you questioning me, Carlie?"

"Sorry, Lex. I just didn't expect you to ask something like that."

"Well, this is my city. If something is happening to our people, I want to know what it's all about."

She narrowed her eyes suspiciously. Then she smiled. "Yeah. Okay. I'll get them for you. Why don't I bring them to you over lunch?"

Lex sighed. "Carlie..."

"Oh, come on, Lex. I am doing you a favor. The least you can do is treat me to lunch."

"I brought you coffee."

She scoffed. "That just got you the five minutes that I'm now late for my meeting with Ryan."

Lex chuckled. "All right. I'll see you at the Specter at noon."

She tossed her head. "See you there."

He was surprised to meet his brother at the elevator. "Nico? What are you doing here? I thought you met Ryan yesterday."

Nico lifted a sardonic eyebrow. "I could ask you the same, big brother."

Lex sighed. "I was asking Carlie to lunch."

"Ah, back on that, are we? I thought you had given her up as a guilty roll in the hay once in a while."

"Don't talk about her like that, Nico."

Nico rolled his eyes. "Well, Mother will be pleased, at any rate."

"What are you doing here?" Lex repeated.

His brother scowled. He glanced over his shoulder. "Digging up information on our maverick ADA."

"Leave him alone, Nico."

"He is creating problems for me. He threatens to embarrass our family."

"Well, if you kept on the right side of things, none of this would be a problem."

"Is this really the appropriate venue for a lecture of this nature?"

Lex shook his head. "No. No, you're right. This is not the time or place."

"And I believe we both have to get back to work, don't we? Creed Corp can't

44

run without its CEO, can it?"

"Nor its VP."

"Don't patronize me, Lex."

Lex sighed. "Care to share a cab?"

Nico shrugged. "Yeah, all right."

It was a gloomy day. Most of the days in Spectra City were gloomy. A large crowd was gathered on the white stone steps outside the Spectra City Courthouse. It looked as though they were waiting for something. When the Creeds stepped out of the courthouse side by side, all eyes turned to them in interest. Lex and Nico glanced at each other.

"Well, Lex and Nico Creed," Libby Gore greeted, striding towards them with an eager expression. "I wouldn't have expected to see you two here this morning. Do you have some business at the courthouse?"

Behind Libby, the dark-haired freelance photographer from the Daily snapped photographs of the crowd outside. She joined Libby presently. She looked politely interested, as though prepared to take a photo if required. She nodded to Lex. He smiled at her.

"We're just visiting some friends, Miss Gore," Lex replied smoothly.

"Is that ADA Tabb? Or maybe the new ADA, Barbosa." Libby smiled sweetly.

Nico narrowed his eyes at her. Up close, his face was chiseled like a fine sculpture. His eyes were just as cold and lifeless. "D.A. Rutherford, actually. He is a close, personal friend of the family, you remember."

"Oh, yes. Of course. But I heard you're not so friendly with ADA Barbosa."

Nico smiled that sculpted, charming smile. "Rumor, Ms. Gore. You know how dangerous those can be."

Libby's smile was brittle. She stepped back as though to allow the men to pass. "Enjoy your day, gentleman."

"I think we will," Nico replied smugly. "Thank you."

Lex paused in front of Cerys. She looked startled at this personal attention. She touched her long, wavy, chestnut brown hair self-consciously. "Well, hello to you again. Miss Knight, is it?"

"Cerys."

"Yes. Thank you for the photographs of the party. My mother was extremely pleased. She says no one has ever quite captured her good side like you."

Cerys smiled. "I am very gratified, Mr. Creed."

"Everyone just calls me Lex." She nodded. He lifted an eyebrow. "What is the Daily doing here this morning? Fishing for a scandal?"

"That is always appreciated in the journalistic world. We're awaiting the verdict in the Frank Adley trial."

"Ah, yes," Nico put in. He had been watching his brother with his jaw set rigidly. Now he smirked slightly. "The Mobley Enterprises executive accused of embezzlement."

"A terrible business, that," Lex said pointedly.

"Yes," Nico drawled. "A shame to think you can't trust your own people."

"I imagine it is hard to trust many people when you are in a position of power," Cerys put in.

Nico's eyes fell upon her. A chill ran up her spine. "Cerys, is it?"

"Yes."

"Nico." He offered his hand to her. His grip was severe. He turned away from her dismissively and jerked his head at his brother. "Lex."

Lex nodded. "Of course. Well. It was nice to see you again, Cerys. I hope you get your story. I'm sure you'll make Adley look good, guilty or not."

She laughed. "Thank you. Goodbye, Lex."

* * *

Lex rubbed his neck wearily. He rose from his desk to pour another cup of coffee. It was late. He needed to sleep. The police reports on the creature attacks seemed little more than a collection of sarcastic renderings of the wild tales of drunks or vagrants. He'd read them over and over. Despite the general underlying tone of complete skepticism in the reports, they were consistent. It wasn't mass hysteria. It was almost never mass hysteria.

There had been six attacks. They had happened in the poorer districts of the city, where anyone foolish enough to be out on the streets was dangerous enough to take care of themselves. Ten people had come forward to detail the attacks. They had all seen the cloaked creatures gliding through the darker, seedier poor districts. Some of them described the creatures as having twisted, grey, mottled features. Some of them saw them hovering inches about the ground. Some of them saw the creatures spread fire wherever they went.

Three of them saw the creatures seize an innocent person off the streets and toss them away as though they were nothing more than a rag doll. Large sections of the reports were blacked out. Lex knew what they described. The witnesses had seen people fight them. They had seen their eyes roll back. They had seen their lips move rapidly. Strange words had poured from them as if from some mysterious source deep within them. They had seen them fall into a trance.

They had seen the creatures converge upon them as they chanted. They had seen them surround them and carry them off between them. Sometimes it happened two nights in a row. Sometimes days or weeks went by without any attacks. Sometimes the chanters didn't come to fight them. On those nights, they simply disappeared, leaving smoldering wreckage in their wake and terrified vagrants cowering behind dumpsters.

Lex pushed his chair abruptly away from his desk. He pinched the bridge of his nose. Someone was taking chanters off the streets. He rose to pace swiftly from one end of the handsome office to the other. But why? And where were the creatures coming from? He paused in front of the wide window to peer out towards Mobley Mansion. It was quiet.

The Creeds and Mobleys weren't the only chanters in Spectra City. There were more. There were many, many more. None of them mattered. Dread roiled in his belly. He glanced up, as if he might see his little brother above him through the ceiling. Something wasn't right about Nico. Something had changed. He had never been so determined to destroy the Mobleys. Perhaps he'd finally found a way.

"What are you doing, Nico? You had better not be behind this."

* * *

The office of the Spectra City District Attorney was quiet. Nearly everyone had gone home for the day. Balthazar Barbosa squinted wearily at the file on his desk. There were stacks of invoices with unusually high dollar amounts paid to Creed Corp by a company called Bower Research out of the Cayman Islands. It wasn't much. It was something, though, if only Barbosa could locate an employee of Bower Research. There didn't seem to be any. The lawyer in whose name the corporation did business was as impossible to reach as the President of the United States. Of course, the President was actually a real person.

Barbosa's private investigator in the Caymans hadn't turned up much yet. Bower Research possessed no physical premises. The other companies with whom the mysterious company did business didn't seem to have physical locations, either. He knew a money laundering scheme when he saw one. An idiot would know a money laundering scheme like this when he saw one. The companies were dummies through which Nico Creed was laundering his illegal money. Barbosa only needed to prove it. He sighed.

There was power in money, though. If he greased the right palms, someone might start talking some sense.

Barbosa rubbed his eyes. He tucked the invoices and the reports from his private investigator into his briefcase. "Balthazar."

He started. D.A. Rutherford looked just as surprised to see Barbosa there in the cube farm outside his office. "Hello, Ryan," he replied calmly.

"Are you still here?"

"It would appear so, sir. I was just finishing up some paperwork."

Rutherford looked uneasy. He passed a chubby hand across his moist forehead. "It's good you're here, Balthazar. I wanted to speak to you about something."

Balthazar raised his eyebrows and stood to join the D.A. in his office. "Sure, boss. What's up?"

Rutherford carefully closed the frosted glass door intricately engraved with his name, though there was no one else in the office to overhear them. Rutherford lowered himself into his chair with a sigh. His expression was amiable, as though he were preparing to deliver some fatherly advice. "I heard you've been sniffing around the Creeds."

"Sniffing around, sir? I prefer to think of it as investigating certain financial discrepancies in their book keeping practices."

"Discrepancies you discovered or dug up?"

"Does it make very much difference?"

Rutherford peered at him in silence. For a moment, his eyes were as transparent as the thin, pink skin of his chubby cheeks. He lived well. He liked power and designer suits. He wasn't going to let them go. "Look, Balthazar, I know you're new to the office and you want to make your mark, but might I suggest an alternative method of doing so?"

"Alternative method, sir? I'm not sure what you mean."

Rutherford frowned. "What I mean is, it might be in your very best interest as a member of this office and this city to remember who's running things."

"Lex and Nico Creed, you mean."

"I said no such thing. I am merely suggesting that you focus on real cases, rather than staining the reputation of someone who has put his life and soul into making this city the great place it is today."

"Regardless of the reputation of the alleged perpetrator, I am sure you wouldn't wish for justice to be ignored, would you, Ryan? You wouldn't want the people of our good city to think that you might ignore the law when it comes to certain individuals?"

The D.A. stiffened. His eyes flashed angrily. His cheeks flushed a ruddy scarlet. "Now, you want to be careful, Balthazar. This is still my office, and you are just an ADA. Keep in mind who runs things around here."

Balthazar smiled, unabashed. He inclined his head politely. "And I am sure you will keep the law and justice in mind, as I have always known you to do. Well." He rose abruptly. "I'd better get home. So should you. It's late. See you in the morning."

The door closed behind Barbosa. Rutherford picked up his phone and dialed hastily.

* * *

"What is it, Ryan?" Nico demanded irritably. He pushed the papers on his desk aside. He leaned back in his tall-backed leather chair with a sigh.

"I spoke to Barbosa this evening regarding his ill-advised investigation."

"And?"

There was a pause. "I don't think he's going to back off, Nico. He's got a bee in his bonnet over you, and he means to see it to the end."

Nico's voice was perfectly calm. "I understand, Ryan. You have done your best. Don't trouble yourself over it anymore."

"What are you going to do, Nico?"

"Nothing, of course. You know as well as I that I have nothing to worry about. There's nothing he'll be able to pin on me. I have done nothing wrong." He smiled. "Just go on home, Ryan. Don't think about it anymore."

Rutherford exhaled heavily in the phone. "Yeah. All right, Nico. Whatever you say."

"Have a lovely evening, Ryan."

"Thanks. You, too."

Nico snapped his phone shut. He tossed it angrily down on the surface of his desk. He stormed out of his office. Lex ducked out from the empty guest bedroom across the hall and followed him silently. Nico didn't notice him. He threw open the door of his private sanctuary and slammed the door behind him.

Lex had forgotten all about the room. He'd almost forgotten it was there. He frowned, pressing his ear against the door. He heard Nico's voice speaking inside, but the words were muffled and strange. He couldn't make any of them out. Damnit, Nico, what are you up to?

Lex waited. For several long moments, nothing happened.

He nearly fell against the door when Nico pulled it open once more. Nico didn't look surprised to find his brother there in the hallway waiting for him. He smirked at him. "Looking for me, big brother?" he asked sardonically.

Lex followed him silently into the library. His expression was dark. "What's going on, Nico?"

"Whatever do you mean?" Nico's pale marble cheeks were slightly pink. He looked more cheerful than Lex had seen him in some time.

The more innocent he behaved, the less Lex trusted him. "Has something happened?"

"I think, big brother, that there is absolutely nothing more we need to worry about. It is back to business as usual." He swallowed the amber liquid in his glass in one gulp. He grinned at Lex's suspicious expression. He strode out of the room without another word.

He left a distinct sense of foreboding behind him.

CHAPTER 7

There was a commotion outside his office door. Lex rose from the enormous mahogany desk. He scowled irritably, throwing open the door to peer out at his assistant in the vestibule outside. She looked harassed as she tried to stop the man attempting to enter the office. "You cannot go in there, sir! Mr. Creed is with a very important client!"

Balthazar Barbosa was impervious to her protestations.

"What is going on, Marisa?" Lex snapped.

She spun to him with large, anxious, amber-colored eyes. "It's your brother, sir. This man insists on interrupting his meeting with Mr. Riccone."

Lex lifted a hand to send her off. "It's all right, Marisa. Go back to your desk. Hold all our calls." He strode forward to offer his hand to Barbosa, who stood grinning in the lavish vestibule. "What can I do for you, Mr. Barbosa?"

"I have a few questions for your brother regarding Bower Research."

There was no change in Lex's face. "I'm afraid I don't know what you're talking about."

Barbosa raised his eyebrows. "No. You really don't, do you? Good for you." He side-stepped Lex and moved forward toward the room labeled Conference. Inside, Nico strode confidently around the room, talking animatedly to their client.

Lex blocked his path. He could be a dangerous man when he needed to be. "Hold on. You can't just walk into our office and harass us, Mr. Barbosa."

Barbosa paused. "I assure you, Mr. Creed, harassment is not my intention. There are several issues about which I must speak to your brother. You wouldn't obstruct an investigation, would you? It certainly wouldn't look good to the press."

"The press isn't my concern. Nevertheless, I am willing to cooperate with your investigation. Mr. Riccone is a very important client, and I do ask that you refrain from interrupting Nico's presentation. It is a very lucrative account for Creed Corporation. I am sure Ryan would be displeased to learn that one of his assistants went rogue and jeopardized it just to ask a few questions about a corporation of which we've never heard."

Barbosa smiled contentedly. "I don't mind waiting a little while, as you please."

Lex inclined his head graciously. "May I offer you some coffee?"

"Thank you."

"Marisa? Can you bring Mr. Barbosa and me some coffee, please?"

The frazzled secretary jumped up immediately. Barbosa seemed perfectly at ease as they awaited her return. "Cream and sugar?" she asked breathlessly.

Barbosa shook his head. "I prefer mine black. Just like you, eh, Mr. Creed?"

Lex nodded absently. He barely tasted the coffee. He glanced towards the conference room. He could hear Nico and Riccone laughing together heartily. Lex looked back at Barbosa. "Would you care to step into my office?"

"Of course."

Lex's office was huge. He might have fit the entire District Attorney's cube farm inside. The room was lined with handsome bookshelves and rich furnishings. Balthazar lowered himself comfortably in one of the thick, smooth leather wing-backed chairs in front of Lex's desk. "Can you tell me a little about this corporation you intend to ask Nico about?" Lex asked, sitting across from Barbosa in an elaborate leather executive chair. It might have been more at home in a monarch's throne room. The office itself might have been a throne room.

"I was hoping to learn more from your brother."

"But you must have some information, if you have come so far as to question Nico about it in the middle of a work day."

Barbosa studied him a moment. "Well, I know they are one of Creed Corp's clients."

"Are they?"

"Do you not know all of your clients?"

"I'm afraid I don't. We offer many services to many companies all over the world. We have account executives to deal with them, and I can't possibly know who they all are."

"This one seems to be a large source of the company's revenue, and yet the CEO is not aware of them?"

Lex frowned. "I confess I am a very busy man. Can you tell me a little about them?"

"They're based in the Cayman Islands. They seem to order a large quantity of specialized encryption software and security services."

"Many of our clients do."

"Yes, but this one pays about ten times as much as the average client."

"Some clients require more specific service. We do customize these services to suit their needs."

"I see you have an answer for everything."

"I know my business."

"Do you really?"

Lex's blue eyes narrowed. "What exactly are you implying here, Mr. Barbosa?"

"It is not what I am implying, Mr. Creed. It is what the numbers imply."

"And what is that?"

"That Bower Research is a dummy corporation."

"For what purpose?"

"For Nico to launder illegal income."

Lex scowled deeply. Barbosa did not quell under his dangerous gaze. "And what proof do you have that Nico is connected to this corporation?"

Barbosa smiled calmly. "I am sure it will all be cleared up once I've spoken to Nico."

"So what you mean is, you don't have any."

"I did not say anything of the kind."

"Look, Mr. Barbosa, if you have some proof Nico is involved in a money laundering scheme, I assume you would have presented it to the D.A. by now. Are you certain you want to continue along this course of action?"

He inclined his head. "I assure you, Mr. Creed, I know exactly what I am doing."

Through the door, they heard Nico's boisterous laugh. Lex glanced at Barbosa and stood to greet his client. Mr. Riccone was a short, thin man with dark, beady eyes. His suit was black pinstripe, lavish and expensive. Diamonds glittered on his thin fingers.

When he saw Lex, his narrow mouth stretched into a grin. "Ah, Lex! There you are."

Lex inclined his head to him. "Mr. Riccone. I assume the meeting went well."

Riccone clapped him on the shoulder. "Just great. We've come to a very profitable arrangement for both our companies this afternoon. You brother was just telling me about a great gentlemen's club in the Art District. Care to join us for a little celebration?"

"I am pleased to hear things went well. But no, I'm afraid I have other plans this evening. I do hope you'll enjoy yourselves without me."

Riccone laughed heartily. "Always a stick in the mud, but I like the way you do business." He nodded to the brothers cheerfully. "See you later, Nico. Lex."

When he'd gone, Nico turned to Barbosa, who stood silently in the doorway to Lex's office, watching the exchange with interest. Nico's expression changed so quickly, it was as though he'd transformed into a different person. He stared coldly at Barbosa. His jaw was rigid. "Nico, Mr. Barbosa has some questions to ask you about one of our clients. Bower Research."

Nico's expression didn't change. His eyes were empty. "Does he. And he considered the middle of a business day an appropriate time to ask them, rather than simply asking me while I was already at his office?"

Barbosa smiled. "Mr. Creed, I'm sure we can clear everything up if you'd just be willing to give me a little of your time."

"I don't have any time. I am extremely busy, as you can see."

"Nico, I think you should answer his questions," Lex said in a low voice. "We wouldn't want to appear uncooperative, would we?"

"No. Of course not, Lex. I have nothing to hide." Nico gestured. "Why don't you step into my office, Mr. Barbosa?"

He smiled. "Happily."

* * *

When he emerged an hour later from Nico's office, Barbosa did not appear as cheerful as when he'd entered. There was a slightly smug quirk to his thick mouth. Perhaps he'd meant only to shake Nico up. If it worked, Lex couldn't tell. His brother's face was completely blank when Lex entered his office.

"What the hell was that all about?" Lex growled.

Nico lifted a shoulder negligently. "I have no idea."

"Money laundering, Nico?" Lex pushed his hands through his pale hair. He paced in front of Nico's desk in agitation. "Is this something he can pin on you?"

Nico's gaze was on the door Barbosa had lately exited. His eyes narrowed in preoccupation.

"Nico!"

He scowled. "What?"

"Did you do this? Is Bower Research a dummy corporation to launder dirty money?"

"What a ridiculous question, Lex. Of course it isn't. They're merely a client with a particular need for delicacy."

"Are you sure about that?"

"Just what exactly are you accusing me of?"

"I just don't want to see this family's name dragged through the mud because you got careless!"

"Of course." Nico's tone was disdainful. "It's all you care about, isn't it? The family name. If I wasn't carrying it the same as you, would you give a damn what happened to me?"

"Dirty money, Nico? Don't you have enough?"

Nico scoffed. "There is no such thing as enough, Lex."

"Do I want to know where it's coming from?"

"I don't know why you even bother to ask."

"If you've done something we need to clean up, I need to know about it."

"There is nothing about which you need to know."

Lex scowled. "Fine. But if this charge sticks to you, I won't bail you out this time."

Nico rolled his eyes. "Of course you will. That's what you do. Big Brother Lex, cleaning up all our little indiscretions. Mom's DUI, Grace's shoplifting. There's nothing you like better than saving our asses and lording it over our heads like the sanctimonious patriarch."

"You're out of line, Nico. I have done nothing but try to protect you and our family."

"Right. Well, you just keep on doing that. Let me worry about myself."

"Nico..."

"I am sure you know your way out."

* * *

Lex paced rapidly between the bookshelves in the Creed library. He heard his mother enter. He didn't pause. "What is going on, Lex?" she demanded..

He glanced at her. She wasn't wearing any makeup this evening. She looked old and strained. She held a glass full of amber liquid. "Nothing, Mother. Everything is fine."

"Don't patronize me. I am not a child, and I am not an idiot. The entire city is gossiping about an ADA visiting the office to ask about a dummy corporation in the Cayman Islands."

"Mother, there is no dummy corporation."

She lifted her eyebrows sardonically. "Are you sure about that?"

He scowled. "I don't know what's going on, Mom. Nico won't talk to me. It's like we're enemies, not brothers."

"Alexander, you have to get your brother out of this."

"I know, Mom! I am doing what I can, but it's not enough if he won't let me in."

Peyton sighed. "Your brother is a man after your father's heart. You're different. You were always different. But your father would not have been happy to see his second son go down like this."

"He won't go down. You know that. We have enough pull in the system to get him off."

"It doesn't matter!" she hissed. "Our family name has never been besmirched, and I don't intend to see it happen in my children's generation."

"What, exactly, do you want me to do, Mother?"

"I want you to fix it. I want you to find out what Nico is up to and stop him."

"How do you expect me to stop him?"

She waved her hand dismissively. "I'm sure you'll find a way. You have always been the cleverest of all my children. And you have always been the best."

He sighed. His mother was right. If anyone was going to stop Nico, it would not be an upstart Assistant District Attorney with more impudence than sense. Lex spun out of the room abruptly. He strode up the stairs. He paused in front of the unobtrusive door behind which he'd seen Nico disappear.

Nico was chanting again.

If he'd intended to use his trances against the new ADA, they hadn't worked. Whatever he was doing tonight, it was worse. When Lex touched the door, he recoiled. It had shocked him. It was hot and charged with energy. He took a deep breath. There was something going on in Spectra City. It probably originated directly behind that scorching door.

Lex didn't close his eyes. He felt a brief burst of energy in his belly. Then he felt nothing. As he chanted, the air around him shimmered. His eyes rolled back until they were pure, glowing white. He saw nothing. In moments, the trance stopped. He blinked. He wasn't at home.

It was a dark night, but it wasn't raining. He was in an alley in one of the dangerous poor districts of Spectra City. He panicked. He dove into the shadows. His heart raced. It would not do for a Creed to be seen wandering around the poor districts. It would be worse if he was seen in the throes of a trance.

But there was no one about. The air was silent and still and ominous. Even if the official police force did not acknowledge the creature attacks, the denizens of these seedy, neglected districts knew there was something wrong. They knew not to be out on the streets at night.

He hadn't meant to travel. He hadn't realized he could. When he'd been a child and experienced his first trance, he had practiced transporting himself around the house. He and Nico had played games, moving themselves from one part of the Manor to another. Their father had always encouraged them to practice their chanting. Unlike other children whose first trance at the onset of puberty came as a complete shock and wreaked havoc upon their families, the Creeds had always known what they would become.

Since Caleb had passed, Lex hadn't practiced at all. He rarely used his powers. It was safer that way, in a city like Spectra where being a chanter was the same as being a dangerous lunatic. He didn't have any idea how he'd ended up in a dark alley in the darkest part of the night. He shouldn't have been able to do it.

He'd only meant to discover what Nico was doing behind that door. In seconds, he knew.

A low, droning hum echoed off the brick walls around him. He peered out from the shadows. They were coming. The creatures. He hadn't really expected them to be real, not the way they'd been described in the reports. He hadn't wanted them to be. They were. The strange, thin creatures glided inches above the ground. Black hoods covered their faces. He knew what he would see underneath. They would be grey and mottled and twisted.

There were half a dozen of them. They did not pause or seem to react at all to their surroundings. They were focused and driven. Lex didn't know what they were after. They hadn't found it yet. He followed them. They drifted quickly through the alley. No one peered out their windows or ran out of their houses to see them. They knew not to.

The creatures hummed as they moved. The sound was more terrifying for being so toneless and insensible. In the alley ahead, amongst a pile of rubbish, something moved. The creatures reacted as though an internal switched had been flipped. They moved as one toward the scruffy, filthy vagrant, who was so startled to see them, he tumbled backwards into the garbage.

The creatures converged upon him. The strange, droning hum intensified. He disappeared between them. He shrieked. Lex's blood chilled. He rushed forward, toward them, unsure how to save the man but sure he must. He threw out his arms. He shouted. He chanted.

Nothing happened. The creatures did not even seem to notice he was there at all. He tried to grip one of the creature's shoulders. There was nothing there. No. It was there, but he couldn't touch or grip it. He felt hot, thick air in the space where the creature appeared to be, as though he were moving his hand through a hot, sultry cloud. They weren't real. They were only wraiths. They could still hurt people.

Then there were more people in the street. They weren't vagrants or drunks stumbling home from a night of drinking. There were three of them. They were chanters. He didn't know any of them. They surrounded the creatures. Their eyes were white and glowing. Their lips moved rapidly. Lex couldn't hear them. He wouldn't have understood them if he could.

A short, wiry man in a long black coat raised his hand toward the creatures. Suddenly, one of the creatures shrieked as terribly as the unfortunate vagrant. He disappeared in a puff of shimmering air.

The creatures turned as one. They moved toward the wiry chanter. Lex shouted to him, to warn him of the creatures. The chanter could not hear him. He could not see the creatures. His trance made him insensible to his surroundings. The creatures caught him up between them.

They spun away as quickly as they had appeared. Lex could not hear the chanter screaming between them anymore. They glided away. Lex chased them. The other chanters hadn't broken from their trances. They didn't know the creatures were gone. They didn't know one of them had been taken.

The creatures were gone.

Lex ran up and down the alley. There was nothing. He cursed. He doubted he could find a cab out here so late at night. Even if he did, it was probably best no one saw him here. He'd done it once tonight. He might be able to do it again.

When he stopped chanting, he was in front of Nico's door again.

There wasn't any sound this time. There was no chanting, no humming, no shrieks from the abducted chanter. There were no wraiths. There was, though, something more serious going on in his house than money laundering.

A sharp, searing pain lanced through his skull. He clutched his head, gasping. He fell to his knees. Black dots exploded in his line of sight. Behind the door, there was soft, muffled thump. He surged to his feet. The pain nearly brought him back down again. He ignored it. He needed only to make it up the stairs to his bedroom.

He didn't make it to the bed. He collapsed on the floor and the black dots became his whole world.

CHAPTER 8

It was mid-morning before Lex awoke. His face pressed into the soft, plush cream carpet of his bedchamber. He wore the same suit he'd been wearing when he'd moved from one side of Spectra City to the other in the blink of an eye. His head still ached. He groaned. He pushed himself to his feet. He lurched for the bathroom. He vomited until his head pounded and his throat felt as dry as sandpaper.

When he stepped out of the shower, he checked his phone. There were no messages. He frowned. His eyes were still shadowed as he knotted his tie. He considered phoning the office. His head throbbed. He couldn't remember where he was supposed to be this morning. It must not have been important. His secretary phoned him if he wasn't five minutes early into the office.

Peyton met him on the stairs. "I called your secretary," she told him. "I told her you were ill this morning."

Lex blinked at her. There was something different about her this morning. He didn't know what it was. There was something in her eyes. She wasn't holding a drink. "Mom?"

"Nico's gone on to the office. He's in meetings all day. Tully's in the kitchen with his wife. It's his morning off."

Lex's brow furrowed in confusion.

Her voice was sharp. "Lex. There isn't much time."

He opened his mouth to respond. She spun away from him before he could. He watched her descend the stairs. He understood.

The door was locked. He had expected it to be locked. Whatever Nico was doing in that room, he wanted to keep it to himself. Lex took a deep breath. His head still hurt. There wasn't much time. He chanted. The air shimmered. The trance didn't last. The pain did.

The lock clicked. Lex tried to handle again. It swung open easy. He hadn't expected it to work. He stepped inside the room. It wasn't, ostensibly, the lair of an evil super villain. Lex wasn't sure Nico was, in fact, an evil super villain. The room was nothing more than a large study. It had never been anything more than a room in which Nico had stored his things. Lex had almost forgotten it.

When they were children, Nico had always been inside, working away at whatever hobby he'd picked up that week. He'd performed chemistry experiments that had resulted in various explosions and hideous stains on the walls, ceilings and carpets. He used to play music in here. Lex used to listen outside the door as Nico banged away on various the instruments their father had bought for him. He'd been particularly gifted with the violin. He hadn't kept up with it.

It was now a sort of monument to his childhood. Inside were still the remnants of his youthful interests. In one corner, neat stacks of books and chemistry sets sat upon a small, wooden table. Propped against the wall were several instruments which seemed not to have been touched in years. In the center of the room was a large, beaten wood worktable.

Nico's current interests were different. There were old, dog-eared books upon the table that looked as though the pages would crumple if they were handled too indelicately. Crystals littered the surface in small, neat piles. They seemed to have been separated for different purposes. Lex didn't know what they were. A silver wand with a crystal on either end lay upon a silk cloth in the center of the table as if in a place of honor.

Lex touched it. It was cool and smooth to the touch. Something about it caused him to recoil. It was as though the metal had moved under his fingers. As though something were inside it. There were no creatures. There were no chanters. There was nothing to indicate that Nico was performing any dark, dangerous magic in here. He might only have been practicing alchemy or charms.

A small stack of dirty dishes sat upon a chair pushed up against the wall. Lex stared at it a moment in surprise. Nico was very neat. A stack of dirty dishes was unheard of in his ordered life. Perhaps he was doing something important here, if he was taking meals in his workroom and forgetting to clean up after himself. Or perhaps his man merely had yet to make it to the room to tidy it up. Nico was neat. He did not lift a finger to clean up around himself. He expected that would be done for him.

Lex paused. He spun around the room. There was something off about it. It didn't seem right. He'd been in there before, once or twice, when he and Nico had been children and still played together. Something about the room had changed. It felt strange, but Lex had felt Nico's magic often enough to recognize its delicate flavor in the atmosphere. That wasn't it. Had it always been this small? He seemed to remember such a large space. Perhaps it had seemed larger when he was smaller. He supposed it had been so many years since he'd been inside, he'd never seen it as a grown man.

There was a noise. Something thumped softly against a wall in another room. His heart leapt. He listened. Sharp, smart footsteps clicked on the polished marble floor below. They were moving closer. Tully was coming.

Lex did not waste time. He tripped over a chair in his haste. He righted it quickly. He rushed out the door. He had forgotten to lock it behind him. Tully's footsteps echoed in the magnificent corridors one flight below. Lex turned back to spin the lock on the doorknob. He pulled it closed.

He heard Tully mount the stairs. He was in the library before the servant reached the door. Lex leaned against the heavy double doors, panting. He hadn't learned much. It was enough. Nico was doing something he probably ought not to be.

Lex only needed more time to figure out what it was. He wasn't sure he had it.

* * *

A low, sensual, bluesy melody drifted from a jukebox in the corner. The Sanctuary Bar was dark and smoky. No one spoke much at the Sanctuary. There was no excited chattering or whoops of laughter from the small groups gathered in tall, secluded booths along the dark walls beneath half-moon sconces that glowed as red as blood. At the bar, Cerys peered meditatively into her empty glass.

The bartender moved towards her slowly. He didn't seem to want to go near her. She looked up. He met her eyes and sighed. "Get you another drink?"

Cerys nodded. She pushed her glass across the bar at him. He placed another in front of her. She caught his wrist. He looked down at it, startled. "Do you know anyone named Tamsin?"

He blinked. He snatched his arm back. He eyed her cagily. "Why do you want to know about her?"

"You know her."

He frowned. For a moment, she was sure he was going to flee.

"I think she might know my brother Cedric," Cerys told him quickly.

The bartender sighed deeply. "You should stay away from people like Tamsin. She's trouble. She brings trouble on everyone around her."

"Like my brother?"

"I don't know anything about that. I don't know about him." He leaned forward. His expression was curiously compassionate. "It's best to stay away from that girl. Don't ask so many questions."

Cerys scowled. "I don't know what you're so scared of, but I need to know who she is. I need to find her. I won't mention you at all if that's what you're worried about." He looked away. Cerys slapped her hand abruptly on the bar. He jumped. "I know you know her. You obviously know enough to frighten you."

He frowned. "Yeah. I know her. You do, too."

"What?"

"You met her the other night when you were in here asking questions."

"The blonde?"

"Yeah. The blonde with the big mouth."

Cerys considered. "Have you seen her tonight?"

He shook his head. "No. Not tonight. Not for a couple nights." He glanced towards the door. When he looked back at her, he looked uneasy. "People are disappearing."

"You think she might have something to do with it?"

He blinked in complete astonishment. "Tamsin? No. I think...I think she's trying to stop it."

"She's a chanter."

"I don't know anything about chanters." His tone was harsh. "Chanters don't talk about being chanters. It's not safe. Do you know what they do to chanters around here?"

"Tell me."

His eyes darted anxiously around the bar. "They don't like them."

"Who doesn't?"

"The city folk. They're afraid of them."

"But there are some that do good."

"Yeah, well, not everyone sees it that way. For every good deed a chanter does, there are dozens of bad ones, and that's all the people remember. People might not say or do anything to them, but they are disappearing, and there isn't much to wonder about why."

Cerys chewed her lip pensively. "You think that's what happened to my brother?"

"If he was a chanter, don't go around telling people about it. Not unless you want to go the same way."

She nodded. "I understand. Thanks." She slapped a banknote on the bar. She paused. "You know anywhere else Tamsin hangs out?"

He nodded eagerly. She suspected he was anxious for her to go. He would probably be happy never to see her again. If she found Tamsin, he wouldn't. "Yeah. She goes over to the Phantasm Bar every now and again, I hear."

"Thanks."

"I didn't say anything."

Cerys smirked. "No. You were totally unhelpful. I don't know why I bothered."

The Phantasm Bar was a block away from the Sanctuary along the dark alley of the infamously sordid Arts District. The only lights came from the faintly buzzing neon signs in windows and over the entrances to the bars and nightclubs along this main strip. Even the vagrants were in hiding tonight. No one stepped out of the shadows to stop her. If they did, they would regret it.

Tamsin wasn't inside the Phantasm Bar when Cerys found it moments later. There were few people inside the dark, morose, smoky bar. Even the most determined drunks and loneliest of the lost souls preferred to drink alone, safe in their own homes, on a night like this. They might not even be safe there. A sense of desperate dread hung over Spectra City. In this place, it was the strongest.

Anyone out on the streets tonight, Cerys decided, was looking for a fight. She was.

She moved towards the bartender. He was a tall, reedy man. There was no hair on his head. His dark eyes were shadowed and anxious. He glanced cagily around the bar. He paced to the window and peered out. Cerys strode towards him. He knew something. If he didn't, he knew enough to be afraid.

He looked at her warily when she reached him. She smiled. He did not return it. "Drink?" he asked shortly.

She opened her mouth. Her reply was drowned by a loud, explosive noise outside. It was too loud to be a car backfiring. It was too expansive to be a gunshot. It echoed through the alley, off the crumbling brick walls and rattling fire escapes. The bartender ducked behind the bar. A frightened murmur filled the bar like the buzzing of bees.

"Chanters."

"The creatures."

"Fire."

Cerys turned away from the bar. She sprinted towards the door.

The alley was alight when she stepped outside. Fire streaked along the street, as though someone had trailed gasoline from one end to the other and dropped a match. Screams rent the former silence of the night. There was a gang of hooded men moving towards the unfortunate people who emerged from the taverns and bars to see what was happening.

But they weren't men, the hooded creatures. They were floating inches above the ground. It was them. The wraiths. They were real. She'd always known they were real. Cerys raced towards them. One of the wraiths caught up a young man with gnarled, skeletal grey hands. It lifted him high up into the air. The young man struggled. The creature's hood fell back.

It had no hair at all on its blotchy grey head. Its features were twisted and hooked. It opened its mouth so wide, it might have unhinged its jaw. The young man keened. The creature holding him suddenly disappeared in a puff of acrid grey smoke. The young man dropped to the hard asphalt. He vaulted to his feet and raced away.

Cerys snapped her head around. There were others now in the alley with her. They were chanting. Cerys ran towards them, but the creatures cut her off from them. The chanters struck down two more of the creatures. A block away, Cerys caught sight of the petite blonde woman for whom she was searching. She was fighting beside the others.

"Tamsin."

The creatures were humming. It was a loud, intense drone that filled the air and drowned out the shouts of the chanters and the screams of the victims. The creatures moved towards Tamsin. Cerys was faster.

"Tamsin, look out!" she shouted as the creatures neared her.

The blonde woman blinked several times, drawing out of her trance. She saw the wraiths moving towards her. Her eyes widened. She chanted so quickly, Cerys did not see her lips move. Tamsin disappeared. Cerys cursed.

Tamsin reappeared just as quickly on the other side of the creatures. They hadn't seemed to notice that she was gone. Perhaps they had no eyes. They paused, as if in confusion. The droning hum didn't stop. Cerys wasn't paying attention to them. She raced towards the blonde chanter. When she saw her, Tamsin turned and ran the other way.

"Tamsin! Wait!" Cerys shouted desperately. "I need your help! Please!"

Tamsin did not stop or turn back to her.

"I'm looking for my brother!" Cerys took a deep breath and lifted her hands. She tried one more time. "I'm a chanter!"

Tamsin paused. She half turned her head. Then she pitched forward. Cerys knew she was not going to stop.

Cerys threw back her head. The alley disappeared. Inside her, a familiar heat gathered in her belly. Her eyes rolled back. As her lips moved, the heat inside her intensified until it spread out through her whole body. For a moment, it felt as though she would explode. She didn't.

A wall of raging, blazing fire rose up in Tamsin's path. The blonde chanter reared back, spinning towards Cerys.

She wasn't there.

Cerys squeaked in surprise as an arm wrapped firmly around her waist and a hand clapped over her mouth. She struggled. Her assailant was much larger, much stronger than she. He spoke urgently in her ear as he dragged her backward, into the dark doorway of a tenement building. "Shh! Be quiet. Don't scream. Don't chant."

She spun around to face him. She went rigid with shock.

"If pull my hand away, will you be quiet?" Lex Creed asked in a low voice.

She glared at him.

"I'll explain everything. Just don't say anything! No chanting. They're here for chanters. If you chant, they will find you, and they will take you. Do you understand?"

She scowled. She nodded slowly. He took a step back from her. As soon as she was free, she opened her mouth to speak.

Lex held up his hand. "Don't scream. If you bring the chanters, the creatures will catch them."

She snapped her mouth shut. She watched him peer out into the alley. Fire still raged along the streets. The creatures moved around aimlessly. It was as if they were blind.

"What do you mean they're here for chanters?" Cerys hissed.

"It's what they're made for, I think."

The drone neared the doorway in which they stood. Lex glanced out of the doorway again. In a single, sudden move, he pressed her backwards into the wall, covering her with his body.

"Shh! They're coming."

She felt his breath stir the fine stray hairs on her forehead. "Let me go! We have to do something," she hissed.

"Be quiet!" His lips moved against her ear. "Just because they're only here for chanters doesn't mean they won't kill you to draw the others out."

"What about you?"

"They didn't come for me."

"How do you know?"

"They can't. They can't detect my magic."

"Then why don't you do something?"

He shook her head. "I can't."

"Why not?"

"The same reason they can't detect me, I think."

"Lex, what are you talking about?"

He leaned back. For a moment, he stared silently into her face. "We're part of the same thing."

She shook her head in confusion. "What does that mean?"

He didn't reply. He was peering out of the doorway into the alley. "They're gone."

She stepped forward to look. He held out an arm to stop her. She hissed at him. "You said they're gone."

"Wait."

He stepped out of the doorway abruptly. Before Cerys realized it, he was halfway down the alley. She sprinted after him. "Lex, wait!"

He spun to her. "Just stay off the streets," he growled. "Don't chant. Don't use magic. Not in Spectra. Get out while you can, Cerys."

"Wait—Lex!"

This time he did not pause. She started after him. A small, delicate hand caught her wrist from behind. Cerys jumped and spun around to face the blonde woman for whom she'd been searching all evening.

"Thank god I found you!" Tamsin gasped. "I thought the wraiths had taken you."

Cerys shook her head. "Someone saved me." She considered a moment. "You won't believe who it was."

Tamsin lifted her eyebrows. "Come on. We'll talk on the way."

"The way?" Cerys asked. She did not resist Tamsin as she led her towards the main thoroughfare.

"To HQ. There's someone there who will be very interested to meet you."

CHAPTER 9

There were no streetlights on the dark, narrow road. There weren't any street signs, either. Tamsin did not speak to Cerys as she steered the black sedan through a maze of old, abandoned and occasionally burnt out warehouses and dilapidated tenement buildings. Cerys wondered for a moment whether Tamsin intended to drop her amongst the crumbling old buildings and leave here there. She had taken Cedric this way. He was missing now. At least it might give Cerys a clue to where he'd gone.

Tamsin veered suddenly onto a narrow side street. It twisted away from the industrial district, along a winding drive. Large, thick trees overhung the drive, forming a canopy that blocked out the moonlight. Cerys glanced at Tamsin. The blonde woman did not look back at her. The trees broke. Cerys could see a tall, dark house looming in the distance.

As they neared it, it grew taller and taller. It was several stories high, built up rather than out. It was surrounded on all sides by a black iron fence. The fence had sharp, narrow points on the posts. Cerys could make out two monstrous gargoyles on the peaked roof, hanging over the edge to leer down at approaching visitors.

No lights burned in any of the windows. It looked utterly abandoned, dismal and creepy. Tamsin stopped the car. Without speaking to Cerys, she hopped out. There was a tiny, black box protruding from a low bush against the fence. Tamsin punched several numbers on the keys. The gate slid open swiftly without making a sound.

Tamsin glanced at Cerys when she got back into the car. Cerys didn't ask where they were. She already knew. The snaking path towards the house was overgrown with trees, bushes and verdant wildflowers. "This place needs a gardener," Cerys muttered.

Tamsin snorted. "You should see the back of the house. The courtyard is amazing."

Cerys wasn't sure if amazing in this case meant a vast, impenetrable wilderness or that there was, in fact, someone who cared for this old, gothic mansion. It might have been a magnificent house once. It seemed desolate now, as though a great tragedy had occurred to drive its once proud occupants to terrible, listless madness. Someone, Cerys thought, ought to burn the whole place down and start over somewhere else. Perhaps somewhere sunny.

Tamsin pulled around the circular driveway to the front of the house. There were a few cars already parked there, around the stone fountain in the center. It was green with moss. It looked as though it hadn't spouted water in several decades. Cerys looked up. She could not see the roof of the house from the front step. A gargoyle peered back at her past a balcony wrapping around the third floor of the house. She shivered slightly.

Tamsin did not knock on the front door. She pressed the door buzzer for a long moment. Inside the house, a melody echoed through the halls. No one came. Tamsin didn't seem to mind. She pushed the door open. She glanced at Cerys. Her dark eyes twinkled slightly.

Cerys blinked in shock. The vestibule into which they stepped was brightly lit by hanging crystal chandeliers. It opened into a grand hall with staircases winding up several flights of stairs on either side. Whatever the owners of the house may have neglected on the outside, they had spared nothing on the lavishness of the interior.

A tall, dark haired man pushed open the heavy oak double doors directly in front of them, beyond which appeared to be a magnificent collection of bookshelves and plush, comfortable arm chairs. His dark eyes were anxious.

Cerys stared at him in utter astonishment. When he caught sight of her, his eyes flashed. There was something so alight within them, they seemed to smolder despite the arctic expression on his even features. He looked at Tamsin. Cerys watched him.

"Zar, this is Cerys."

"I've seen her before. I know who she is."

"Balthazar Barbosa?" Cerys said incredulously. "You're Zar? You're the leader of Chant?"

He scowled deeply. "I don't know how you know about that. Tamsin, why did you bring a reporter into my house?"

"I'm not a reporter. I'm a photographer."

"That is slightly worse."

Tamsin was unrepentant. She lifted her chin. "She's a chanter."

This did not seem to move Barbosa in the least. He scowl remained fixed.

"Her name is Cerys Knight," Tamsin said emphatically.

Barbosa blinked. "Knight?"

"She's Cedric sister, dummy."

His expression changed instantly. He looked at Cerys in surprise. "Is she?"

"I came to Spectra to find my brother. In his letters he told me he'd joined up with Chant. He mentioned your names." Cerys lifted a shoulder. "Obviously, not your real ones or I would have found you sooner."

"Yes. Yes, of course. Cedric." He sighed deeply. He looked troubled.

"You know where he is."

"We...suspect."

"What does that mean? Was he taken by those creatures we saw tonight?"

Barbosa gestured towards the winding staircase on his left. "Come upstairs. We have a lot to discuss."

Tamsin grinned as though she were highly enjoying the scene. "You won't believe what she has to say, either." Barbosa paused. He glanced back at Tamsin. "Lex Creed was in the Art District tonight. In the alley."

Barbosa lifted his eyebrows keenly. "Doing what?"

"Helping, I think."

"The creatures?"

"No. Us."

"He stopped me from chanting," Cerys put in. "He said it attracts them."

"Yes, we had already figured that out," Barbosa replied.

"But what is their purpose?"

"We don't know. They are collecting chanters for something."

"And my brother was one of the chanters?"

Barbosa sighed again. "Come."

They did not speak as they climbed the stairs. Cerys was eager to receive the answers for which she'd come. Still, she remained silent. When they reached the fourth floor, Barbosa paused in front of another set of double doors. He pushed them open. Tamsin flitted into the room ahead of him. He did not call her back.

"Cerys, check this out," Tamsin said.

The room was a small, modest library, much smaller than the one she had glimpsed downstairs. The walls were piled to the ceiling with bookshelves. A few chairs were scattered around the room. A small table with half-empty bottles of liquor sat in the center of the chairs. There were no windows.

Tamsin paused in front of a bookshelf. She yanked one of the books forward. It did not fall from the shelf. Instead, the entire shelf seemed to move forward and slide sideways, in front of the shelf beside it. Cerys moved forward in interest.

Behind the hidden panel in the wall was a huge room. It hummed. Enormous glass screens hung suspended from the ceilings in a large, shimmering, transparent octagon. Some of the screens were blank, awaiting instructions from the glass panels beneath, upon which a man with short, spiky black hair was furiously typing. Streams of incomprehensible data moved rapidly across the others, as though the pale, gaunt, black-haired man needed only to touch the panel to understand the computer's language. He rolled back and forth between them on a wheeled chair. He barely glanced up when they entered.

"X."

The man looked up. When he saw Cerys, he rolled backward in his chair, as though attempting to escape the stranger. "Who is she?"

"X, this is Cerys," Barbosa told him off-handedly. He moved inside to stand in the center of the room, spinning around to view the screens.

"She's Cedric's brother," Tamsin told him in a low voice. X nodded. His expression did not change.

Several small, red X's marked an aerial map of the city. There was one large, green X in one corner, larger than the others. It glowed as though it were a point of great significance. "What are those?" Cerys asked.

"Some of them are the areas in which the creatures were seen."

Cerys nodded. "What's this one? The green one up here, away from the others?"

"You don't seem very surprised by any of this," X told her disapprovingly. "This is probably the most state of the art computer system in the entire world. I built it myself. You should be more impressed."

She glanced at him. "I've read enough comic books. I know what this place is. Cedric came looking for Chant, and he found it. I know where I am. I know what you do here."

X spun away from her sullenly. Barbosa gestured them out of the lab into a small, glass enclosed conference room. He slid a bottle of scotch across the table towards Cerys. Her dark blue eyes were sharp. Barbosa sighed. "Your brother was one of the chanters who were taken."

She exhaled heavily. She had expected it. She had hoped she was wrong.

"He volunteered to use himself as bait."

Cerys shot to her feet. "And you let him?"

Barbosa sighed. "I had no choice. We had to discover where the creatures were coming from."

"And you learned?"

"Yes. We learned. Cedric was equipped with a tracking device the night he was taken. It gave us his location. It was the green 'X' you asked about on the map."

"What's there?"

Barbosa and Tamsin exchanged a meaningful glance. "Creed Manor."

Cerys closed her eyes. "So the Creeds are chanters, after all. The rumors are true."

"Yes. And they are more than that. They're villains."

Cerys passed a hand across her face. "So Cedric is in Creed Manor."

"Yes. Or he was, when the GPS blipped. It only lasted a moment and then it was gone. We haven't received any other signal. There's no telling where he is now."

"You can't just go in?" Cerys demanded. "He's in there!"

Barbosa sighed. "This operation isn't exactly legal, Cerys. Even if it was, we couldn't use a momentary blip on a GPS as evidence to storm the house."

She frowned. "What will happen to my brother if he isn't found?"

Barbosa exchanged another look with Tamsin.

"It's bad, isn't it? Will he die?"

"No. He won't die. At least, not right away."

Cerys sighed in relief. Barbosa's expression chilled her blood.

"It's almost as bad, Cerys," Tamsin murmured grimly.

Barbosa rose to his feet. "Come. There is more to see."

Cerys followed them further into the hidden laboratory. Past the conference room was a medical lab. Several beds had been set up on one side of the room while the rest was filled with a collection of various expensive-looking equipment, glass screens and a worktable upon which were spread microscopes and other testing equipment. Cerys didn't know what any of it was used for. Barbosa led her towards the beds.

She wasn't entirely sure she wanted to see.

The man upon the bed looked eerily deflated. He was as thin as a skeleton. There seemed to be no muscle or sinew in his body. His pale, wrinkled skin hung upon his bones as though his insides had been sucked out and only partially, hastily replaced. There were electrodes and wires coming off every inch of exposed flesh. He was breathing, barely. Each breath rattled like his last. Cerys stared at him in horror.

"This is Eddie," Tamsin told Cerys grimly. She laid a hand gently upon his delicate brow.

"He was one of the first taken by the wraiths," Barbosa explained. "A month later, he showed up at our door. He was raving and insensible. It was a wonder he made it to us. Something happened to him. We just don't know what. We've been keeping him under sedation while we study him and try to find a way to cure whatever it was that did this."

"Have you had any luck?"

"No. There's something strange in his brain activity." Barbosa paced to one of the glass screens. Upon it were two images. They were x-ray scans of two different human brains. "See here. That is a chanter brain." It was bright, brilliant and colorful. The colors swirled around constantly, as though it were in a state of rapid activity. The one beside it was still and grey. "The other is Eddie's now."

"He's alive," Tamsin put in. "He isn't exactly brain dead. There are things going on in there. But all the major activity is just...gone."

"Is it his power?" Cerys asked.

"We think so. X isn't a chanter. He has an extraordinary brain, but it isn't colorful like this. It's active and healthy, but it's not special, not in the way a chanter's is, anyway."

"So his power has been taken."

"It seems so."

"The Creeds are taking the chanters for their powers? But how are they

74

getting it out of them? How are they doing this to them? And why?"

Barbosa shook his head. "We don't know the answer to any of those questions. Not yet. We haven't been able to get close enough to them to find out."

Cerys spun away from Eddie to pace several feet away. "But why doesn't anyone notice? Why isn't anyone doing anything about it?"

"A lot goes on in Spectra City that no one really wants to talk or think about. The PD has stacked up the reports of the creatures, but no one seems to want to actually investigate them. The official line is it's just mass hysteria."

"That's ridiculous."

"Yes, well, it's not bad for us, really. It leaves us to investigate our way without any interference." He turned away from Eddie abruptly. "Tell me about Lex Creed. You said he helped you."

"Yes. Well, it seemed that way, anyway. I was about to chant. He stopped me. He said chanting attracts them. He said that's what they were there for; to take chanters."

"Did he attack the wraiths?"

"No. He couldn't. He said he couldn't, anyway. He said his power doesn't work on them. And theirs doesn't detect him. He said...they're part of what he is."

Tamsin and Barbosa peered at each other for a long time, as though they were communicating silently. "What was he doing there, if he couldn't do anything to stop them?"

"I don't think he was trying to stop the wraiths; I think he was trying to stop us being taken by them."

"Perhaps big brother isn't entirely on board with what Nico's up to," Tamsin murmured thoughtfully.

"Assuming it's Nico," Cerys remarked.

"Well, it's not likely to be Grace or Peyton. Neither one of them seems to put down the bottle long enough to have an original thought that doesn't include what they're wearing that night."

"Tamsin," Barbosa scolded mildly.

"I wouldn't underestimate any of them," Cerys said darkly. "I don't think any of them are what they appear. They didn't keep the truth about their family hidden this long without being very skilled at deception."

"We don't know for sure the girls are chanters," Barbosa added reflectively. "It doesn't necessarily run in the family. It just usually does. Sometimes it skips people."

"I don't really think it matters much which of them is involved."

Tamsin shook her head seriously. "It does matter. It matters a lot if Lex isn't."

They considered this. Cerys sighed. "Is this why you're investigating Nico?"

Barbosa blinked. "You know about that?"

"I'm in the media. And I hang out in a lot seedy bars. I know about everything."

Barbosa chuckled dryly. "Yeah. I'm working on getting something solid on him."

"How is that going to help us find Cedric and the others?"

"If I can get enough on him, it will be enough to execute a search warrant on the house and his other properties."

She frowned. "Can't we just go in?"

"I'm a chanter. I'm not a criminal. That's not what we do. Besides, I'm a DA. I can't go around breaking into people's houses. We have to stay above board."

"But we aren't all DA's. What about the rest of us?"

Barbosa looked at her skeptically. "You've been to Creed Manor. Do you think anyone can get in there uninvited?"

Cerys sighed. "No, I suppose you're right. What are you doing, then? What have you got on Nico?"

"We have someone in the Cayman Islands--one of us. He's investigating the Creed's accounts and corporations there. There's evidence that suggests Nico is involved in laundering dirty money through dummy corporations."

"Money laundering? Seriously? We've got wraiths running loose in the streets, kidnapping chanters, and you're trying to get him on money laundering? What about the dirty money? Where's it coming from?"

"Do you think if I knew that, I would be wasting my time on this? It's the best I can do right now! Al Capone was finally put away on tax evasion. You take what you can get. It will be enough to arrest him and execute a warrant. We just need it to get us into the house."

"How much time does Cedric have?"

"We don't know. I'm sorry. A few have returned, and you can see how that turned out. The rest are still missing. We just don't know. We have no idea what's happening to them right now."

Cerys spun away, taking a deep, hitching breath.

Barbosa touched her shoulder gently. "I am working on it, Cerys. I am doing everything I can. We'll find him."

"Will it be in time?"

"We have to believe it will or all this won't mean anything. Cedric gave himself to get something against the Creeds."

"It is just like him to do something so stupid!"

"He was a hero!" Tamsin said angrily.

Cerys glanced at her. "Yes. He always was." She looked at Barbosa. "So, that's your plan? Find a way to get him through the legal system so you can get inside the house?"

"Yes, so far that's the best we've got."

"It isn't any good."

"I know!" Barbosa growled. "We can't get him for the wraiths, even if we're sure it's Nico. Chanting isn't illegal; the courts don't acknowledge we even exist. And if it was illegal, a blip on a GPS isn't enough. We've got nothing to go on."

Tamsin perked up slightly. She looked at Cerys meaningfully. "There might be a way. A chink in Nico's armor."

Barbosa frowned. "Don't be cryptic, Tam."

"Well, big brother saved Cerys in that alley. He didn't try to stop me or any of the rest of us chanting. Maybe he likes her. It might be a way to get inside. Maybe he'll help us."

Barbosa turned to eye Cerys interestedly. She glanced away uncomfortably. "I don't know, Tam. I've seen Lex show up more than once to hush up one of his brother's mistakes." He spun suddenly, sweeping his hand across a small table beside Eddie. Metal tools and gadgets tinkled against the tile floor. "I just cannot get to his guy!"

Cerys strode forward. She laid a hand on his arm. "No one is untouchable. I won't accept that. There has to be a way. Lex was scared tonight. Whatever it was he's afraid of, I suspect he isn't involved in the wraith attacks. He wants to stop them. I will do anything to get my brother back, even if it means doing it through Lex."

Tamsin looked up at them thoughtfully. "There may be something else. We might not be able to get into the Creeds' place, but maybe we can get close enough."

"What are you talking about, Tam?" Barbosa demanded impatiently.

"The Mobleys."

"What about them?"

"Well, they live next door, don't they?"

"You want to break into the Mobley's place?"

"No. There are a lot of rumors about a blood feud between the Creeds and the Mobleys. It's been going on for decades."

Barbosa nodded slowly. "Yes. I have heard that. They're always polite when they're seen together in the city, but I have noticing something not quite right there. But how can that help us?"

"They are chanters, too. Maybe they've seen something. Maybe they know something about what's going on. They can't exactly come forward about it. But they might know more about this than we do. If nothing else, it would be helpful to have them on our side."

"How do you expect to get to them?"

Tamsin shrugged. "I don't know. I'm sure I can be subtle."

"You, subtle?"

"I'd like to hear how that conversation goes," Cerys put in. "Will you start with the bit about them being chanters or being in a feud with the Creeds? I suspect if either of those things is true, they aren't going around telling strangers about it."

"There are a lot of rumors around the city, Tam," Barbosa told her. "It could all be nonsense."

"Maybe so. But it's worth looking in to. Besides, I need something to do. I want to find Cedric and the others as much as you. I want to help."

Barbosa looked dubious. Cerys nodded. "I'll talk to Lex. Balthazar, you keep doing what you're doing. Tamsin can check out the Mobleys. If she can find out something from them or find a way to the Creeds through them, it's worth a shot."

Tamsin smirked. "I thought you were leading this operation, Zar?"

Barbosa scowled at Cerys. She lifted her chin, unabashed. Finally, he sighed. "I think, under the circumstances, Cerys has more stake in this than us." He held out his hand to her. "Welcome to Chant, Cerys."

Her grip was firm. She nodded shortly. "We don't have a lot of time. Cedric doesn't have a lot of time."

"I know, and we won't waste it. But there's nothing more you can do tonight." He laid an arm across her shoulders. "Come on. The others should be here soon. I'll introduce you."

CHAPTER 10

"Where are the others?" Cerys asked. Behind her, the hidden panel was open. X's computers hummed happily. He did not join her and Barbosa in the library.

"They went after the wraiths. Not all of them have made it back, but if what you and Tamsin said is true, they should be here. No one was taken tonight." Barbosa filled his glass. He offered her another drink. She nodded absently.

She tilted her head towards the computer lab. "What is he doing in there?"

Barbosa smiled. "X?"

"Yeah. What's his name?"

"Just X." She rolled her eyes. "He's just watching."

"Is that all he does?"

"I can hear you, you know," X said impassively.

"Yeah, that's all he does."

"All the time?"

"No, not all the time. He sleeps sometimes, mostly during the day." Barbosa smiled slightly. "There's not a lot of chanting going on during the day."

"Doesn't he ever leave the house?"

"No," X replied for himself.

"X is an agoraphobic. He prefers his computers to the outside world." As though he sensed her pity for the strange young man, he added, "He's happy this way. He has everything he could want."

"How did you meet him?"

"He hacked a government computer system. I caught him. I offered him a deal, and then I offered him a job."

"Ah."

"It's the closest I can get to being a superhero," X said quietly.

"A lot of boys seem to want that job."

Barbosa laughed. "Yeah, well, some of us are lucky enough to have it."

She eyed him. "Who are you?"

"Balthazar Barbosa. Assistant District Attorney by day, leader of Chant by night."

She rolled her eyes. "I know who you are. I mean, how did you become the leader of Chant?"

"Ah. Right. My parents died when I was very young, like yours. I don't remember them well. I was raised by a foster family. They were good to me, but they weren't chanters. When my abilities surfaced, I hid them from them."

Cerys nodded. "Cedric and I did the same. Our aunt and uncle were not chanters. We never knew if our parents were."

"I didn't have a brother or sister when I discovered my powers. I knew I had to hide what I was. I didn't tell anyone. The only people I could relate to were comic book characters."

She laughed. She cut off abruptly. Barbosa was serious.

He smiled. "It sounds silly, I know. It's the truth. They helped me find my path. It just seemed natural to use my powers to help people and to stop bad chanters from doing harm. It never occurred to me to do anything else. So, I went to law school, got my degree and came back home to Spectra City."

"To join the D.A.'s office."

He lifted a shoulder. "It is a little trite, but it seems like the most convenient job for someone who wants to fight crime, doesn't it?"

Cerys laughed. "I suppose I can see your point."

"No one remembered me or my family when I returned, but our family home was still here."

"It's lovely."

Now he laughed. "It doesn't look like much on the outside, I know. I prefer it that way. The house has been an eyesore for decades. No one comes near it. There are rumors it's haunted or cursed. It suits us all right. No one bothers us or pays us any attention. As a headquarters, it has everything we could want. X designed the systems. I designed the rest of it with the help of a very discreet contractor. We have a doctor who manages the infirmary."

"It's pretty impressive."

"It suits our purposes. After that, I used my job to discover chanters doing harm or good. I learned about the Creeds and the corruption in the government systems. X designed a system to track chanter activity within the city. He used me as a test subject until he found the right frequencies. If someone chants, he sees it on his screen."

She raised her eyebrows. "How?"

"One day you can ask him to explain it to you. If you can understand it, explain it to me, will you?"

She laughed.

"I started to follow the activity. I found chanters. Some of them were bad, and I fought them. Others were good and I brought them here. I discovered some of us in the police department and the courts. Some of them joined us. Others are too afraid to risk exposure, but they help when they can. There are a lot of us, Cerys. More than you could ever possibly imagine."

"Then why can't they do something to get the others back?"

"None of them have any more ability to do so than we do. None of them can get inside the house to search it. You must be patient, Cerys. I promised you I would do all I could."

Cerys nodded sullenly. She did not reply. The door swung open. Tamsin strode inside. She was accompanied by three women and a tall, burly blonde man in a rumpled black suit. Barbosa stood as they entered.

"Are you all right?"

A tall, slender woman with short, dark hair nodded. "Something was keeping the wraiths from capturing anyone."

Cerys lifted her eyebrows. "How do you know?"

The woman shook her head. "I don't know. It was like someone was protecting us. They were attracted to us, and then they just moved on as though they didn't notice us."

Tamsin looked at Cerys pointedly. "See. He was helping. He was protecting us."

"I don't understand. He said his power doesn't work on them."

"Not on them. Maybe on us. Maybe he was using it on us. Hiding us from them somehow."

Barbosa looked thoughtful. "If that's the case, we may have a way in, after all."

"What are you all talking about?" demanded an extremely pretty woman with long, pale hair tied back in a severe ponytail. She looked weary and weather-worn. She did not seem to appreciate the unexpected guest at all. "Who is this?"

"Ah. Yes. Of course. Sorry." Barbosa said. "This is Cerys Knight."

They all peered at her in interest. "Knight?" the first woman asked.

"I'm Cedric's sister."

"No kidding," the tall, blonde man said. He smiled and offered his hand. "Abel Dane. Detective, Spectra City PD. He told us about you. It's good to meet you at last, although I'm not keen on the circumstances. I assume you came here looking for him."

"Yes. I knew he'd joined up with you. I knew about the wraith attacks. When I didn't hear from him in a few days, I got worried and came looking for him. I wasn't wrong."

They were all grim. "We're sorry. It's terrible," the third woman said. She was small with bleached white hair. Her nose and lip were pierced. Several tattoos peeked out on the exposed skin of her arms. "What's been happening." She held out her hand to Cerys. "Tae Winkler."

"Tae owns a bookstore downtown," Barbosa explained. He nodded towards the dark-haired woman. "This is Kate Windsor. She's our doctor. She's helping us figure out what's happened to Eddie and the others."

Kate inclined her head at Cerys. The other woman was Isobel Singer. Cerys was surprised to learn she was a firefighter. Isobel looked delicate and gentle. She was not as she seemed. In Spectra City, she was discovering, most people were not as they seemed.

Cerys glanced at Tamsin. "What about you, Tamsin? What is your secret identity?"

Tamsin shrugged. "I don't have one."

"You don't have a job?"

"This is my job."

"Tam used to be a bartender," Barbosa put in.

"I thought this was more important than slinging drinks in a seedy bar," Tamsin said darkly.

"There aren't many of you," Cerys observed. She joined the others in the circle of chairs. "I expected there would be more."

The chanters glanced at each other solemnly. "There used to be," Tae told her grimly. "Some of the others were taken by the wraiths. More of us have left. They're afraid."

"I don't blame them," Isobel said darkly. "Nothing good can come of going after the wraiths."

"There are more of us," Tamsin added bracingly. "They're just not here. Some of them are working. Others are checking the city to be sure the wraiths aren't coming back."

"We're all trying to stop what's happening, Cerys," Barbosa told her, as though he sensed her disappointment in the dwindled number. "We're all doing what we can to get your brother and the others back."

Abel nodded. "There isn't much of use in the police reports. About a dozen people have reported them, but no one seems interested in investigating it. They helped discover the pattern of locations the wraiths have attacked, at least. It's mostly poor districts and areas where crime occurs. Whoever is sending them--"

"It's Nico Creed," Barbosa replied firmly.

"Nico is targeting areas in which chanters are likely to be."

"No one has seen where they come from and where they go," Isobel added. "That's when Cedric decided to try the tracker."

Cerys scowled. "It worked," Barbosa replied.

"How long since Cedric was taken?"

"A couple weeks," Tamsin said grimly. "I was there."

Cerys looked at her in surprise. "I didn't know."

"It was awful. They just--he just disappeared between them. He didn't even scream."

"Tamsin," Abel said. "Cerys doesn't want to hear that."

"I do want to hear it. I want to know what we're dealing with."

"Now you've seen them."

"Yes. And if they took my brother...I just hope he's still alive."

"We have every reason to believe he is," Kate told her matter-of-factly. "Nico is using them for something. He's had Rory and Bobby for over a month. He took

Mary Anne and Luther around the same time as your brother. None of them have come back yet, and no one has discovered their bodies."

"He might be burying them somewhere," Isobel muttered.

"That isn't helping anyone," Barbosa growled.

Cerys ignored them. "How many of them have come back?"

The chanters exchanged another glance. "Three."

She frowned. "Where are the other two? There was only one in the infirmary."

Barbosa hesitated. "Emily is home with her mother. She's a chanter, too. She wanted to take care of her daughter herself. There isn't much we can do for her here. But she's alive."

"What about the other one?"

They sighed. "He didn't make it," Kate answered. "He went into shock. What happened to him was the reason, but it wasn't the cause of death. What Nico is doing to them isn't necessarily fatal."

Cerys sighed deeply. "We have to do something. We can't just sit here talking about it."

"We are doing something," Abel replied somewhat indignantly. "We're doing what we can. Barbosa and I are working on taking Nico down. Some of the others are tailing him, trying to get some ideas of what he's up to. We haven't gotten anything solid yet. Everything seems to slide off the son of a bitch."

"Not this time," Barbosa said. "This time, I've got something solid."

"But what if it's someone else controlling the wraiths, Zar?" Isobel demanded. From the tone of her voice, Cerys suspected it was a subject that had been broached before.

"Lex Creed confirmed it," Tamsin told Isobel, scowling. "It's Nico."

"What do you mean Lex Creed confirmed it?" Kate said.

"He didn't confirm it, not exactly," Cerys argued.

"He as good as confirmed it. He was in the alley tonight," Tamsin explained. "He stopped Cerys from chanting. He told her it attracts the wraiths."

"We already know that. That isn't any confirmation. It just means he's seen them before," Isobel replied.

"Yes, but he can't chant against them, and they can't detect him. He said they are part of what he is."

They all considered this a long moment. They looked at Cerys in interest. "Why would he tell you that, Cerys?" Isobel asked suspiciously.

Cerys lifted her shoulders. "I don't know."

"Do you know him?"

"I met him a couple times."

"That doesn't seem like something he would tell a stranger."

"Well, he did," Tamsin told her shortly. "And you don't really know him, do you? So you don't know what he would say at all."

"What it means is, Lex believes Nico is responsible for the attacks," Barbosa said mildly. "And if he was protecting you in the alley, he doesn't want the attacks to continue."

"If you think we'll be able to get Lex Creed to turn on his brother, you must be out of your mind," Abel said. "He's as much a family man as their father. He'll do what he can to protect Nico."

"It's worth a shot, Abel," Tamsin hissed at him. "We haven't got anything better."

Cerys sat back in her chair. She took a sip of her drink. "I would have thought a real superhero organization would have better ideas," she observed wryly.

Barbosa sighed. "This isn't a comic book, Cerys. There are consequences for our actions. We have to act within the confines of the law or we'll be no better than the Creeds and the villains we fight."

"I know. But at least we'd have my brother back."

* * *

Nico cursed. He paced impatiently back and forth. Tully waited unwearyingly at his side with his hands behind his back. "Where are they?" Nico growled.

"Sir?"

"They should have been back by now! Where are they?"

"Perhaps they are held up, sir."

"Held up? By what? They've been created to be back to me by now. Something stopped them."

"Perhaps the chanters did not take the bait tonight, sir. They may have become aware of the creatures' purpose."

Nico glared at him. He spun away to stride the length of the room once more. He paused abruptly. "Tully, did you move this chair?"

Tully glanced at him in surprise. "I beg your pardon, sir? Move the chair?"

Nico stared suspiciously down at the wooden chair near the door. "Yes. This chair. Did you move it?"

"No. Of course not, sir. You are very specific in your arrangement. I would not presume to adjust it without your permission."

"Has someone been in here?"

"Sir?"

"Someone's been in here." Nico spun on him. His brilliant blue eyes blazed. "Did you let anyone in here?"

"Of course not, sir. Your instructions are very specific."

Nico spun abruptly towards the wall. He ran his fingers along a seam. A panel slid away. Behind it, four cubicle cells were occupied. The chanters, curled up in their filthy, stinking clothes, slept peacefully, kept sedated through intravenous needles stuck in each of their arms.

Nico sighed in relief. It was not enough. "Tully. We have to move them. It isn't safe here anymore."

Tully inclined his head. "As you wish, sir. Right away."

* * *

Lex pushed his disheveled blonde hair away from his face. His skin felt dusty and dirty, as though the filth of the Art District had settled into his pores. The wraiths were gone. They hadn't taken anyone. Despite his exhaustion, Lex was somewhat relieved he'd been able to do something, small as it was. He was afraid to risk using his magic to bring him home tonight. He couldn't face another headache like he'd had the last time. He'd had to hail a cab.

His footsteps were slow and drudging when he arrived at Creed Manor. It was late. No light burned in the house. He didn't move directly to his bedroom to shower the night's horror from his body. His nerves were ragged and singing. He needed a drink.

Nico was already in the library when Lex pushed open the doors. He lounged sullenly in a wing backed leather chair. His long legs were sprawled in front of him. He was holding a glass of amber liquid. He peered into the glass reflectively. When Lex entered, he looked up. His expression was utterly blank.

"Ah. Big brother. Where have you been?"

Lex eyed him warily. He strode to the small bar. He poured himself a drink. He swallowed it in one gulp before he looked back at his brother. "Out."

Nico raised his eyebrows. "Out," he repeated.

"Yes. Just out."

"You look like hell."

"It was quite a night."

"Really. While you were out."

"Yes." Lex spun to face him wearily. "Do you want something, Nico?"

"Do you?"

"I just wanted a drink."

Nico smiled. "Me, too."

"Good. I'm tired. I'm going to bed."

His brother's smile didn't waver. It was as cold as ice and sharp as a blade. "Good night, Big Brother."

"Good night."

Nico stared after him when he was gone. His smile faded.

* * *

Lex emerged from the Spectra City Bank. The steps were slippery with rain. The sun peaked unexpectedly through the dank, dark clouds swirling in the sky. Its rays glinted off the wet ground. Raindrops sparkled on the trees around the building. He paused, peering up at the sky. The clouds looked ominous. The sun wouldn't hold them off for long.

He stopped short in front of his sleek, black Jaguar. A tall, slender woman with long, dark, wavy chestnut brown hair was leaning against it with her arms crossed over her chest. Her dark blue, almond shaped eyes watched him narrowly as he approached.

He frowned at her. "Yes?"

Cerys lifted her eyebrows. "That's all? That's all you have to say to me after last night?"

Lex's expression was blank. "I don't know what else you expect."

She straightened and strode towards him. "What was that, Lex? What is going on? I know you know something about what's going on."

He did not respond to this. He moved around her to stride to his car.

Cerys stepped in front of him. Her dark eyes flashed. He scowled at her. She lifted her chin. "I want to know what that was all about."

"I don't know what you're talking about."

"Don't. Don't bother. We both know what happened. We both saw those things. And we both know it has something to do with you." Cerys moved closer to him until their faces were inches apart. He felt her breath on his cheek. "If you didn't want me to know you were involved, why did you stop me using magic?"

"Cerys," he growled. "Keep your voice down." His eyes darted around them, as though afraid someone might overhear.

"Please, Lex," she said in soft, pleading tones. "Those things took my brother. I have to know what they are and why they're taking chanters."

He blinked at her. His cold blue eyes softened slightly. "Let's not talk about this here."

"Where?"

He considered. "Dinner. Tomorrow night."

Cerys took a step back in surprise. "What?"

"Let me take you to dinner tomorrow night.."

"Are you asking me out?"

Lex thought about this. "I suppose I am."

She frowned suspiciously. "Are you putting me off?"

"I just asked you to dinner. Does that sound like putting you off?"

She stared at him a long moment, as though she were unsure how to respond to this unexpected offer. "You'll tell me what you know about the creatures?"

"I already told you I don't know anything."

She opened and closed her mouth stupidly for a moment. "All right. Pick me up at the Warren Hotel at eight."

"The Warren?"

"Yes."

"Ritzy place."

She narrowed her eyes. "I like a nice view."

He smirked. "I'll see you tomorrow."

* * *

Isobel was leaving when Cerys walked into Chant headquarters without awaiting an invitation.

"Hey, Isobel," Cerys greeted. She smiled hesitantly. The pretty, pale-haired woman did not smile in return. Isobel grunted in reply. Cerys ignored this. "Is anyone else here?"

Isobel jerked her head toward the stairs. "In the glass box."

"It's not so much a box as an octagon."

"If you want to banter, do it with Tamsin. She's upstairs." Isobel strode past Cerys without looking at her. "I have to get to work."

Cerys sighed. She and Isobel were not going to be friends. She watched the ill-tempered firefighter leave. Isobel slammed the door behind her. Cerys turned away. She did not pause to admire the sumptuous surroundings or the opulent furnishings of Barbosa's family home. She mounted the stairs quickly, two at a time. In the small library, she yanked on the red book that would reveal the hidden laboratory. The panel slid sideways.

Inside the laboratory, Barbosa and Tamsin stood silently side by side, as though they were waiting for something. X rolled back and forth between his consoles, typing furiously upon the glass keyboards and sweeping his hand across the screens to manipulate the words, images and random numbers. None of them glanced up at her as she entered.

She jerked her thumb over her shoulder. "Is she always like that?"

Tamsin flicked her eyes at her. "Isobel?"

"Yeah."

Tamsin sighed. "No. She's actually usually pretty nice. Her husband, Rory, is one of the chanters who were taken."

"Oh, that's--"

"Shh!" X and Barbosa hissed at them. "We are working here."

A low, melodious, almost sensual voice echoed through the glass room. "...See you tonight, then. I'll bring the wine."

Cerys lifted an eyebrow. "What have you all been doing in here?"

Barbosa and X looked up at her in surprise, as though they hadn't even realized she was there until that moment. "It's Nico Creed," Tamsin announced proudly.

"We've tapped his lines," X told her matter-of-factly. "I'd tell you how, but you wouldn't understand."

Cerys rolled her eyes. "Is that illegal?"

Barbosa waved his hand dismissively. "Strictly speaking, but the feds and the SCPD do it all the time. It just isn't admissible in court. We might hear something that will help us or at least give us an idea where to find evidence we can actually use."

"Hear anything good?"

"Not much yet. He's just been talking dirty to his girlfriend."

"Anything else from your man in the Caymans?"

"Nothing new. He's still trying to track down the lawyers who supposedly run the dummy corporations paying out to Creed Corp." He sighed. "I might just have to buy the bank."

Cerys blinked. "Can you do that?"

Barbosa shrugged. "Sure. Why not?" He paused a moment, as though considering it for the first time. "Excuse me a moment. I need to make a call."

They turned to watch him stride out of the room. Cerys looked at Tamsin doubtfully. "Can he buy a bank?"

"He can buy whatever he wants."

"I see. Have you learned anything about the Mobleys?"

Tamsin sighed deeply. "No. They are harder to get to than the Creeds." Her lips twisted sourly. "How about you and Lex? How did it go?"

Cerys averted her eyes. "It went all right. We're going out tomorrow night."

Tamsin smirked. "See? I told you he likes you."

"I don't know if he likes me. I confronted him about what happened last night."

"Did he say anything?"

"Of course he didn't."

"How did you come around to going out?"

Cerys shrugged. "I really can't claim any credit for being crafty. He just asked me. It was somewhat easier than I expected."

Tamsin sighed mournfully. "What can't I find a gorgeous rich guy who wants to take me out?"

"Why don't you ask Colin Mobley? From what I hear, he's both extremely rich and extremely gorgeous."

Tamsin laughed. "I wish. I don't stand a chance with him. I can't even get close enough to find out if he's a chanter."

Cerys frowned. "When did we start considering the Creeds and the Mobleys as dating potential?"

"I don't know that we ever did until you made a date with one."

"Ah. Yes. It's not quite how I saw this all going when I set out to find my brother." Cerys frowned. "Dating isn't my first priority here, Tam. It's the means to an end. I want to find Cedric."

Tamsin sighed. "I know. I'm sorry." She dropped into an empty chair near X. The pale, dark-haired man stared up at his screens and acted as though he was completely alone in the lab. "I just wish I could do something else."

"You are doing something. And if Balthazar can get a lead off these wire taps, maybe we'll have something to go on that will get us into the Creed's house to search for the missing chanters."

Tamsin sighed. "So far, all we've heard on the taps is him making calls to clients and ordering flowers for his girlfriend. Remarkably, he seems to really like her. It's weird but not exactly illegal."

"Why is it weird for someone to like their girlfriend?"

Tamsin eyed her. "If you'd spent as much time watching Nico Creed as we have, you start to notice things. He doesn't like anyone. Not his friends or his family or his clients. Yet, he seems to genuinely like Simone Stowe."

"Who is she?"

"The usual type of socialite. Her family is old money. They've been around

Spectra City a long time. She was a fashion model for a while, and then she started her own clothing line. She has a little boutique in the Historical District."

"Is she a chanter?"

"I don't think so. We've never heard of anything like that running in the Stowe family. Of course, you never know. Some families are better at hiding things than others."

"What's she like?"

"How would I know? I've never met her."

"You've been eavesdropping on her phone calls."

"Yeah, well, only her calls with Nico, and they are racy."

Cerys laughed. "Well, I don't suppose it matters much."

"Yeah, why are you so interested? Trying to find out what kind of lady the Creed men like?"

"I don't think Nico's taste in women is necessarily indicative of his brother's."

"You never know."

"Anyway, I don't care what sort of lady Lex likes. I care what he knows about the wraiths and where my brother is."

"I hope you find out something, then. At least maybe you'll get a fancy dinner."

"That would make it worth my time." Cerys sighed deeply. She sat down in one of X's chairs and rolled to face Tamsin. "Tell me about Cedric."

Tamsin blinked in surprise. "What?"

"Tell me about my brother. About when he joined Chant. Cedric and I were best friends all our lives, but when he came here, all I got were letters and a few phone calls. I want to know what he was like with you."

Tamsin's dark eyes slid away. She smiled wistfully. "He was amazing. He was so brave. He wasn't afraid of anything. He was always first on the front line when there was something to fight. He lived for it."

Cerys smiled. "That sounds like my brother. How did he join Chant?"

Tamsin laughed. "About the same as you did. I should have known right away who you were. You're a lot like him, you know. You even look alike. Almost exactly alike."

Cerys smiled. "I know."

"I miss him," Tamsin whispered. "I miss him so much. I didn't want him to do it. I didn't want him to risk letting the creatures take him, but no one could stop him when he got it in his head to do something."

Cerys eyed Tamsin shrewdly. "Were you involved with my brother?"

"What?"

"Were you and my brother romantically involved?"

"Why do you ask that?"

"Just something in your eyes."

Tamsin looked away. "No. We weren't. But I think we might have been, if he hadn't gotten himself kidnapped by Nico Creed." She looked up into Cerys' eyes. "I am as anxious as you to get him back unharmed."

"I appreciate that."

"I mean it, Cerys. I'll do whatever I can to help."

"Thank you. Right now, I think we're doing all we can." Cerys sighed deeply. "I just hope it isn't too little too late."

CHAPTER 11

Cerys was waiting outside the huge, lavish white stone Warren Hotel in the loading zone when Lex's sleek, black Jaguar sedan slid into the parking lot. He slowed the car as he saw her. The automatic window rolled down. Lex raised his eyebrows wryly. "Would you prefer to just hop in as I slowly drive by?"

Cerys laughed. "You will get out of the car and open my door for me."

He smirked. "Well, at least this is a date, then."

She waited as he climbed out of the driver's side and circled the car to open the passenger door for her. He gestured grandly. He offered his hand. She took it. She smiled as he closed the door gently behind her.

"I would have picked you up at your door. "Lex said. He steered the car out of the parking lot towards the main thoroughfare.

"I wouldn't want to inconvenience you. Besides, I never told you my room number."

"I don't mind a little inconvenience now and again." He glanced at her. "I am Lex Creed, you know. Do you think I couldn't get your room number?"

Cerys smirked. "I gave very specific instructions regarding giving out my room number when I checked in."

"There are few things I want that I cannot get. I take it you didn't want me to know it."

"A woman likes to have a little mystery about her."

"You have that right enough. I already know you're in the penthouse suite. Staying at the Warren is like putting out an ad in the gossip pages." He glanced at her. "I wouldn't have marked you as a lady with such expensive tastes."

"It was the only room left." She glanced sidelong at him. "Speaking of expensive tastes, I would have expected you to drive a sports car. Something Italian and sexy with a speedometer that goes up to screaming emoticons."

Lex snorted. "I have one. I didn't think it was the appropriate vehicle in which to take out a respectable lady. It seems to draw the sort of woman I'm not interested in catching."

Cerys laughed. "I suppose I can understand that." She glanced at him again.

He was dressed comfortably in jeans and a black sweater. They were designer jeans. The sweater was cashmere. The watch on his wrist had probably cost more than a month's salary at the newspaper. She lifted an eyebrow. "I suspect it doesn't matter much what you drive."

He shrugged. "Sometimes it does."

"That sounds a little cynical."

"Maybe I am a little. It's hard to know what people are after sometimes."

She did not reply to this. She peered out the window for a long moment. She watched the city pass quickly by. She didn't recognize the streets. All the streets in Spectra looked the same. Even in the darkness of night, the storm clouds lightened the sky to a cold, steel grey. Buildings loomed up around them like dark, monolithic sentinels. The lights streaked past the window in brilliant flashes of color.

The sky rises of the city center gave way to a lavish, green residential area. The houses were huge and brightly lit, spaced far apart to allow the gardens to grow lush and verdant between them. Lex didn't seem to mind her silence. Soft, moody jazz filled the quiet.

Lex did not stop in the residential area or the small, quaint strip of shops and restaurants in the Historical District that streaked past as quickly as the other sights. Soon, the buildings appeared less frequently. Lex steered the Jaguar along a winding, overgrown road. Suddenly, the dark, churning sea appeared before them.

Cerys looked at him. His profile could have been chiseled from marble. There was no expression on his face. He did not glance back at her. "Where are you taking me?"

"Are you nervous?"

"Should I be?"

Now he smirked. "I suppose it depends on your perspective."

"Are you going to tell me what was going on the other night?"

"No."

She sighed. Her stomach roiled slightly in apprehension. Perhaps she was nervous. If his intentions were less than pure, he would find her an extremely formidable opponent. He didn't try anything. He veered off the main road. He drove for several minutes through a thick copse of trees.

The trees broke. The sea raged outside the window beneath the swirling clouds. Directly in front of them was a huge, brightly lit sailboat. It appeared to have gone to ground against the rocky, speckled beach. It was slightly slanted. A large, roughly hewn log held it up on its precarious right side. An old-fashioned, hand-painted sign read The Wrecked Ship. That was precisely what it was. It was in remarkably good shape. The rustic red and brown paint looked fresh.

Cerys looked at Lex in amazement. She laughed.

He smirked. "Did you expect I was taking you somewhere sinister?"

She smiled. "Perhaps for a moment."

"I am not actually a super villain, you know."

She shrugged. "I don't know very much about you. Just what I hear on the streets."

He did not respond immediately. He parked the Jaguar in the makeshift lot around the boat. He climbed out of the driver's seat to open her door. He held out his hand. She took it. "And what sorts of things do you hear on the streets?"

She smiled. He didn't release her hand. He seemed to be waiting for her reply. "All sorts of things. I hear your family is involved in those mysterious creature sightings and kidnappings."

"That's crazy talk." His tone was perfectly even.

She smirked. He tugged gently on her hand. Inside, the Wrecked Ship had been hollowed out. The various sections of the original vessel had been replaced with long, rough-looking wooden benches carved from thick tree trunks. Small groups gathered upon the benches, laughing and talking quietly as they ate.

Lex glanced at her. "I suppose I should have asked if you like seafood."

"I'm allergic to shellfish."

His face fell. "I'm sure they have...other things."

She laughed. "I'm sorry. I was joking. I live in the Pacific Northwest. Of course I like seafood."

Lex rolled his eyes at her. His confidence seemed slightly shaken. When the hostess approached him, smiling, a bit of his swagger returned. She nodded to him deferentially. She already knew him. "This way, Mr. Creed, if you please."

The table to which the hostess led them was small, set for two under dim, soft light. It faced a porthole. The sea moved outside. It seemed almost as though they were upon the water, floating serenely over the waves. There were no other guests around them. Lex Creed, of course, warranted special treatment.

Cerys sighed softly when they were seated. She leaned back in her chair. "It's beautiful."

"You don't mind the rain?"

"I've always liked the rain. Even when there's so much of it."

"You've come to the right place, then."

She smiled. Lex did not ask her opinion about the wine or the food. He ordered with an easy, unaffected confidence as someone assured his judgment was the only one that mattered. She didn't mind. His taste was sure to be exquisite. They did not wait long for their order. The waitress returned in mere moments with plates of steaming shrimp and crab cakes.

Cerys studied Lex in interest. He seemed perfectly at his ease. He poured her a glass of deep, scarlet wine. He waited for her to sample it. He did not ask if she approved. He expected that she approved. If he was trying to impress her, he wasn't showy about it. He behaved as though she were as used to this special treatment as he was. She did not intend to disappoint him. "Why did you ask me here tonight?"

Lex smiled. "I wanted to spend time with you."

"Really."

"Yes. No games, no ulterior motives. You have one, though, don't you?"

She lifted her chin. She sipped her wine. It was rich and woodsy. It seemed to dissolve on her tongue like puffs of smoke. She sampled the shrimp. They were plump and sweet and unexpectedly spicy. They tasted so fresh, they might have been fished off the pier outside. She had been right. His taste was exquisite.

"Why did you come with me?"

Cerys placed her glass delicately on the polished wooden table top. "I want to know where my brother is."

"I already told you I don't know."

She inclined her head. "Yes, and I am actually inclined to believe you."

Lex lifted an eyebrow. He leaned back in his seat as comfortably as a king upon a throne. "Then why did you come?"

"I was curious."

"About?"

"You. I've heard a lot around the city about you and your family, but I know nothing about you."

He smiled. "I see." He considered a moment. He leaned across the table. His expression was earnest. His blue eyes glittered in the light of a small, sweetly scented oil candle. "I'm thirty-five."

Cerys laughed.

"I was born in Spectra City."

"I know all that already. I work in the media; I know the official line."

He considered a long moment. "My favorite food is peanut butter and jelly sandwiches."

"Smooth or crunchy?"

"Crunchy."

"I did not expect that."

"I like to surprise."

"Ever been married?"

"No."

"Wanted to?"

He hesitated an ephemeral instant. "Yes."

She lifted an eyebrow. "Recently?"

"No."

"Is it open for discussion?"

"No."

"Okay. Kids?"

He laughed. "No."

"Do you get along with your family?"

He blinked. "Some of the time."

"Pets?"

"No. These are easy questions."

"Would you prefer I asked harder ones?"

"You can ask whatever you like. I reserve the right not to answer."

She smiled. She considered him a long moment. The candlelight danced across his face. It softened his marble features. His hair glowed like a halo around his head. She could almost believe he wasn't a super villain. Of course, no super villains actually looked like super villains. Except in comic books, anyway. "What do you do in your spare time?"

He shrugged. "I don't really have any."

"You can't work all the time. What do you do when you don't have anything you have to do? How do you spend your free time?"

He considered. "I like music. And dancing."

"Do you go out a lot?"

"Sometimes. I used to go out a lot more than I do now. When I'm at home on my own, I like to read books."

"What kind?"

He smiled. "All kinds. Popular fiction, horror books, mysteries, the usual."

"What kind of music do you listen to?"

"I like all kinds of music."

"But what do you listen to the most?"

"I like classic rock."

"Really. I would have suspected you'd be a jazz or Sinatra type."

"Oh, I am, but I love old rock music. The Doors, Pink Floyd, Aerosmith. The stuff that drives my mother crazy. You?"

"Oh, yeah. I like all those. I'm a big Billie Holiday fan."

"So you like jazz?"

"Sure. And old big band and swing music."

"Nice. Maybe sometime I'll take you to a jazz club. Spectra City has one of the best in the world."

She smiled. "I would enjoy that."

"So, what about you? What do you do in your spare time? You must have quite the life. Flying all over the world? Photographing everything you see?"

Cerys sighed. "I guess. Yeah."

"You must see a lot of the world."

"Seeing it through the lens of a camera isn't the same as living it. Sometimes it's all about getting the shot. I forget to put down the camera and pay attention to what's going on around me."

He lifted his eyebrows. He considered this. "Does that make you enjoy it less?"

She thought about it. "I suppose it doesn't. Not less. Just differently."

He nodded. "Friends?"

She shrugged. "Yeah, sure, a few. There are people I hang around with, mostly co-workers or colleagues."

"Do you even like them?"

She looked away. "I like them all right. We have a nice time together and have plenty to talk about."

"Work stuff."

"Yes, work stuff."

"It doesn't sound like you have a life. It sounds like you have a job."

She smiled. "I like my job. It's hard to find people I have things in common with. It's hard to make connections with people when you have to hide what you are."

He didn't seem to hear her. He smiled wryly. "I know how it feels. To just have a job."

"Did you always want to be a rich and powerful CEO?"

For a moment, his smile faltered. It returned so quickly, she thought she might have imagined the slip. "No. I never wanted to be."

She lifted her eyebrows in interest. "Really?"

"It wasn't my choice. It was a condition of my birth. I don't know that I would have been allowed to be born if I had refused the job."

Cerys laughed. There was an edge of sadness in his voice. For a brief moment, she pitied him. It seemed ridiculous. "What did you want to do, then?"

"A lot of things. None of them were realistic. I always knew what I would be, so when I dreamed, I could be as outrageous as I wanted."

"Well?"

He didn't look as though he were entirely comfortable sharing. He did, anyway. "I wanted to be a cowboy. A Wild West gunslinger or a U.S. Marshall." She laughed. "A lounge singer."

"Really? Do you sing?"

"Not well. I performed a set for my family when I was six, and it went over quite poorly. For a while, I wanted to be a private detective. Then I wanted to be a superhero." He smirked slightly. "I wasn't cut out for that."

"Why not?"

He considered. "I don't really care for lurking about in alleyways looking for trouble to come along."

"And yet...isn't that how we met?"

His expression was bland. "No. We met at my mother's birthday party."

She sighed. She wondered if he intended to spend the entire night pretending their meeting in the streets, amongst the din and chaos of the creatures, had never happened.

"What about you then, Cerys?"

"What about me?"

"Did you always want to be a famous photographer?"

She laughed. "I'm not exactly famous."

"No? I've heard a great many things about you. Your work is quite highly revered in Spectra."

"Spectra isn't the entire world."

"It is if you're in Spectra."

She considered this. "Yes. It seems to be the only place in the world when you're on the inside. Anyway, I got some lucky shots, and I have a gift for talking my way onto projects."

He laughed. "I'm not surprised. Is that what you did this time?"

"Yes. I needed to be in Spectra City." He looked expectant. She smiled. "I didn't want to be a photographer. I mean, I didn't not want to be one. It just wasn't on my list."

"What was, then?"

"I wanted to be an artist. Cedric, my brother, used to spend his entire allowance on comic books every week. He'd bring them home, and we'd read them together. I wanted to be a comic book artist."

"Why didn't you do it, then?"

She smiled sadly. "I'm a terrible artist. I tried to learn. I took classes and everything, but I had no knack for it. I took up photography instead. I am better at that." She sighed. "It was Cedric who wanted to be a superhero."

Lex was quiet. It appeared as though he was waiting for more. When he got it, he didn't appreciate it.

"He thought it was why we were given these gifts. To use them for good."

Lex stiffened. He darted a look around the room, as though afraid they would be overheard. "You shouldn't be so open about it."

"Open?" She laughed humorlessly. "I have spent my whole life hiding what I am. I shouldn't have to."

"But you do. It's what we do to stay alive."

"And on top?"

He shrugged. "I never wanted power."

"You just have it?"

"I would have preferred to live my own life, to choose my own path."

"You still can. You don't have to keep doing it."

"Yes, I do. It isn't so easy to run away from your family and your position." He glanced away. His eyes were distant. There was a strange, glittering resentment in them. "You don't know what it's like to have responsibilities you never asked for and can't get out of."

She sighed. Her own resentment abated slightly. "I don't know. You're right about that. I have always chosen my path."

"You're lucky."

"I don't feel lucky."

"Why?"

"Because the person I care most about in the world is gone, and I can't find him."

Lex reached across the table. He folded her hand in his. She looked down at it in surprise. His hand was pale and flawless. His fingernails looked freshly manicured. He'd never seen hard labor in his life. "I'm sorry you've lost him."

"I haven't lost him. He's been taken."

Lex blinked at her as though he understood her for the first time. He didn't say anything to this. In fact, he did not say much as he motioned the waitress. He did not pay the check. Perhaps men like Lex Creed simply paid a bill at the end of the month like others paid for their utilities. Perhaps, she considered absently, he owned the place. She was sure he owned many places for which he claimed no proprietorship.

He rose abruptly. "I'd better get you home."

She blinked. She was not going to reveal her surprise to him. She inclined her head. She rose to walk beside him to the Jaguar. Perhaps she had pushed him too far. She had intended to handle the situation delicately. She had been about as delicate as a battering ram.

He did not speak much on the drive home. It seemed much longer than it had on the way to the Wrecked Ship. She studied him in the passing lights as they wove deeper and deeper into the center of Spectra. His expression was perfectly blank, but his jaw was rigid. He looked troubled.

"I'm said something to upset you."

He did not glance at her. "No, you didn't."

"Didn't I?"

He steered into the circular drive in front of the Warren Hotel. He stopped the car. He glanced at her. His eyes were guarded. "No."

She opened her mouth to say something. He did not wait for it. He vaulted out of the car and circled to open the passenger door. He offered his hand. She ignored it. She stepped out. When she did, Lex was inches away. She dropped her head back to look at him. There was something different in his glittering blue eyes. Her pulse leapt. She exhaled heavily.

"I want to see you again," he told her in a low voice.

"Do you really?"

"Yes."

She eyed him speculatively. "When?"

"I'm not sure. I'll call you."

She didn't roll her eyes. She wanted to. He stepped back to allow her to pass him. She lifted her chin as she strode towards the door.

Lex caught her arm to tug her back towards him. "I meant it, Cerys. I will call you."

She nodded doubtfully. He smirked. She opened her mouth to reply. He did not give her the chance. He leaned down and pressed his lips against hers. It was a brief, chaste kiss. It felt strangely sweet. He didn't tell her he'd had a nice time. She wasn't sure he had. He didn't tell her anything. He pulled away from her. He moved silently to the driver's side of the Jaguar. He got in and drove away without looking back.

She watched him go. She thought she'd actually had a pretty nice time, even if he hadn't. Lex Creed had not been what she'd expected at all.

CHAPTER 12

Nico was in the library when Lex arrived at home. His younger brother looked different. His dark hair was mussed. His electric blue eyes glittered almost manically. He slouched in a leather chair, his leg spread out haphazardly in front of him. He still wore the same rumpled suit in which he'd conducted his last meeting hours ago. Lex stared at him. "Nico, are you drunk?"

Nico looked up at him. He didn't look drunk. Something else was wrong with him. He looked half-crazy. When he spoke, his tone was so even and normal, Lex was uncertain the voice actually came from the disheveled man before him. "Of course I'm not drunk. Genes like ours? I don't think it's physically possible for us to actually get drunk. At least you wouldn't think so, the way Mother always manages to remain in control. Where have you been?"

Lex narrowed his eyes. "Why are you so interested in where I'm going lately?"

"Is there something wrong with taking an interest in my big brother's life?"

"Wrong? No. Unusual."

Nico smirked. "Were you out with a woman?"

"For your information, yes."

Nico did not look surprised. "Carlie?"

"No, not Carlie."

"Ah. The photographer."

Lex blinked. "How do you know about that?"

"I know a lot more than you think, Lex."

"Do you."

"And I suspect you know more than you're letting on."

"I really don't know what you're talking about, Nico. What's this all about?"

Nico smiled luminously. "Nothing. Of course. I didn't mean anything. I was only joking around with my big brother."

"It went a bit awry."

"Nico, what are you doing in here? I thought you were just getting a drink and coming to bed," Simone said from the doorway. She was wrapped in an ivory silk robe. Her long, blonde hair was slightly mussed.

Nico looked up at her innocently. "Nothing. Just making sure my big brother got home all right."

Simone glanced at Lex in interest. "And where have you been, Lex?"

"He's been on a date," Nico told her.

She lifted her eyebrows. "Has he indeed?" She rounded on Lex. He shrank back from the strangely ravenous expression in her pale eyes. "With whom?"

"Simone..."

"That photographer from Mother's birthday party. The one from the Daily."

Her eyebrows traveled disdainfully toward her sleek, side-swept fringe. "A reporter?

Lex sighed. "She isn't a reporter. She is a freelance photographer. She's just doing some work for the Daily while she's in Spectra."

"And why is she in Spectra, Lex?" Nico asked. His tone was deceptively smooth.

His brother glanced at him with a guarded expression. "I am not sure what you mean. I thought I just said why."

"No. You said she was working while she's here, not why she's here."

Lex considered him silently. "I understand they made her a very good offer."

"But why her?"

His eyes narrowed to slits. "What do you mean? What is this about, Nico?"

Simone rolled her eyes. "Nico, please, why are you so interested in what the Daily is up?"

"I'm interested in why they would seek out a photographer from San Francisco when we have our own people who do just as well without expecting special treatment."

"She's very good. Besides, I don't think she expects special treatment."

"She's just staying at the Warren because everywhere else was booked?"

Lex smirked. "That is what she said, actually."

"Why did she come here?"

"I'm sure Lex will ask her the next time he sees her," Simone replied languidly. She lifted her arms above her head and yawned dramatically. "Come to bed, darling. It's late. We both have an early morning."

Nico smirked. He rose abruptly to his feet. He strode toward Simone and wrapped an arm around her waist. He smiled at her. Lex could have sworn it was a genuine smile. "Of course, dear." He met his brother's eyes as he closed the door.

It wasn't over. He meant to find out exactly what Cerys was up to. When he did, she was going to be in trouble.

* * *

Nico had gone ahead to work to meet a client from New York City. Tully had left the manor an hour ago. Grace had spent the night in her flat in the Historical District. Peyton hadn't emerged from her room yet that morning. Lex was alone in the house.

The door to Nico's work room--or lair or den or whatever it was he was calling it these days--was not locked. Lex frowned. He had expected resistance. He had anticipated the splitting headache and nausea that accompanied his trances. None of it was necessary. The knob turned easily under his hand. It didn't bode well.

He stepped into the room and sighed deeply in frustration. It was completely empty. Only the old, neglected instruments remained. There were slight indents in the carpet to mark the place the table and chairs had been. The room was as lonely and forsaken as the sad, out of tune instruments.

Nico knew. He knew someone had been inside, and he probably suspected it was Lex. It couldn't really have been anyone else. Lex cursed and spun away. Things were not going well. When it came to Nico, nothing ever really did.

* * *

Lex ducked low behind the steering wheel of the old, battered Honda. Nico hadn't yet emerged from the Webber Core Technologies building, though night had already fallen. His sleek, silver Maserati was double parked in front of the building. A police car slowed as it passed the car. When the officer recognized it, he accelerated quickly away.

While he waited, Lex made a phone call.

Cerys answered on the third ring. "Hello?

"Cerys."

"I didn't really think you would call."

Nico strode out of the building. His lips twisted up slightly in a smirk. His gait was confident and relaxed. The meeting had gone well.

"I told you I would."

Nico slid into the driver's seat. He stamped on the accelerator. Lex swung into traffic behind him.

"I thought you were just being nice."

The Maserati drew easily ahead of the other cars. The old Honda Civic struggled to keep up. Lex didn't pay attention to the course Nico was taking through the winding streets and back alleys. He simply kept up.

"Can I see you again?"

Cerys didn't say anything. Lex glanced around him. He had seen this neighborhood before. He couldn't recall when. It didn't look like the sort of place Nico would be keeping an army of chanters. Then again, Lex rarely understood his brother's plans.

"Was I such a bad date?" he prompted.

Cerys laughed. "No. You were a good date."

"That is not a very ringing recommendation."

"Somehow I doubt you'd be satisfied with a woman who worshiped the ground you walk on and didn't give you anything to think about."

Lex laughed. Seconds later, he frowned. Nico slowed his car to a crawl. "You are right about that."

Nico swung abruptly into an underground parking structure. Lex slowed his own vehicle and stared up. He suddenly recognized the swank, glass and metal apartment building. He dropped his head against the steering wheel. He felt like a fool.

"Lex? Are you still there?"

"Yeah. I'm here."

"How about tomorrow night?"

Lex glanced up at Simone Stowe's building and cursed softly to himself. "Tomorrow isn't good. How about Friday?

"Sure. See you then."

Lex flipped the Honda around. Unless Nico's girlfriend was keeping the chanters in her small, penthouse flat, he'd hit a dead end.

"Yes. See you Friday. Good night, Cerys."

"Good night, Lex."

"Oh. Cerys?"

"Yeah?"

"Dress up."

* * *

Cerys snapped her phone shut. Balthazar and X averted their eyes as though they had not been listening to every word. She rolled her eyes. She leaned back in her chair in the computer lab. "Is something going to happen, or should I just head home?"

"You don't have to stay," Balthazar told her. He did not sit down. He stood as perfectly motionless in the center of the room as he had for the past two hours. He crossed his arms over his chest. "It doesn't seem as though we're going to learn anything tonight."

Cerys sighed. "I'll stay. If something does happen, I want to be here."

Balthazar inclined his head. "The life of a super hero isn't exactly what you expected, I suppose."

She smiled. "It does, at least, beat lurking around in dark alleys waiting for petty criminals to come along."

X frowned. "Speak for yourself. I spend all day in here monitoring these screens. Sometimes I long for dark alleys and petty criminals."

She snorted. Balthazar frowned at him. "If you would prefer to respond to the next creature attack, X, I would certainly not stop you."

X held up his hands. "You know I can't. Even if I could leave the house, I don't think I'm cut out for field work. I can't even chant."

"Then stop complaining. The work you do here is important."

"There haven't been any more creature attacks," Cerys muttered darkly. "We can't even send someone else in."

"It wouldn't do any good," Barbosa mused. "If Cedric went in and still hasn't come back, no one else is going to do any better."

"At least I would be with my brother."

He frowned at her. "That would not do anyone any good. You are better off here where you can help us fight the war."

"There isn't any war. There isn't anything. We're just floundering here."

"If you don't like the way we operate, you don't have to work with us," X told her indignantly. "But we're the only show in town."

Cerys sighed. "I'm sorry. I'm frustrated. I know we're doing all we can, but it seems as though it's all useless."

X opened his mouth to reply. He snapped it shut again abruptly. A soft, barely audible hum filled the room. A line opened on Nico Creed's cell phone. "Finally," Barbosa breathed.

X and Cerys shushed him. The phone rang once before it was picked up on the other end. "Good evening, sir," said a low, serene voice. They did not recognize the speaker.

"Find out who owns the number," Balthazar ordered quietly.

"Did you do as I asked?" Nico demanded tersely.

"Yes, sir. As requested and not a moment too soon."

"Do you have the owner?" Balthazar asked.

X sighed. "It's Nico."

"Damnit."

"Yes, I suspected as much," Nico said over the line.

"You will find everything meets your specifications, sir," the serene voice told him.

"Thank you, John. I knew you could be relied upon. Text me the number."

"Of course, sir. Enjoy your evening with Miss Simone, sir."

Nico seemed to be smiling when he replied, "I think I will."

The call was over almost as quickly as it had begun. Cerys sighed. "Who's John?" Barbosa demanded.

X lifted his shoulders. His fingers moved rapidly across the glass keyboard in front of him. "There are about fifty Johns who work for Creed Corporation. It could be any of them."

"Yes, but it isn't. He must have some connection to what is happening here. Cross reference them with Bower Research."

"There is a John Hubble in Accounting. He signed off on the invoices to Bower Research."

Barbosa stroked his chin thoughtfully. "Maybe we could talk to him. He might know more than he told the White Collar guys who questioned the employees."

Cerys shook her head. "I don't think so. This might have nothing to do with Bower Research. That doesn't have anything to do with the creature attacks, does it?"

Barbosa frowned. "No, not so far as we have been able to tell. If there is a link, it's not an obvious one."

"This might have to do with the missing chanters."

"It could have something to do with anything. It might be his dry cleaning, for all we can tell. It isn't exactly incriminating," X told them.

"He's smart," Cerys murmured. "He might not say anything plainly on the phone. This could be a waste of time."

"It isn't a waste of time. Eventually, we'll get something. We just need enough to point us in the right direction."

"I don't think this is it."

Barbosa sighed. "It's something. I can feel it."

"A feeling isn't going to help us find Cedric!"

"I know. I know! I'm doing everything I can. I know it isn't enough."

Cerys lowered her head. She sighed deeply. "I'm sorry. I know you are. We all are. I'm just worried about him, Balthazar."

"So am I." He stared at the screens. His dark eyes were distant. "I'm worried about all of them."

"I'm afraid it's already too late."

He spun to her. "Don't think like that, Cerys. It's not helping anyone. We have to believe this isn't all for nothing."

"I'm trying to remain optimistic here, Zar, but all we've got are some cryptic phone calls, a PI in the Caymans who can't turn up anything, and one really awkward date with Lex Creed!"

"At least you'll have another go at the awkward date," X put in. He did not look away from the screen in front of him. Words and images flew across it so quickly, they looked like a jumbled blur.

"Calm down, Cerys," Barbosa barked. She scowled at him. "You should go home. There's nothing more to do here. You need to get some sleep."

"I haven't slept in days."

"I can tell. Go home. You can't do anything else here tonight."

She sighed. She looked as though she might refuse.

He strode forward to grip her shoulders. "X and I will work on finding out who this John is. At least it might help us narrow down what they might be talking about."

"But—"

"If anything happens, I'll call you. I promise."

"What if there is another attack?"

"You'll be closer to the scene at the Warren than if you're here."

She sighed. "All right. I'll go."

Barbosa smiled tightly at her. As she rose, he wrapped an arm around her shoulders. "Even if we can't figure out who John is, we might have enough to shake Nico's tree."

Cerys glanced up at him in interest. "Shake his tree?"

"I am good at shaking trees. Go home. I'll call you tomorrow."

"Okay. Just don't shake his tree too hard. We don't want to put him on guard."

Barbosa smirked. "I think I can be subtle."

* * *

A figure in a dark suit paused in front of his desk in the cube farm. Barbosa glanced up at Nico Creed. He lifted an eyebrow. "Good afternoon, ADA Barbosa," Nico greeted. His smile was as sharp and deadly as a rapier.

Barbosa lifted his eyebrows. "Well. Mr. Creed. I wouldn't have expected to see you here."

"No? I'm just meeting Ryan for a friendly chat. He requires my council on a few business matters."

"Really? And what would those be?"

"I don't believe that's any of your concern."

"I don't suppose it's regarding banking laws in the Cayman Islands?"

"I do not appreciate your implications, Mr. Barbosa."

"No. I don't expect that you do."

Nico smiled at him. "You may try whatever you like, Barbosa. The Creeds always come out on top."

"Do they? Then you clearly have no reason for concern."

"No, I don't believe I do. Nevertheless, I prefer not to see the family name dragged through the dirt."

"I assure you, I have no interest in your family's name."

"I can see that. There will come a time when you wish that you had."

"Perhaps." Barbosa smiled at him. He rose from his seat to close his briefcase over a stack of case files. "If you don't mind, Mr. Creed, I have a lot of work to do."

Nico's eyes narrowed. "Of course. I wouldn't wish to keep you from trumping up charges and waging personal vendettas."

Barbosa laughed. He started towards the courthouse. He paused and spun back to Nico. "Oh, Nico." Nico stopped. "I do hope you enjoyed your evening last night."

Nico blinked. He lifted his eyebrows. "I enjoy most of my evenings."

"I'm sure that you do, though I expect it must be difficult, with such exacting specifications as you must have."

"I'm not sure what you mean."

"Oh, simply that it must be difficult to find employees who are adept enough to execute your requests in the nick of time." Barbosa smiled.

Nico stared at him. His eyes were utterly blank. "Well, in my business, we are often under tight deadlines, as you know. A capable and timely employee is always highly valued."

"I'm sure they are. Well. Do enjoy your lunch. The Specter's special is glazed salmon today. I hear it's quite worth the wait."

Nico smirked. "I assure you, Mr. Barbosa, I never have to wait for anything."

Barbosa laughed. He nodded briskly to Nico. "Until next time, then, Mr. Creed."

"I'll be looking forward to it.

* * *

Nico did not wait for his brother to answer the sharp rap upon the bedroom door. He strode into Lex's room. His blue eyes glinted angrily. Lex paused in the act of buttoning his shirt. He looked at Nico in surprise.

"What's up, Nico?"

Nico paused in the center of the room. He glared at Lex. "Have you been speaking with Carlie?"

"What? No. What are you talking about? I haven't seen Carlie since we had lunch last week. What's going on?"

"It's Barbosa." He said the name as if it were a dirty word.

"What about him?"

"Something's going on."

"What do you mean?"

"He said something...nothing. It's nothing." Nico spun away abruptly.

"It's not nothing or you wouldn't have come in here."

"It's nothing," Nico repeated emphatically. He turned back to his brother. He lifted his eyebrows in interest. "Where are you off to?"

Lex smiled and turned to the mirror to brush his pale hair from his forehead. "I'm going to pick up Cerys."

"The photographer? You're seeing her again?"

"Yes, if you must know."

"A second date already? That isn't like you."

Lex shrugged. "Maybe it's different this time"

"Maybe. Or maybe it's something else."

Lex looked at him in surprise. "What do you mean? What else would it be?"

Nico shrugged. "Nothing, of course."

He spun on his heel and strode from the room without another word. Lex watched after him in bemusement. He frowned. There was something very, very wrong with Nico. He had never seen the paranoid, half-crazed look in his eyes before. He was going to do something. Whatever it was, Lex was pretty sure cancelling a date with Cerys over it would lead to more questions than he was prepared to answer. Nico would have to clean up his own messes tonight.

CHAPTER 13

Cerys jumped at the rapping on her door. Oh, damn. She looked wildly around the penthouse. "Just a minute!" she shouted. She darted towards the door. Lex peered back at her through the peephole. He was early. Just early enough to catch her before she had left the suite to meet him downstairs, in fact. She cursed.

"Cerys, come on. Open up."

She spun around the room. She snatched her handbag from the coffee table. She glanced anxiously at the large board beside the door. It was covered now with all the notes and photographs she'd collected. Lex stared out at her from every corner of it. She didn't think he'd appreciate the tribute.

"I'm coming!"

She angled the board away from the door. She turned the knob slowly. She peered out into the hall. Lex smirked at her. "Are you going to ask me in?"

"You're early."

"I thought I'd meet you at your door. It's ungentlemanly to pick up a woman outside a hotel."

She slipped carefully into the hall. She pulled the door shut behind her. She smiled brilliantly at him. "I appreciate your efforts."

He lifted his eyebrows wryly. "Do you?"

"Shall we go?"

"You look nice," he told her as they stepped onto the lift.

She glanced at him, patting her long, dark curled hair self-consciously. "Thanks. So do you."

"Is there some reason you don't want me to see into your room?"

"I'm a very poor housekeeper. The cleaners have abandoned me completely."

He laughed. He did not look at all convinced by this. "All right. I know you like to have your mysteries."

She smiled. "You look nice, too, but I suspect you know that."

He laughed. "Do you think I am so conceited?"

"I think you are a man who wears his confidence well."

"I think I will take that as a very weird compliment. You, on the other hand, wear a black dress very well."

"Where are you taking me tonight, then? I assume it is not another out of the way restaurant at the end of the world."

"Not tonight. I thought we might try something a little different."

She lifted her eyebrows. "I suppose I'm up for anything."

He laughed. "Are you?"

"I'm wearing my big girl heels and feeling adventurous tonight."

"I'm very glad to hear it." He led her out into the crisp night and assisted her into his car. He smiled at her as he steered the Jaguar out of the Warren's lot. "You're looking unusually cheerful this evening."

"I thought I looked nice."

"They are not mutually exclusive. Quite the contrary."

"Perhaps I am feeling quite cheerful."

"Should I flatter myself that you are simply happy to see me?"

"If you like."

He laughed. "What has got you in such a good mood, then, if it isn't me?"

"I didn't say it wasn't you."

He snorted. "I hadn't realized you were so keen on me yet."

"Well, you seem to be a very likable guy."

"Oh, I am. I am a very likable guy."

She smiled. She watched out the window as he drove through the brightly lit streets of the Diamond District. Men and woman strode languidly along the sparkling, cobblestone walks outside the upscale restaurants and clubs. The couples and small groups along the thoroughfare were dressed to the nines. They might have walked straight from the cover of a fashion magazine or runway. The clubs were the sort you had to wait outside for hours to get in. That is, unless you were someone like Lex Creed. She doubted the Creeds ever had to wait in line anywhere.

Lex stopped the car in a red zone before a packed club. A long line of people wrapped around the block to get inside. Cerys looked up at the bright, red neon sign above the unassuming black door. It read: Mama Louie's. She had heard of the place before. What she'd heard was her co-workers complaining that they'd waited outside for three hours without ever getting inside to see whatever wildly famous jazz band was playing that night.

She glanced at Lex. "A jazz club."

"Not just a jazz club. It's the most famous jazz club in Spectra."

"People wait hours to get in here, but I don't suppose Lex Creed waits for anything."

He laughed. "Being a Creed does come with some privileges." He looked at her. "If you would rather go someplace a little less high-profile, I wouldn't mind. I do know a few nice restaurants you might not have heard of."

She shook her head. "Oh, no. If I'm going to go out with a Creed, I might as well enjoy the perks. I've always wanted to see this place."

He laughed. "Excellent."

"But I do know you're only trying to impress me."

"Don't be so conceited. They have amazing ribs."

A red-coated valet strode out to meet them. He was young and stiff backed. His expression was extremely self important. He started to speak before he leaned down to peer into the driver's side window. "The lot is full." He paused when he caught sight of Lex peering back at him. He cleared his throat. "Mr. Creed, sir. I apologize. I didn't recognize your car. Of course there's a place for you, sir."

Lex smiled. "Thank you, Jimmy."

Cerys snorted. She waited for Lex to climb out of the car and hand his keys to the sheepish valet. She took his hand as he opened the door to assist her out. Lex led her directly to the front door where a large, black man in a sleek black suit stood at a red velvet rope. Lex inclined his head to him and held out his hand.

The doorman took it and shook it vigorously. "It's good to see you, Lex."

Lex smiled. "You, too, Sam. How's the band tonight?"

"Just setting up. They came from New Orleans. I heard them sound check earlier. You'll like them." He opened the rope and stepped aside to allow them in. He nodded politely to Cerys. She saw him tuck a few bills into his jacket pocket. She rolled her eyes.

The hostess greeted them cheerfully. "Good evening, Mr. Creed. We've been expecting you."

"Hello, Polly."

"Your usual table is prepared. If you'll just follow me."

"Thank you."

Cerys leaned against Lex as they climbed a short flight of stairs around the side of the club. His usual table was small and candlelit. It was among only a few other empty tables on a balcony overlooking the large, brightly lit stage. Below them, a jazz quintet was setting up on the stage. The tables and chairs in the main room were already filled to bursting with men and women who laughed, sipped drinks and talked animatedly.

Lex pushed in her chair as she sat. She looked at him archly as he sat across from her. "Well, the VIP treatment isn't so bad," she told him.

"I take it you are impressed."

"A bit. You don't have to impress me, though, Lex."

"I know that. You have other reasons for coming out with me. I just wanted to show you that I don't."

She glanced away from him. Her cheeks heated slightly. She was relieved when a young, beautiful waitress paused at their table. She smiled sweetly at them. "Good evening, Mr. Creed, Miss Knight. I'm Layla. I'll be your server tonight." She bent down slightly to speak quietly to Lex. "Polly made me aware of your specifications, Mr. Creed. Can I start you with wine?"

He glanced at Cerys. She inclined her head. "White, please. Your house will be fine."

"Lex Creed ordering house wine?" Cerys asked, smirking.

"It's better than any bottle I've ever had. In any case, you said I didn't need to impress you."

She laughed. "You don't. But not for the reasons you think. I don't go out with people because they can get me into exclusive clubs or drive me around in expensive cars."

He did not have a chance to reply to this. Layla returned with two glasses and a decanter of crystal clear white wine. She placed it before them. "Would you like to hear our specials?"

He glanced at Cerys again. She smiled. "Didn't you say the ribs were amazing here?"

Lex grinned. "They are."

"Then I'm glad I wore black. I'd like some of those."

He laughed. "Me, too."

"Of course, sir, ma'am."

"I like a lady with simple tastes."

"Well, I eat most of my meals at the Warren. One can only live on gourmet food for so long before they just want to eat beer and pizza like a normal person."

He inclined his head. The jazz band upon the stage struck up a spirited tune. For a long moment, he watched them in silence. Cerys studied him. He didn't seem to mind her scrutiny at all. She leaned across the table to speak to him. "Did you bring me here to avoid having to talk to me?" she asked suspiciously.

Lex laughed. "No. I brought you here because I thought you might enjoy a dance."

She lifted her eyebrows. "A dance."

"Sure." He rose and held out his hand to her. "What about it?"

She smiled and took his hand. There was already a large crowd of people on the floor, dancing spiritedly to the quick, light-hearted music. Lex spun Cerys around with an unpracticed ease. He was a good dancer. She laughed as he swung her carelessly around the floor. She could barely keep up with his energetic steps. "Where did you learn to dance?" she asked breathlessly.

He grinned. He spun her away from him and then tugged her back into the circle of his arms. "Oh, Mother insists the Creed men are expected to be good at a great many social particulars. It wouldn't do for us to be seen doing anything badly."

She laughed. "I suppose not. You do excel at looking good."

"That's quite a compliment. You don't do too bad yourself."

"I'm not a very good dancer."

"You're not bad. You don't have to be good. You just have to be able to follow."

"I think I can do that. At least in this case."

He smirked. "If it becomes too difficult for you, I'll let you lead for a bit."

She laughed. She was relieved when the band ended its set. She was flushed and breathless. They clapped appreciatively with the rest of the crowd. Lex whooped loudly. He offered his hand. "Come on. There are probably cold ribs waiting for us on the balcony."

"Surely not. I expect Lex Creed would never be served cold ribs. They'd simply take them back and bring new ones."

He considered. "That is actually true."

She was right. When they returned to their table, Layla appeared with two steaming plates of ribs, as though she had been anticipating the moment they would be ready for them. Cerys looked at Lex archly. "Pretty good service here."

He smirked. "Well, they do know what I like." She rolled her eyes. "I never eat my dinner until after the first set."

They did not speak for several moments. They tucked into their dinner voraciously. The dancing had left Cerys famished. She barely took care to spread a napkin over her lap before picking up her first rib. Lex grinned. He watched her eat for several long moments. When she realized he was watching her, she flushed slightly and wiped her mouth. "So you come here a lot?"

"I used to. Not so much anymore."

She lifted an eyebrow. "You bring a lot of dates here? You seem to enjoy impressing a woman."

He waved his hand. "I don't go on many dates."

"I find that extremely hard to believe. You are a very good date, all things considered."

He chuckled. "All things considered? I'm not sure exactly what that means, but I'll take it. I do try." He lifted a shoulder nonchalantly. "Most of the women in Spectra know what they're getting with me. And if they want it, they want it for the wrong reasons."

Cerys considered this. "Not everything that comes with being a Creed is a perk, then?"

He sighed deeply. His electric blue eyes shifted away. "No. Not everything."

She studied him. His features were perfectly blank. There was something in his eyes, in the way a shadow seemed to pass over his face, that struck her. She suspected it had nothing to do with the women in Spectra. "Lex, are you all right?"

He blinked. "I'm fine. Why wouldn't I be?"

She narrowed her eyes. "No. You're not, are you? Something is up. What is it?"

He glanced around them. He didn't need to. They were completely alone on the balcony. The band was hopping onto the stage for another set. No one was paying them any attention at all. When Lex Creed wanted to be left alone, she suspected, he got what he wanted. "It's just this stuff with Nico," he admitted finally in a low voice.

She blinked in surprise. She hadn't expected him to bring up his brother. She waited, breathless, for him to go on.

"This new ADA Barbosa seems determined to smear him."

Cerys stared at him in shock for a moment. Then she understood. He wasn't referring to the creatures or to Chant at all. Of course he wasn't. She'd been a fool to think he would bring them up at all, let alone in such a pubic venue. "Of course."

He lifted an eyebrow. "I suppose you know all about it, working for the Daily?"

"Yes, well, I do hear a lot of things." She leaned back in her chair to sip her wine. "Is there any truth to it?"

His lips turned up slightly at the corners. He didn't seem to mind her audacity at all. "Honestly, I wish I knew. I might be able to do something about it."

She narrowed her eyes. "To stop him and help the D.A. or clear it up for him?"

Lex frowned thoughtfully. "We have to take care of our own, Cerys. You of all people understand that."

"I do understand it. But clearing up his mistakes isn't helping anyone. Sometimes you have to do what's right."

"It's not always easy to know what that is."

"Yes, Lex, it is. There is a very clear cut difference between right and wrong."

He lifted an eyebrow. "That is easy for you to say. Your brother was a hero, wasn't he?"

"Is. He is a hero."

"You don't have to face tough decisions about what side to take. Don't judge me for wanting to protect my family. You would do the same. You're lucky you don't have to."

"Don't I?"

He sighed. For a long moment, he stared at her. "I'm sorry. That was insensitive of me. Have you learned anything about Cedric?"

She blinked at him in surprise. She met his gaze in silence. "You really don't know where he is, do you?" she asked suddenly.

For a split second, she thought he looked hurt. "Did you really think I did?"

"Yes."

"Really?"

"Yes. At least I thought you could find out."

He considered her a long moment. "Is that why you went out with me?"

She sighed. "No. I went out with you because I wanted to see what you were like. I wanted to see what would happen."

"And what am I like?"

She smiled. "I think you're...nice. And interesting. You're not what I expected at all."

"No?"

"No."

"Nice?"

"Yes."

"No one has ever described me as nice."

"Well, maybe you aren't nice, really. But you're not bad."

"Did you think I was?"

"Well, I have heard things."

"And who has been saying these things?"

"Many people. Word on the streets."

He laughed. "You really can't trust the word on the streets."

"Sometimes it's the only thing you can trust."

"Do you spend a lot of time with your ear to the ground?"

She shrugged. "So to speak."

He smiled. He studied her silently for a long moment. "I'll see what I can find out about your brother."

She stared at him in shock. "Will you?"

He lifted a shoulder. "Maybe I am a little nice, after all."

"Is that the only reason you're doing it?"

"Why else?"

"All right. I'll leave it at that. I suppose it doesn't matter why."

He reached across the table. He laid a hand upon hers. "I like you, Cerys. If I can do something to make your pain go away, I will."

She looked at him in silence for a long moment. She smiled. "Thank you, Lex."

An hour later, they were standing outside the penthouse suite at the Warren Hotel. Cerys peered up at him. She suddenly wished they were back in the noisy boisterous club. She wasn't sure what to say to him here. He didn't seem to have anything to say, either. He stared down at her in silence. Perhaps he'd already said more than he'd ever meant to.

"Well, I--" She shut her mouth. This was awkward. "Thanks for tonight."

He smiled. "I do hope you didn't mind all the fanfare."

"It's nice once in a while. Maybe not all the time."

"Next time I'll take you to the burger joint around the corner."

She laughed. He leaned towards her. She knew what was going to happen. She tilted her face up to him. His lips were soft and gentle against hers. She sighed softly. She wound her arms around his neck. He caught her around the waist and drew her up against him. Seconds later, he pulled away from her. He smiled.

"Good night, Cerys."

"Good night, Lex."

He stepped away from her. She slid her keycard into the lock.

"Cerys."

She spun around. He advanced on her so abruptly, she gasped. He caught her face in his hands. He kissed her. His lips moved against hers. They were hot and moist. His tongue slid across her lower lip. She opened her mouth. She exhaled in a soft moan and wrapped her arms tightly around her neck. His tongue stroked languidly against hers. Her stomach fluttered.

He pressed her back against the door. He leaned into her. She could feel his arousal hardening against her belly. She pulled him more tightly against her. He responded with an enthusiasm that startled her. He reached down to lift her thigh up to his hip. His hand slid slowly over the soft bare flesh of her leg beneath her dress. She dropped her head back and moaned low in her throat.

He trailed hot kisses across her neck. He tugged her against his arousal, lifting her slightly to press closer to him. His fingers brushed teasingly over the lace of her black panties. Heat pulsed through her. Her heart raced. She rolled her hips as though to bring herself closer to him. He exhaled heavily against her neck. His other hand skimmed across her left breast. He plucked gently at the taut, sensitive nipple through her silk black dress. Her head thumped softly against the wall as she dropped it back.

Arousal flooded her, and she whimpered almost inaudibly. He must have felt the heat pulsing between her legs. His fingers brushed her inner thighs along the line of her panties as though he were waiting to slip them inside, into the hot depths of her desire. He didn't. She moaned in anguish.

He lifted his head to look down at her. His eyes were bright and glittering. His lips were deep, scarlet red. He smiled. "Why don't we take this inside, Cerys?"

"Hallway's good."

He chuckled low in his throat. He dragged his tongue over her throat in the same moment he worked his fingers under the hem of her panties. He didn't touch her, not the way she wanted him to. He waited. "No. Cerys. Let me inside." He squeezed her breast slightly less gently than before, rolling the nipple between his fingertips.

She bucked her hips and clutched at the nape of his neck to draw his mouth back to hers. His tongue plunged into her mouth and explored it more thoroughly. He slipped his fingers further under the panties. She gasped. She felt him smile against her mouth, and then he drew a fingertip lightly across the swollen, sensitive slit between her legs. He encountered moisture there and groaned from low in his throat. She inhaled sharply. Her hands clenched around his neck.

He pressed closer to her and dipped a finger inside the slick moisture of her arousal. She moaned and moved into him. "We can't do this out here."

"There's no one else on this floor."

"Cerys." He withdrew his hand from her, and she groaned in disappointment. He lowered her thigh. She blinked at him through hooded eyes. He smiled and kissed her softly on the mouth. "I won't do this in the hallway. Let me in."

Her breath was short and ragged. She nodded blearily and reached for his hand. He caught her wrist and pressed her palm against the tight front of his trousers. His arousal strained against his pants. It was long and hard. He cupped the side of her face in the other hand and kissed her earnestly. She closed her eyes and melted into him. She reached back to grope for the door with her free hand.

Then her eyes flew open. The board. She hadn't even covered it up. Damn. She dropped her hands to his chest to shove him gently away from her. "I don't think that's a good idea."

His brow furrowed in confusion. He blinked at her in surprise for several seconds. "What? Why not?"

"I'm, um...I'm not that sort of girl."

He lifted his eyebrows. "You're not that sort of girl." He narrowed his eyes at her. "Is there something in there you don't want me to see?"

"I had a really good time tonight, Lex."

He stared at her for several long moments. He looked as though he wasn't sure what to say to her. Then he laughed. "Okay."

"Okay?"

"Okay. We're moving too fast. I won't go inside. Keep your secrets." He leaned towards her again. His kiss was soft and chaste. If he was feeling the strain of their interrupted interlude, he didn't let on.

She wouldn't either, then. "You're angry."

"I'm not angry. I'm not that sort of guy."

"I'm sorry."

"Whatever you're hiding in there, maybe you'll hide it better next time."

"I told you; I'm not hiding anything."

"Right. Well, I'll see about sending a cleaner up to your room the next time we go out."

She laughed. "Good night, Lex."

"Good night."

She didn't wait to watch him stride towards the elevator. She slipped inside her room. She fell back against the door with trembling legs. She glared murderously at the dry erase board beside her. "I don't like you anymore."

CHAPTER 14

It looked as though Barbosa and X had not moved since the last time she'd seen them in the computer lab at Chant headquarters two evenings ago. Barbosa stood in the center of the glass octagon with his arms crossed over his chest. He stroked his chin thoughtfully as he stared at the words and pictures flying across X's screen. She paused beside him.

"Anything good yet?"

He did not look remotely surprised to see her. "No. But purchasing a bank in the Cayman Islands is not as difficult as one might suspect. I'll have something on Nico soon. Enough to move things along anyway. It doesn't matter if it sticks to him or not."

X did not spin around to look at her. His eyes darted rapidly from side to side as he read the data in front of him. "You sound cheerful. That's new."

Barbosa raised his eyebrows at her. "The courting going well, then?"

"Yes, thank you for asking."

"Has he invited you over yet?"

"I am not that kind of lady, Balthazar."

"Then become that kind of lady, Cerys."

"It's a delicate task. It requires a bit of finesse."

He gave her an incredulous look. "I am sure a woman like you can talk the man she's dating into bringing her home if she really wanted to."

Cerys blushed furiously. "It's not so much that as...well, he seems keen on coming into my place, anyway."

"I suppose it's better than nothing, if it all leads to the same thing."

"I don't feel comfortable discussing this with you two."

"It's just business."

"That's easy for you to say. It's not your sex life we're discussing as if it were nothing more than an exchange of goods and services."

He considered. "Yes, when you put it that way, it does seem a little insensitive."

"Now it's awkward," X put in.

Barbosa glanced sidelong at Cerys. "You aren't starting to like him, are you, Cerys?"

She frowned. "I don't know how I feel about him. I'm not sure what he is yet."

"Just don't get too carried away. We need you to stay focused on what we're doing here."

Carried away. She was lucky she hadn't gotten carried away last night. She nearly had. She spun a glare on him. "Believe me, I haven't forgotten. I wouldn't even be here if I wasn't looking for Cedric. I'm not going to forget about him because some man took me out on a couple dates."

"Right. Sorry."

"Anyway, I might have another way into Creed Manor."

"Don't tell me you pick pocketed his keys."

"Don't be ridiculous. I wouldn't even know how. I've got an assignment for the Daily. Libby Gore's writing up a feature about the prominent families in Spectra. She's interviewing them in their homes. They put me on the feature yesterday."

"They're taking an interview in their home?"

"Yes."

"That seems out of character."

"Yes, well, I think we have you to thank for it. They've always been reticent with the press, but since you got on Nico's case and started dragging the family name through the mud, they seem keen to put on a good face."

Balthazar smirked. "I knew I was good for something."

"Come on, Zar, we all think you're very good," X told him calmly.

They ignored him. "So you can look for clues while you're there," Balthazar said.

Cerys nodded. "Yes. Or at least maybe we'll get an idea of what we're dealing with. I don't expect they will lead the press into Nico's evil lair, but maybe we can get an idea of where in the house it might be."

"Well, it's worth a shot, anyway. Let me know if you turn anything up." He glanced at her in interest. "Does Lex know?"

"No. I think it will be a nice surprise for him." She smirked. "Anything new on the taps?"

"No, not really. Nico seems to be opening up a new location. But for what, I have no idea."

Cerys frowned. "Could it be important?"

"Yes. Maybe. I can't be sure."

"Where is it?"

"I don't know. He never says over the line. He doesn't say much. It's all ambiguous." He sighed. "He probably suspects he's been tapped. He's been a lot more careful since our last conversation."

"See, that is why people don't shake trees. Sometimes things fall out of them and hit you on the head."

He rolled his eyes. "I don't think it would have mattered much. He isn't stupid. He knows we can tap him. Surely he'd suspect that we had."

"Maybe he thought D.A. Rutherford would tell him."

"I am pretty certain that he would have."

Cerys sighed. "You should go after him next."

"It had crossed my mind. In any case, we aren't getting much on the taps."

"Well, don't scare him off before we find Cedric and the others. If he thinks you really have something, he might run or hide them or worse."

"I know. I know, Cerys. When we have something solid, we'll take him down without giving him a chance to do anything about it."

"I hope you're right. I hope he hasn't already done something."

Balthazar considered this a long moment. "I guess I hadn't really thought about that. I thought if I kept the heat on, he would stop the attacks."

"He has. At least for the moment. We haven't heard of any in a few days."

"Yes, but...if he thinks I might actually have something on him, he might do something rash."

Cerys sighed deeply. "It's possible."

He looked at her for several long moments. His brow furrowed. "I think maybe I should back off. Take the heat off. Maybe let Rutherford think I've given up and dropped the investigation."

"If he thinks he's safe, he might do something careless and we can get something on him."

Barbosa nodded contemplatively. "It's worth a try. So far, railroading him hasn't done much good for anyone."

"Lex said he'd help me find Cedric."

"What? Why didn't you just say that before?"

"Because...while his resources might be helpful under normal circumstances, I think it means he really doesn't know where he is."

"Ah. Do you think he believes Nico has them?"

"Yes. I think he does. But he won't talk about him at all. He only mentioned the investigation for the first time last night, and then it wasn't anything new. He doesn't talk about his family specifically, and when he does it's usually about the past, not now."

"But if he really wants to help find him, we may be able to bring him over to our side."

"Maybe. I'm not sure. The last time I talked to him, I got the impression... well, I think the reason he doesn't mention what's happening is he doesn't want to have to choose between me and them. I don't think he can go against his family."

"He can. He just won't."

"It all amounts to the same thing. I want to find Cedric, but I want to stop Nico just as much. Even if Lex helps us get Cedric back, it doesn't necessarily mean what Nico's doing will stop."

"Then we just have to give him a reason to turn on his brother."

Cerys sighed. "It would have to be a really good one."

"We'll just have to think of one, then. Who knows? Maybe we'll get lucky and Nico will give him a reason all on his own."

"That would be lucky. But I don't think I'll hold my breath for it."

* * *

Nico glanced into the rearview mirror. The battered old Honda Civic was several cars behind him on the dark thoroughfare that wound through the Industrial District. He smirked. He slowed the Maserati. Two cars passed him. The Honda slowed. Nico had to hand it to his brother. He was dogged, anyway.

Nico's cell phone chirped. He swung the Maserati abruptly into a dark, empty parking lot. A single light burned in the quiet, featureless warehouse. A night watchman peered out the window into the night. Nico did not turn off his lights. He picked up his phone. A text message lit up the screen.

He is behind you.

Nico chuckled. "Somewhat late, Tully, but I appreciate the sentiment, anyway."

Nico replied, I know.

I am on my way to the pen.

I trust you will take care of things in my absence.

Of course, sir. Is there anything else you require?

No. Thank you. See you in the morning.

Nico snapped his cell phone shut. He backed out of the parking lot. The night watchman strode out of the warehouse towards the Maserati. Nico lifted a hand to him and stamped on the accelerator.

Behind him, a battered Honda Civic switched on its lights and rolled slowly after him. Nico laughed. He was enjoying giving Lex the run around. "Just another hour or so through the Industrial District, big brother," he said blithely. "Tully has some work to do, and I can't have you interfering. Then we can both enjoy a nice glass of wine while we pretend I don't know you've been tailing me all over town every night this week."

* * *

It was not Cerys' first time at Creed Manor. Nevertheless, the wrought iron gates and massive trees were as impressive and imposing as when she had first seen them. Libby didn't seem fazed by the extravagant security measures the Creeds employed to keep out solicitors, reporters, rumormongers and other unwanted visitors. She idled her car at the closed gate and languidly held up her press pass to the camera.

The gate crept open with a screech. In the daylight, Creed Manor was a brilliant, sparkling monolith of white stone. The trees and gardens surrounding it were lush and verdant. Libby steered the car along the winding road without paying any attention to the beautiful grounds. Clusters of rose bushes lined the drive. The blossoms were huge and well-tended. There were so many different unique colors, Cerys wondered if they had been created exclusively for the Creed's garden.

Libby parked the car in front of the house. A man in a smart, charcoal grey suit was waiting on the front steps. He stood so stiffly, he might have been a statue. He wasn't. When they stepped out of the car, he turned towards them. Cerys blinked. She wondered how long he had been standing there waiting for them.

He inclined his head. "Misses Gore and Knight."

Cerys lifted her eyebrows. "Yes."

He turned smartly and gestured them towards the door. He opened it. Cerys and Libby exchanged an amused glance. The man bowed them in with an exaggerated flourish. "Miss Peyton is waiting for you in the sitting room. If you would come this way, please."

Cerys allowed Libby to precede her. She glanced around at the stunning entrance hall. She had seen it before. She hadn't had a chance to study it at the party. Now, she took her time. The hardwood and marble floors gleamed. Fine art and elegant furnishings decorated every room. It wasn't a comfortable home. It was a beautiful home, but it wasn't the sort of place children played or families ate together in front of the television. It was like living in an art museum or a palace. It was truly no wonder all the Creeds had such a maladjusted view of the world and everyone around them. It was like growing up in a beautiful gilded cage.

Peyton Creed was lounging on a chaise in an elegant silk pants suit of shimmering ivory when the butler showed them into the sitting room. Her long, sleek red hair was combed back in an elaborate twist. She wore so much makeup, her smile seemed brittle and stiff. She rose gracefully from the chaise and greeted them effusively.

"Good afternoon, Miss Gore. I'm so pleased to see you again." She looked at Cerys. "Oh! You've brought a photographer. I hadn't expected. Miss Knight, is it?"

Cerys smiled at her. It was difficult not laugh, for she doubted the woman turned out so elaborately every day. "Yes, ma'am."

"Please. Call me Peyton. Your photographs of my birthday party were simply beautiful. I don't suppose I could convince you to email me some of them?"

"Sure. I have some I didn't use for the spread. You might like to see them."

"Terrific. I'll have my man give you the family email address on the way out." She gestured around the room. "You may take photos of whatever you wish."

Cerys smiled. "Why don't we get a shot of you by the mantle?"

"Oh, well, if you insist." Peyton moved to the large, stone fireplace. Upon the mantle were several family photographs. Above it was a large, beautiful oil painting of the house. Cerys was disappointed not to find a huge portrait of some long dead ancestor peering creepily down at them like she'd seen in films and old television shows. The landscape was slightly more tasteful.

Cerys took several shots of Peyton as she posed beside her beloved family heirlooms. Libby took advantage of the matriarch's good cheer. "Tell us a little about Creed Manor, Peyton."

Peyton smiled proudly. "It's lovely, isn't it? I was nineteen when I married Caleb and moved here. He was the eldest of his two brothers. When his younger brother, Aaron, married, he and his wife left the house. Caleb's parents died before my eldest, Alexander, was born. They house has been ours since. It will be Alexander's eventually."

"Not Nico's?" Libby asked in interest.

"Lex is the eldest, so he is the heir." Peyton smiled. "Of course, he would not turn out his brother. Nicholas loves this place. He will probably spend the rest of his life here."

"How does he feel about Lex being the heir?"

Peyton blinked. "Well, I'm sure he's perfectly content. He has all he could possibly want."

"I can see that. It is a beautiful house. I understand it was built about a hundred years ago?"

"Yes. My husband's great great grandfather, Nicholas, built it in the early 1900's. Nico was named for him, of course. He was born in the late 1800's. He went west during the gold rush. He was lucky. He made a fortune in the mines with his partner, Mordecai Mobley."

"Mobley?" Cerys asked.

"Yes. Nicholas and Mordecai were the closest of friends. They moved north and built their homes here side by side to always be near each other."

Libby glanced at Cerys. Her dark eyes glittered. Cerys suspected there were several questions in the intrepid reporter's mind that she was dying to ask. She also suspected Pete Blake, their editor, had given very specific instructions not to. "They did not go into business together?"

Peyton's glance was slightly sharp. "No. They did not agree on that point. Nicholas was interested in technology. He had a vision for the future. He dabbled in electricity and telephones and the various discoveries of the age. Mordecai had trained as a doctor before moving west for the gold rush. In fact, he worked sometimes as a doctor in the mining town in which they lived. He was interested in developing new medicines and equipment to help people."

"Did they quarrel?"

Peyton laughed. "I wouldn't know. I'm afraid I wasn't there, but they remained close and each was very successful in their ventures. The Mobleys still work in medical advancement, and Creed Corporation is a leader in technology and computer software. It was Caleb who moved the company towards computers. He saw their potential in the beginning and invested heavily in them. He shared his great grandfather's visions of a bright future."

"Will you tell us a little about Caleb?"

Cerys spun away from her examination of the lovely sitting room. "He was a wonderful man," Peyton said. Her blue eyes slid away wistfully. "He was smart and charismatic and handsome. I think I loved him the moment I saw him."

"How did you meet?"

"At an art showing back in the days when the Art District was thriving. I was an artist. He came to one of my shows. He bought my most expensive painting. He claimed to be a fan." She smiled. "Later, on our first date, he told me it was me he liked, not the art. I wasn't sure whether to be flattered or offended. It was all the same in the end. I married him. He kept that painting. It hangs in our bedroom. He said it always reminded him of how we met. He was sweet sometimes. He was even romantic."

"You were an artist."

"Yes, well, I gave up my art when I discovered there was no money in it." She laughed. "I still draw and paint sometimes. When I married Caleb, I gave it up as a career. My work was here, in the home, raising our family."

"Did you ever regret it?"

Peyton laughed and gestured around her. "Regret it? Would you, if you were given all this in exchange? And Caleb always encouraged me to continue painting. He was very supportive."

"I'd like to see some of your paintings," Cerys told her honestly.

Peyton tittered and waved her hand. "I was never really very good. I would be embarrassed to show a real artist."

Cerys laughed. "I promise you, Peyton, I am no artist. I wanted to be, when I was a kid, but I wasn't any good. I took up photography because I didn't have much of a choice."

Peyton smiled at her. "Well, maybe we can look at them a little later."

"I'd like that."

"It must have been hard on you all when Caleb passed away," Libby said to draw Peyton's attention back to the interview.

"Yes. It was. Very, very hard. I miss him every day. It was hard on Grace and the boys. Caleb was our whole world. We all looked up to him and looked to him when something went wrong or something needed done. He was always there."

"And now Lex is?"

"Yes. Lex is very like his father in many ways. He had to step in and become the head of the family before he was really ready, but he has never let us down. He is everything his father would have wanted him to be."

"What about Nico? Is he?"

"Nico is different than Lex. He likes to live his own life. He is loyal to the family, of course, but I don't know that he'd enjoy the duties of running the family. It is a challenge, indeed."

"I imagine it must be. There must be a lot of responsibilities."

"Nico has never shied from responsibility. He is fiercely loyal to us all. But I believe he enjoys his freedom rather more than Lex. My eldest is a very serious man. His family and his duty always come first."

Cerys' stomach sank slightly. She smiled at Peyton. "Can we see some of the rest of the house? I would love to get some shots."

"Of course. Come. I'll give you the grand tour."

CHAPTER 15

Creed Manor was a huge, labyrinthine collection of rooms so richly and grandly furnished, it might have been the home of a great king. Every surface gleamed. Crystal chandeliers hung from every cathedral ceiling to cast the fine, expensive art, sculptures and furniture in the most impressive light. None of the rooms seemed particularly inviting. In fact, they seemed untouched and lifeless. They were beautiful, but they were not the sort of rooms in which a person might feel comfortably at home or welcomed to spend a relaxing evening. Cerys snapped photographs dutifully.

Libby Gore was an extremely good interviewer. One would not have known it. She allowed Peyton to ramble expansively as the matriarch led them through sitting rooms, libraries, studies and the impressively large, polished ballroom in which Cerys had first met the Creeds. Peyton spent the better part of an hour pointing out and describing various pieces of art the family had received as tokens of gratitude for their extensive charity work. She spoke eloquently of the various contributions her husband and sons had made to the city's schools, museums, and community centers, amongst other things.

Cerys wasn't listening. She suspected Libby wasn't, either. She knew what Libby really wanted to ask about was Barbosa and the allegations against Nico. She might even have wanted to ask about the creature attacks. She certainly didn't want to hear the self-indulgent recommendations Peyton was spinning for her now. It didn't really matter what Libby wanted to ask. They had been given firm instructions.

Cerys didn't mind in the least. She knew all she needed to know about the Creeds, insofar as Cedric was concerned. What she really needed to know was where Nico was keeping him. It didn't seem likely there could be a chanter prison somewhere here in this cold, pristine palace. It didn't seem likely the woman describing her late husband's love of swing dancing could be involved in kidnapping chanters off the streets.

She wondered for a moment how it was possible the family could have hidden their true face for so long. They were very good at hiding. And so where, she thought as she snapped photos of a sunny lounge, would they have hidden the chanters? There were no distinguishing markings to suggest what book to tap, what lever to pull or what sculpture's head to remove to reveal the means to the entrance of an evil lair. There were no moans from behind the walls to indicate where the captive chanters were kept. There was no trick staircase or big red phone in any of the sitting rooms.

She hadn't expected any of that. The least she could have hoped for was an unmarked door and a warning from Peyton to stay out or face Nico's wrath. That would have been something. Peyton seemed perfectly at her ease. She didn't seem to even notice that Cerys moved around the rooms, pulling books from shelves and staring at creases in the walls as though they might reveal a hidden panel in the wall. It would take hours to examine every room. The house was huge.

"What is on the top two floors?" Cerys asked abruptly.

Peyton spun towards her. She struck a pose in front of a particularly vulgar sculpture of a naked cherub holding a bow and arrow. Cerys snapped her picture. "Those are our private chambers."

"Ah." Libby smiled. "I don't suppose we can see them?"

Peyton considered. "I do not think my children would appreciate that. They are rather private."

Now they were getting somewhere. "We certainly wouldn't wish to intrude. It's just it would be very interesting to see how you all live behind closed doors. When you have time to yourselves," Libby said smoothly. Cerys beamed at her.

"Well, I don't suppose it would hurt terribly. It is the purpose of the feature, isn't it? We are normal people, just like everyone else." Peyton smiled radiantly at them. She lifted a hand to gesture towards the wide, winding staircase to their right. "We wouldn't want to seem as though we're hiding anything."

Cerys lifted her eyebrows. She managed not to snort in disbelief. Libby's smile was admirably bland. They climbed the stairs. Peyton had anticipated their request. Her chambers were as beautiful and sterile as the rest of the house. The four poster bed was draped in a sheer, blue canopy like a queen's. Tasteful art hung along the walls. Beyond the bed was a large dressing room with two enormous walk-in closets filled with gorgeous, expensive clothes. The other was filled with shoes. Cerys suspected she had enough to fill several shops.

Peyton laughed as she caught her examining them. "We women. We do like our shoes. I have to say, my passion for them is slightly out of control."

Cerys laughed. "No woman could judge you for that."

Peyton smiled. "My daughter Grace has rooms across the hall, but she spends most of her time in the city in her own apartment these days. Her event planning business is so successful. She has very little free time, and she finds it easier to be closer to her work."

Someone had been tidying Grace's rooms in her absence. They were feminine and sweet, as though she hadn't changed the decorations since she'd been a child. The counterpane was soft pink. Several brighter pink lace accent pillows were piled high on top of it. It didn't look as if it had been disturbed in several days. Peyton strode inside. She seemed lost in thought a moment. Her hand fluttered over the pink curtains. She sighed.

When she turned back to them, it was as the moment had never occurred. "Would you two care for a drink? Being a reporter isn't like being a police officer, right? You can drink on duty."

Libby laughed. "If you couldn't, there wouldn't be a lot of point in taking the gig."

Peyton smiled. "I'll show you the library. It seems to be the most popular place in the house. We spend a lot of time there together."

Cerys raised her eyebrows. She had gotten the distinct impression the Creeds didn't spend a lot of their time together anywhere, unless they were within view of a camera. They followed Peyton through a long, winding corridor. She spoke as she walked. "The boys' rooms are upstairs. They like their space. They each have a set of rooms up there in which they can engage in—well, whatever men do when they are without their women."

Libby laughed. She paused in front of a single door near the stairs. It was oddly placed, as though it were purposely separated from the other rooms on the floor. Cerys paused in front of it. Libby noticed. She lifted an eyebrow. "What's this room, Peyton?"

Peyton glanced at it. She seemed surprised, as though she hadn't known it was there. "Oh. That used to belong to the original Mrs. Creed's lady's maid. She kept her own rooms apart from her husbands, I understand. She kept her lady close at hand." She smiled. "Grace and I prefer to attend to ourselves. I believe Nico took it over years ago as a music room. He dabbled, I remember, in many instruments. He was particularly gifted at the violin."

Her eyes drifted away wistfully for a moment. She continued. "He gave it up. He was an intense child. He threw himself into everything he did. The trouble was, he never stuck to any one thing for very long. I don't know the last time he was in here."

Cerys' pulse leapt. "Are any of his old instruments still in there?"

Peyton considered. "I don't really know. I suppose they must be. I never saw them anywhere else."

"Can we see it?" Libby asked eagerly.

Peyton hesitated for an ephemeral instant. Her expression didn't change, but Cerys thought she saw something flicker in Peyton's blue eyes. "Nico likes his privacy. He usually keeps his rooms locked."

"It's okay," Libby told her off-handedly. "I had no idea Nico was interested in music."

"He is interested in many things. Why don't we just look in?" Peyton smiled. She stepped forward and tried the knob. It wasn't locked.

The instruments, stacked neatly against the wall, were the only things in the room. Peyton let out an almost inaudible sigh of relief. Cerys was disappointed. It wasn't exactly an evil lair. Peyton spun around in a slow circle. A small frown furrowed her brow.

"I seem to remember this room being much bigger." She shrugged and smiled at them. "Isn't it amazing how time twists your memory. Well. How about that drink?"

Cerys didn't want to leave the room. She'd hardly had time to examine each crease in the wall for hidden panels or secret passageways. Nevertheless, she was obliged to follow when Peyton gestured them out of the room. There was something different in the set of Peyton's jaw now. Her smile looked slightly fixed. Cerys suspected they were wearing out their welcome very quickly.

The library was stunning. Books lined every wall. Cerys snapped several photographs of the stained glass window on the far wall. As Peyton strode towards the bar to pour them each a drink, Cerys remarked upon it. "I have never seen a window like that before. It's beautiful."

Peyton glanced at it. She smiled somewhat wanly. "Yes, Caleb put it in after Lex and Nico broke the old one when they were kids. They were playing baseball or something in the house."

Cerys laughed. She took the drink Peyton offered and strode towards it to look out. "You can barely see the Mobley house across the trees."

"It has the benefit of affording us a little more privacy."

Libby joined Cerys at the window. "Can you see it from here?"

"Oh, yes. Our houses are placed in such a way that we can see each other quite plainly from this side of the house," Peyton replied.

Libby squinted her eyes through the blurry glass. "I can't wait to see the opposite view."

Peyton spun to her. "I beg your pardon?" she demanded, frowning.

Libby looked at her. "Well, we're visiting the Mobleys after we're through here."

Peyton's eyes narrowed to slits. "The Mobleys?"

"Yes. We're visiting several well-known families in town. You, the Mobleys, Mayor Rainey's family, the Rutherfords. The usual people," Libby explained.

Peyton's face had changed so abruptly, she seemed like a different person. Her lip curled. Her eyes glared furiously between them. "If the Mobleys are included in this feature, my family wants no part in it!"

Libby and Cerys blinked at her in surprise. "But why? I understand your families aren't close anymore, but I was under the impression you were friendly with them." Cerys asked with such convincing innocence, Libby turned her head to hide her smirk from the incensed matriarch.

Peyton took several deep breaths. "Oh, yes. Of course we are. Of course. I beg your pardon," she said. She fanned herself with her hand. Her cheeks flushed slightly. Her smile returned as though the hateful look had never been on her face at all. "Forgive my outburst. I suppose I became jealous of the spotlight for a moment. I had been enjoying all the attention." The ladies laughed together for a moment. "Silly me. Of course we are friendly. We've lived right across the garden for decades. They're lovely."

Cerys wasn't convinced. She sipped her drink silently. Libby sat down in one of the wing-backed arm chairs to listen to Peyton explain the origins of a collection of very old and rare books. Cerys didn't sit. She moved around the room. She touched a number of books. None of them triggered a spring in the wall. She supposed it was too much to assume the villains would have the same mechanism in their lair as the heroes, even if it was a tried and true classic.

Somewhere downstairs, a door opened and slammed. Peyton lifted her head. She smiled and rose to her feet. "That must be one of the boys."

Moments later, Nico Creed burst into the room. There was a gleam of triumph in his electric blue eyes. When he saw Libby and Cerys, he stopped. His eyes narrowed. "What are they doing here?" he demanded coldly.

"Nico!" Peyton exclaimed. She looked utterly shocked. "Don't be rude. I told

142

you about this, remember? We're being interviewed by the Daily."

Nico stared at Cerys. She did not like the arctic glint in his eyes. "Of course, Mother. I'm sorry. I had almost forgotten."

Peyton looked slightly crestfallen. "Isn't this why you're home early? I asked you and your brother to be here for this two days ago."

Nico smiled faintly. "Yes. Of course it is. I just didn't realize...so what can I answer for you, Miss Gore? I'm sure you've been dying to get your claws in me."

She had been, Cerys knew. It must have killed her to ask the most notorious man in Spectra City about his love life and how it felt to be so powerful and well-liked. It looked painful, anyway.

Nico lifted an eyebrow. "Come on now, Libby. You don't really want to hear about my day to day life as VP of Creed Corp and my endless lunches with clients and politicians and other influential people. You really want to know about the investigation, don't you?"

"Nico!" Peyton hissed.

"Well, she does. I can see it in her eyes. I'm actually impressed you managed to restrain yourself. So, come on. Go ahead." Nico's smile was so charming that, looking at him, it was difficult to believe he was responsible for all the trouble in Cerys' life. Well—maybe not all the trouble.

"Okay. We've all heard the rumors and the allegations of money laundering and dummy corporations in the Cayman Islands," Libby said. Cerys admired her composure. "We've heard the official line from your press people. How about your side of the story? What do you have to say about it?

Nico grinned. "Well, it just so happens I have just left a lunch meeting with D.A. Rutherford. It turns out the Assistant District Attorney in charge of the investigation has been unable to find conclusive evidence that there are any illegal accounting practices connected to Creed Corp. In fact, he has officially dropped the investigation. I expect your office will be hearing from the DA's PR people within the week. ADA Barbosa has agreed to make a public statement to the effect and an apology to me and my family for the trouble."

Libby's mouth dropped open. "Are you serious?"

"Completely."

"Can I quote you?"

"If you like. Here's a quote for you: ADA Barbosa's allegations were outrageous and untrue. It was only a matter of time before he realized that nothing could come of the investigation. My family and I will happily accept his apology and bear no ill feelings towards him."

"Well, I am sure this news pleases your family greatly," Cerys murmured.

"Yes, Peyton, do you have anything to add?" Libby asked eagerly, spinning towards the stunned-looking red-haired woman.

Peyton opened her mouth to speak. Nico cut her off. "You've been seeing a lot of my brother lately, I hear, Miss Knight."

Peyton spun to look at her in surprise. Libby gave her an incredulous look. "Really?"

Cerys lifted her shoulder casually. "We met at Peyton's birthday party. We ran into each other again somewhere."

"Is that so?" Peyton studied her narrowly.

"You've seen each other rather more often than such a lofty explanation would indicate." Nico's smile was as sharp as a razor.

"Well, we have run into each other one or two times subsequently," Cerys replied smoothly.

"Have you, indeed."

Cerys was saved from reply. Lex strode into the room. He paused. He stared around at them all with an expression so void of emotion, he might have been a statue. "Cerys?" he asked, as though her presence in his house was the most puzzling element of the scene before him. Everything else, he could probably have coped with. They others turned to her in interest. "What are you doing here?"

"I see you weren't expecting us, either, Lex," Libby said, grinning.

Lex blinked several times. Then realization dawned in his face. "The story."

"Don't either of you listen to your mother?" Peyton asked archly. She turned a long-suffering look upon the two young women. "Honestly."

Nico was studying Lex with narrow eyes. "Ah, Miss Knight did not tell you she would be here?"

Lex looked at him blandly. "No. She didn't."

Cerys met his gaze. She smiled blithely. "Well, I only just received the assignment. There wasn't the time to warn you."

Lex didn't look as if he entirely believed her. He smirked at her in a way that suggested there would be some penance to pay for her mischief. A tiny thrill raced along her spine. She thought of the last time she'd seen him. Heat lanced through her body from head to toe. "Or perhaps your new friend is trying to dig up dirt on you, eh, Lex?" Nico said, smiling. The expression did not touch his chilling eyes. "It wouldn't be the first time a lady was caught doing that."

Cerys smiled. Lex did not laugh at this. "Well, aren't you suspicious, Nico," Peyton scolded. "I'm sure the young lady is doing no such thing. She didn't ask about Lex at all." She stepped forward to press Cerys' hand. "Why don't you tell me a little more about yourself, dear, since you seem to be acquainted with other members of my family. I had no idea."

Cerys blushed. She opened her mouth to reply. Lex and Nico chuckled. "Mom," Lex said gently. "Perhaps now is not the time for that. I think the ladies want to talk about us, and you know how we like to talk about ourselves." He winked at Cerys. "Cerys, if you would like to dig up dirt on me, how about later tonight?"

She didn't recognize the look in his eyes. She was uneasy. She smiled at him. "All right."

Peyton smiled happily. Nico, however, frowned.

"Eight o'clock all right?" Lex asked calmly.

"Fine."

"Well," Libby said brightly. "This has been fun. Peyton, thank you so much for your time. We've got an appointment with the Mobleys next door, and we wouldn't want to be late."

"The Mobleys?" Nico growled.

Peyton's look was sharp. "Of course, Nico. The Daily is talking to all the old families in Spectra."

Lex glanced at Cerys. He lifted an eyebrow. She shrugged and held up her camera. She turned to Peyton. "Thank you so much for the photographs, Peyton."

"Of course, dear. It was lovely to see you again." She tucked her arm in Cerys' as the party moved downstairs to the entrance hall. "You simply must come see me again. Perhaps you can join us for dinner sometime."

Cerys threw a beseeching look at Lex over her shoulder. He smirked at her. "That would be very nice. Thank you."

"Lovely. Well, good day to you both. It has been very pleasant. I trust you've gotten enough for your feature."

Libby smiled. "Oh, I think we got what we needed. Thank you, Peyton." She threaded her arm through Cerys and tugged. "Bye!"

Cerys allowed Libby to lead her firmly towards the door. "Cerys," Lex called. His voice was a low purr. She imagined she heard amusement in it. "See you at eight."

"Okay. Bye!"

Libby did not even wait until they had reached her car. She pounced on Cerys the moment the door had closed behind them. "I didn't know you were dating Lex Creed! Why didn't you tell me?"

Cerys sighed. She and Libby weren't exactly intimate friends. Not to mention, telling Libby something was like putting out an ad in the paper. She didn't tell Libby this. She shrugged. "We've only been out a couple times. It's not like we're planning our engagement."

"Well, nice one." Libby smirked at her. "He's quite a catch, isn't he?"

Cerys made a noncommittal noise. She glanced back up at the looming house. She wasn't sure what Lex was. She was sure that the Creeds were not what they appeared. Could he be sincere, or was it merely another deception? "Maybe."

"Come on. I can't wait to hear what the Mobleys have to say about the Creeds. It was funny how Peyton fired up about them, wasn't it? You'd think something was going on there."

"You would, wouldn't you?"

"We'd better make this interview quick. If what Nico said about Barbosa dropping the investigation is true and we don't get it to Pete before the evening news, neither one of us will have a job by morning."

Cerys smirked. "Speak for yourself. I'm only a temp."

"Yeah," Libby said darkly. She glanced sourly at Cerys. "Not to mention you have an inside line to the Creeds."

"I wouldn't be too sure about that."

CHAPTER 16

The Mobley mansion was as gorgeous as Creed Manor and built of the same shimmering white stone. The courtyards and gardens that surrounded it on all sides were as luscious. Its balconies were polished and overgrown with ivy and roses. It was oddly brighter than Creed Manor, as though the sun shone upon it even in the gloominess of the afternoon. Looking up at Creed Manor next door, Cerys could almost imagine it lurked beneath a large, dark shadow. Perhaps it was merely the atmosphere of the place, the sense that something sinister lurked behind every beautiful, extravagant room.

The Mobley's house felt positively jolly in comparison. A butler did not meet them upon the step. When they rang the bell, Celeste Mobley opened the door. She greeted them with a sweet, cheerful smile. Her long, dark blonde hair was tied in a careless ponytail. She wore no makeup, but her face was lovely still despite her age. She was dressed in jeans and an emerald green sweater that matched her eyes. She could not have been more different from the stunning, imposing Creed matriarch.

"Ah. Libby, Cerys?" she asked. They inclined their heads and held out the hands to shake. "I'm Celeste. It's lovely to meet you. Come in." The entrance hall of Mobley Mansion was huge and stately. There was a distinct sense of life within the house. A small, gleeful, brown Shi Tzu bounded forward to meet them. He was shaggy and wore a little blue bow on the top of his head. He leapt excitedly at their feet.

Libby stepped back in surprise, holding up her hands as though in surrender. Cerys glanced at her in amusement. "Are you afraid of dogs, Libby?"

"No!" Libby replied hotly. "Not afraid. They just...make me uncomfortable."

Celeste laughed and swept the little dog up in her arms. He licked her face excitedly. "This is Paolo. He's a lover, but I think we'd best keep him in his room for now." She strode towards a small door on their left.

"He has his own room?" Libby hissed to Cerys when Celeste had moved away to deposit the dog behind a tall protective gate spanning the doorway. The room beyond looked like a playroom. There was a ball pen, sandbox and running track. Toys were scattered all over the room in varying stages of destruction.

"Can I take a picture of that?" Cerys asked eagerly.

"Oh, of course. It's Paolo and his sisters' room. Please, take as many as you like."

"There are more of them?" Libby demanded as Cerys stepped forward to snap several shots of the frolicking Paolo. He dove into the ball pen and was immediately lost amongst the piles of multicolored balls. From beneath the balls, they could hear his ecstatic yips.

"Oh, yes. They're with the boys probably or sleeping on one of our beds. Paolo was the only boy in the litter. There are four girls." Celeste smiled and shrugged. "No grandchildren yet, you know. We take what we can get."

Cerys laughed. Libby attempted to conceal her revulsion. Cerys nudged her. She turned smartly to Celeste and put on her most professional interviewer face. She smiled. "So you're eager for grandchildren, then?"

Celeste sighed. "I have wanted grandchildren before I had children." She smiled mischievously. "When you have your own children, you're responsible for making sure they grow up properly and learn their lessons and turn out to be upstanding members of society. When you have grandchildren, you can stay up all night eating ice cream and spoil them rotten, and it's someone else's problem."

Cerys liked Celeste Mobley. She seemed remarkably down to earth for a woman of her wealth and position in the community. There was no pretext in her amiable chatter. She spoke proudly about her husband, Lochlan, and her son, Colin. Libby smiled somewhat slyly. "Is there anything the readers of the Daily might need to know on that front?" she asked. "Any sign of grandchildren in your future?"

Celeste laughed. "If you want to know if Colin is seeing anyone, perhaps you should ask him. I don't know that he'd appreciate his old mom talking to the press about his love life."

"It was worth a try, anyway."

"So what you like to know? The usual line, I suppose? The history of the house and the family? Our charitable contributions and work in the community?"

"We know all that already," Libby told her dismissively. Cerys smirked. She didn't seem nearly as afraid of Celeste Mobley as she had been of Peyton Creed. "What we really want to know is what you're really like. Behind closed doors. Away from the public eye."

Celeste smirked. "I don't know that the entire readership of the Spectra City

Daily could be considered 'away from the public eye.'"

"What do you do when you come home?" Cerys asked abruptly. "When you have free time and get to do whatever you like."

Celeste considered this. She smiled somewhat sheepishly. "The truth is, we play a lot of video games."

"What?" Libby asked, shocked.

"It's true. Lochlan bought Colin a Nintendo when he was a kid, and since then we've all been hooked. Anytime a new system is out, we're right there waiting to buy it. I think we have enough games to open a shop."

"That is highly unexpected."

"Would you like to see the gaming room?"

"Would I?" Libby exclaimed.

There was nothing like this in the museum that was Creed Manor. The room might have been an arcade or a movie theatre. Television screens lined every wall. Handheld games and pinball machines were scattered around the room. A large, plush leather sectional sofa filled the center of the room from which the Mobleys could watch several screens at once. Wireless game controllers stuck out from every cushion as though the players had simply dropped them and hadn't bothered to return them to their rightful places.

"This is where we spend most of our time. We like to make a night of it when the boys are home. We battle each other. I have to say, I think I'm getting to be the best of us all, though Gage gives me a run for my money when he and Riordan are over," Celeste explained. She ran her fingers lovingly over the chocolate brown leather cushions.

"They don't live here?" Cerys asked absently. She snapped several shots of the incredible room.

"Oh, no. Riordan is Lochlan's younger brother. Lochlan got the house when their parents died. He wanted Riordan to stay, but I think Ri wanted to strike out on his own. I was pregnant with Colin at the time, and I think he felt as though he was intruding. He met his wife, and they moved into a place closer to the office. Gage was born a few years later. He and Colin are thick as thieves. He spends a lot of his time here. He has his own rooms and everything."

"It sounds like you're all very close."

She smiled. "We stick together."

"I understand you had a daughter."

Celeste blinked. A shadow crossed over her face. Cerys spun around to look at her. She hadn't known anything about a daughter. Celeste took a deep breath. "Yes," she murmured. "We did. She is gone.

"I'm sorry," Cerys said.

"It was many years ago, but a parent never gets over the death of their child."

"I understand the circumstances of her death were somewhat mysterious," Libby said.

Celeste studied her. "I don't know that they were mysterious. Her heart stopped."

Cerys blinked. She remembered Peyton saying mentioning Caleb Creed's death, as well. Hadn't she said his heart had stopped? "How old was she?" Cerys asked gently.

"She was twenty-one."

"That's terrible."

"Nothing has ever been so hard." Celeste's smile wavered.

"How long ago did it happen?"

"It's been nearly ten years, I think."

"Do you want to talk about her?" Libby asked in a soft voice.

"No. Not just yet. Maybe in a while."

Celeste wasn't as cheerful as she led them through the beautiful rooms of the house. She didn't describe the art on the walls or the history of the house and family with as much liveliness as before. Cerys took several shots of the house and the Mobley matriarch, but her thoughts were distracted. How had a young woman in her early twenties died of heart failure? She supposed a preexisting heart condition might have caused it, but Celeste hadn't mentioned any such thing. Caleb Creed had died similarly. Everyone who had known him had spoken of his great looks, his robustness, the many activities and sports which he'd loved.

There were many things that might kill and leave no traces. In this case, there was probably only one: a chanter. Perhaps Tamsin had been right all along. Perhaps the Creeds and the Mobleys were in a feud. And if they were, they were fighting it with magic.

Libby seemed to be thinking along the same lines. At least, insofar as the feud was concerned. Cerys doubted Libby was thinking too closely about Celeste Mobley being a chanter. "Peyton Creed seemed surprised when she learned the feature included your family," Libby told Celeste mildly.

Celeste scowled. "Peyton Creed is arrogant. She believes the Creeds are the only family that matters. The Mobleys have been around as long and done as much as their family. Our great great grandfathers came here together and built these houses. Everything they did, they did together. Peyton Creed would prefer to pretend none of that happened."

"I get the impression your families are no longer close."

Celeste's expression was suddenly so cold, the air seemed frigid around her. "I don't want any such thing in your story."

"I assure you, Mrs. Mobley, that isn't the purpose of the feature," Libby told her.

Celeste's smile was brittle. "I'm sorry. It's just that our families haven't been close in some time. I do not know when they began to drift apart. I just married in, you see. By the time I became part of the family, it had already begun. We are friendly, but we are not close. It is a shame, really. They are...lovely people."

"Of course." Libby didn't sound as though she believed her.

The women were silent a moment, as though they weren't sure what to say now. In the quiet, they heard a clamor of footsteps on the stairs. Celeste's face illuminated. "That must be Colin."

Cerys spun in interest. Libby's eyes gleamed. Colin Mobley burst into the small, friendly sitting room. He was breathless, as though he'd been seeking them through the house for some time. Colin was a tall, well-built man in a black suit. He did not resemble his mother. His hair was wavy and dark, worn slightly long past his ears. His dark eyes twinkled merrily as he bent to kiss his mother before turning to the reporters with a smile.

He was very handsome. Libby seemed quite taken with him. She batted her eyelashes as she held out her hand. "Colin. Good to see you again."

"Hello, Libby. Always a pleasure." He turned his dark eyes to Cerys. "I don't believe we've met. I'm Colin Mobley."

Cerys shook his hand. "Cerys Knight."

"Reporter?"

151

She held up her camera. "Photographer. May I take a photo of you two together?"

"Come on, then, Colin," Celeste ordered, holding out her hand to her son.

He chuckled and wrapped an arm around her shoulders. He was nothing like Lex or Nico Creed. It was astonishing that people who had grown up so closely together, so irrevocably entwined, could be so different. Cerys wondered if anything in Spectra City was as it seemed. Probably, she decided, it wasn't.

"Why don't I take the ladies from here, Mother?" Colin asked, smiling at her. "You have a meeting with the Ladies Auxiliary later, if I remember."

"Yes. Thank you, dear." She stepped forward to press Libby's and Cerys' hands. "It was a great pleasure speaking to you both. I hope you got what you needed."

"You were a delightful subject," Libby told her. She had eyes for Colin alone, however. She dismissed the matriarch almost instantly to take his arm.

Cerys smiled at Celeste. "Thank you for your time, Mrs. Mobley."

"Don't forget to say goodbye to Paolo on your way out."

She laughed. "I won't."

Celeste waved and left them alone with Colin. He held out his other arm to Cerys. "Shall we, ladies?"

"Why, Colin, I suspect you just wanted to be alone with us," Libby said.

He laughed. "That is true enough. Would you like to see the rest of the house?"

"I am most interested in seeing your favorite part of the house."

"We already saw the game room," Cerys warned him.

He chuckled. "That isn't my favorite part, anyway. That's Mother's. Come on. Let's go outside."

The gardens behind the house were thick and lush. Roses bloomed brightly upon tall bushes that circled a large, marble fountain in the center. Four benches were placed at each corner beneath ivy-wrapped arches. Colin did not move towards the benches. He sat on the edge of the fountain. Clear, sparkling water filled the pool beneath a still and silent spout. He trailed his fingers pensively through the water.

Cerys snapped his photograph. He looked up at her and smiled. Libby sat beside Colin. She peered out over the garden. Creed Manor rose above the trees next door. Libby lifted her hand to point at it. "I didn't realize how close together the houses were."

Colin's smile faded. He looked at her. "Yes. Our grandfathers were great friends. They liked to be close."

"Are you friends with Lex or Nico? Surely you went to school together. Did you play together when you were kids?"

"We just grew up next door to each other," Colin told her. There was an icy edge in his voice.

"But you're not friends?"

"Is this part of the story? Our relationship with the Creeds?"

"No. I just wanted some background information. It is interesting that two such prominent families have such an interesting history together."

"And what history is that?"

"Your great grandfathers striking gold and coming to Spectra."

He blinked. "Ah. Yes. It is interesting to people, I suppose. I have grown up knowing it my whole life. It doesn't seem so remarkable to me. We did not spend much time with the Creeds when we were kids. Our family is very close. I played with my cousin, Gage, and..." For a moment, his dark eyes slid away. "My sister."

"What happened to her?"

Colin stiffened. "She died," he said flatly. "Many years ago."

"I'm sorry, Colin. It must have been very hard."

"Yes, it was. It still is. She was my best friend."

"Was she older or younger than you?" Cerys asked.

"She was younger. Just a year younger. I was twenty-two when she died." He took a deep breath. " I would rather not talk about her, if it's all the same. She's gone, and I miss her every day."

Libby's expression softened. Cerys' heart leapt a bit. Colin Mobley was a very arresting man.

He was an unpredictable man. His expression sharpened suddenly. He looked at Cerys. "I heard you're dating Lex Creed."

Cerys blinked in surprise. "You...what?"

"It may be a big city, but we run in very small circles. People talk."

"It seems to be the topic of the day," Libby said dryly. "Little did I know the real story people wanted to hear was right beside me the entire time. Here I was the last to know."

Cerys lifted her chin. "I have met him a few times."

Colin stared at her for a moment. "The next time you meet him, ask him about my sister."

Cerys blinked. "What?

Libby pounced on this eagerly. "What does Lex have to do with Diana?"

Colin ignored her. His eyes bore into Cerys'. "Just ask him."

Cerys inclined her head. "All right."

"I hear you and Lex are sort of rivals, Colin. Are you considering going up against him in another area?" Libby asked slyly.

Colin chuckled. Cerys felt her cheeks heat. "Maybe."

Cerys looked away. Libby smirked. "Is it true you two really don't get along?"

Colin sighed. "You are determined to continue this vein, aren't you, Libby?"

"Very."

"It's true there is no love lost between us, but my mother and father would prefer us not to mention such things in mixed company." Libby opened her mouth to ask another question. Colin held up his hand. He smiled. "I think I'd better end this interview now before you pry out all my secrets. I am sure you have enough for your column?"

"Oh, yes."

His expression was stern. "I trust there are things that you will leave out of it, Libby."

She sighed. For a moment, she looked as though she would refuse. Finally, she nodded. "Of course, Colin. Anything you like. You know that."

He smiled. He gestured them out of the garden. Libby pressed his hand warmly and started towards the car. Cerys nodded to him. When she turned to follow Libby, Colin caught her arm. He pulled her back towards him. His eyes were intent. His expression was deadly serious.

He spoke in a low voice, as though he feared Libby might return and overhear him. "Cerys, ask Lex about Diana," he said urgently. "See how you feel about him then." He pressed a card into her hand. "Call me if you want to talk about it some more."

She stared at him silently for a long moment. She nodded. "Okay."

He nodded briskly. Without another word, he spun on his heel and strode away. She peered down at the card. She tucked it into her pocket. She wasn't sure exactly what he was about, but she suspected it had little to do with any romantic rivalry with Lex Creed. Perhaps she had just made a very unexpected ally.

She was beginning to suspect she would need one.

CHAPTER 17

Nico eyed Lex as he sipped a tumbler of amber liquid. Lex didn't speak. He peered out the stained glass window as though he might see Cerys and Libby with the Mobleys across the garden. When he turned to Nico, his brother was staring at him with eyes that were cold slits. "That was an interesting surprise," Nico said in a deceptively cavalier voice.

"What was?"

"Finding Mother in here with your photographer."

Lex chuckled wryly. "Yes, it was somewhat unexpected."

"You didn't know she'd be here."

Lex lifted his eyebrows. "No."

"Really."

"What are you getting at, Nico?"

"You've been seeing a lot of her lately."

"And?"

Nico shrugged. "You like her?"

"If I didn't like her, I wouldn't be taking her out."

Nico snorted. "Come now, brother. I know you better than that. You've taken Carlie Tabb out enough times."

Lex frowned. "We both know what reason there was for that."

He smirked. "Yes, well, they can't all be so useful, can they? What is it about her then, brother, that makes her worth your time?"

"Is there something you're trying to say?"

"I'm merely showing an interest in my brother's affairs."

"Since when?"

"Since I became the subject of a kangaroo court."

Lex rolled his eyes. "Don't be so dramatic. Balthazar Barbosa is nothing of the sort. He's just misguided."

"He's dangerous."

"He wouldn't be if you just stayed out of trouble."

"Since when did you become so sanctimonious?"

"I am not the one under investigation!"

"No. Of course you're not. You were always the good son. I suppose this amuses you?"

"Of course it doesn't. I have been working my ass off to shield you from this!"

"Have you? Have you really?"

"Of course I have. What are you suggesting?"

"Nothing. Merely that perhaps seeing me behind bars would be entertaining for you."

"It wouldn't. It would kill Mother, and our family name would be destroyed."

"Ah, yes. The family name. There are some things worth fighting for, aren't there, Lex?"

Lex stared moodily out the window. "I don't suppose you'd fight for anything."

Nico rose abruptly from his chair. His eyes flashed angrily. "You don't know me at all! You've no idea what I'm capable of!"

Lex didn't turn back to him. "I'm beginning to get an idea, Nico."

"Good. Perhaps it's good for you." Nico paused at the door. He spun back to his brother. "By the way, Barbosa is dropping the investigation. I expect a full apology from his office."

Lex spun around in surprise. "What didn't you say that before?"

Nico shrugged. "Just wanted to get an idea of what you're really about."

"Nico, I've had enough of your games."

He smirked. "Well, in any case, I suppose you don't have to concern yourself with Mother and the family name. It seems as if Rutherford has finally earned his keep."

"I'm glad to hear it."

"Are you?" Without awaiting a reply, Nico strode from the room. He did not bother to close the door behind him.

Lex sighed. "Actually, I am."

* * *

"You aren't really going to issue an apology to Nico Creed, are you?" Cerys demanded the moment she stepped into the computer lab at Chant headquarters after the strange interview with Colin Mobley.

Barbosa, Tamsin and X glanced up at her in surprise. Tamsin looked disgusted. "What is she talking about, Zar?"

Barbosa looked offended. "I am lulling him into a false sense of security, not making myself look like a fool in front of the entire city. I'll let Rutherford do the groveling. It's what he does best."

"What are you two talking about?" Tamsin asked again.

"I heard from Nico Creed today that Zar is dropping the investigation. He expects a humble apology and a full admission of your inferiority." Cerys smirked.

Barbosa rolled his eyes. "Maybe we'll get lucky and he'll hold his breath until I prostrate myself at his feet. It would solve our problem completely."

"Except we still wouldn't know where the chanters are," Tamsin said darkly. "Speaking of Nico, how did the interviews go?"

Cerys considered. "It was a bit of a wash, really."

"You didn't see anything?"

"I saw a lot. Creed Manor doesn't exactly look like the sort of place you would expect to find a secret chanter prison in the basement."

"But you didn't see the basement, did you?"

"No. Peyton showed us a lot of it, but it's so big." Cerys sighed. "If they are hidden somewhere in there, it will take a while to find them."

"When we've got Nico by the short hairs, we'll have all the time in the world. At least now you have an idea of the layout of the house. X has got some blueprints from the city planning office. See if you two can make a virtual map of what you know. It might help. Maybe something will come up."

"What, like rooms being smaller than the plans suggest?"

"Well, yes. Exactly that, actually."

She nodded. She was silent a long moment. "There's something wrong in that house."

"Like being the lair of an evil chanter?" Tamsin asked.

"No. Not like that. I mean, yes, like that a bit, but no. It's them. There's something wrong with all of them. They all seem just on the edge of something."

"I'd say they've already tipped over," Barbosa muttered.

"No. That's the problem, Zar. They haven't. Not yet. When they do, it's going to get so much worse."

They were silent a long moment. "We're going to be there to stop them when they do," Barbosa said firmly.

"We're going to try, anyway." Cerys glanced at Tamsin. "You were right about the Creeds and the Mobleys. There's something going on. Peyton was furious when she found out the Mobleys were part of the feature. She didn't directly say they were enemies, but she admitted their ancestors drifted apart sometime in the past. The Mobleys were slightly more candid. Colin told me they did not get along."

"Colin did?" Tamsin asked shrewdly.

Cerys ignored this. "But they didn't exactly say they were in a feud," Barbosa said, frowning.

"No. But Caleb Creed died young of heart failure. He was, by all accounts, a perfectly healthy man. And Colin had a younger sister, Diana, who died of the same thing when she was twenty-one."

Tamsin shook her head. "So?"

"It might have been magic that killed them. If they are chanting against each other, Caleb and Diana might have been casualties of the feud."

They considered this in silence a long time. "It doesn't amount to much," Barbosa said.

"No." She sighed. "But Colin told me to ask Lex about Diana when I see him again."

Tamsin lifted an eyebrow. "What does that mean?"

"How should I know? It just means Lex must have something to say about it."

"Do you think he's suggesting Lex killed her?"

"I don't think he was suggesting anything. I think Lex knows something about it that Colin thinks I should know. Or Lex had some part it in that's important." She considered. "He gave me his number."

"Oh, for god's sake," Tamsin muttered. "Lex Creed and now Colin Mobley?"

"No. I don't think he meant it like that. It wasn't 'call me for a good time.' I think he gave it to me in case I need help."

"Getting away from Lex?"

"I don't know. Just help. There was something in his eyes. I think he knows more about this than he's saying."

"About the creature attacks?"

"Maybe. Or maybe just about Lex."

"Cerys, you know he's dangerous," Barbosa told her in an almost gentle voice. "You do, don't you?"

She looked at him. "I don't know what he is yet, Zar. I don't know if he's a friend or an enemy. It isn't him I'm worried about, though. It's Nico. There was something about the way he looked at me. I got the feeling he doesn't trust me."

"He doesn't trust anyone, I understand."

"No. Not just in general. I mean he specifically doesn't trust me."

"You think he knows you're Cedric's sister?"

She shook her head. "No. I don't think he does, or he might have reacted differently. He was distinctly suspicious of me, like he thought I was there spy around the house."

"You were," Tamsin remarked.

Barbosa ignored her. "You think he knows you're part of Chant?" he asked, frowning.

"Maybe. Or maybe it's just because I'm going out with his brother. There doesn't seem to be much love lost between the two of them, though. They put on a good face for the public, but I have never seen two people so much alike and so much at odds. When Nico looked at me, I got the chills. He looked at me like he wanted to do something to me."

"Oh, god, Cerys, now Nic—" Tamsin began.

"No. I mean something bad. Like he wanted to hurt me."

They considered this a long moment. "So, Colin Mobley might be one shot at them," Tamsin mused.

"I don't know. Maybe. He seems okay. He seems like the good guy, but I don't really know anything about him."

"You could always start dating him, too."

"Don't be stupid. We have enough problems on our hands without that one," Barbosa said disdainfully.

"Anyway, I don't think that's what Colin had in mind. I think he knows what the Creeds are. I think he thinks I'm in over my head."

"Do you think he knows you're a chanter?"

She shrugged. "Probably not. Maybe, I suppose. There are some chanters who have the ability to spot others without seeing them in a trance. He might have it. Maybe he just wants to warn me away from Lex."

"When are you seeing him again?"

"Tonight."

"You don't waste any time."

"We don't have any time to waste!"

Barbosa sighed. Tamsin lifted her eyebrows. "Do you think he will tell you about Diana?"

"No," Cerys replied glumly. "He never really tells me anything. It's as if he's pretending nothing ever happened with the creatures and his brother."

"What do you two talk about, then?"

She shrugged. "Small talk, I guess. Nothing important, really."

"Are you going to call Colin Mobley?" Tamsin asked.

"I guess we'll see after I hear what Lex has to say about his sister. For all I know, Lex is angry with me for sneaking around his house without warning him."

"Did he seem angry?"

"He never really seems angry. He is very adept at hiding his feelings. I am not sure what his reaction is."

"Well, I guess you'll find out. If he dumps you, at least you have Colin to fall back on."

"I really wish you wouldn't make it something it isn't, Tam," Cerys scolded.

"Sure it isn't. Because Colin Mobley gives his phone number out to all the reporters he meets."

"Not all the reporters he meets are dating his arch rival."

"That's true. Lex hates reporters."

Cerys rolled her eyes. "Balthazar, what are you going to do? Are you really backing off Nico?"

He scoffed. "Of course not. You should know me better than that by now."

"You'd better be careful. It won't take much for him. I could see it in his eyes. He's spinning out of control."

"He's already out of control. He just hasn't made his move yet."

"You might be right about that. And I think Lex knows it, too. I just don't know if he's going to come over in time to help us stop it."

Barbosa exhaled heavily. "This plan...it's not working out the way I thought it would."

"It's not working out at all," Tamsin complained. "We haven't learned anything."

"That's not true," Cerys said firmly. "We have learned some things. We've learned that Nico is controlling the creatures. We know the Mobleys might be on our side if it comes to war."

"I think it already is war. It just isn't being fought yet." Barbosa rapped his hand against a glass panel. X stared at him in horror. "Sorry. We have to do something."

"Short of breaking into Creed Manor, I don't think we have a lot of options here," Tamsin put in.

Barbosa considered this a long moment. "Cerys, did you see any way in?"

She blinked at him in surprise. "I wasn't scoping it out for a burglary. I didn't really pay that kind of attention."

"Damn."

"Anyway, no. Not really. I think maybe the Mobleys could get to the house from theirs, but I don't think they'd want to. I think...they have to keep the Creeds' secrets."

"But why?" Tamsin demanded.

"Because if they didn't, they'd have to reveal their own. There are deaths on both sides. None of them are really innocent in this, regardless of how they appear. For all we know, the Mobleys are the bad guys in this feud."

"It doesn't matter which side they take in the feud. What matters is that they are against the Creeds, and so is Chant."

"You want to just go in and ask them all to join? You don't think there would be worse consequences?"

"Nothing would be worse than losing our friends!" Tamsin replied hotly.

Barbosa held up his hand. "Enough, you two. This isn't getting us anywhere."

"None of this is getting us anywhere!" Tamsin hissed at him. "I hate not doing anything."

"We're doing the best we can," Barbosa told her wearily.

"It's not good enough! We haven't found anything on the taps. The investigation is going nowhere! The creature attacks have stopped, but even if we could get someone in the Creed house with a tracker, it wouldn't matter! We've got no way into the house!"

"I don't see you coming up with anything better," Cerys snapped. "You think if there was something else we could do, I wouldn't do it? I would do anything to get my brother back!"

Tamsin softened. She lowered her head. "I'm sorry, Cerys. I know. I forget sometimes that you have as much at stake in this as we do."

Cerys sighed. "Are we friends again?"

Tamsin smiled. "Yeah. Of course. But that doesn't change the fact that we aren't getting much of anywhere. We're just floundering. What good are we to anyone if we can't even save our own when they're in trouble? What the hell good is being a chanter if we're powerless?"

"We aren't powerless," Cerys told her in a low voice. "We are just facing a more powerful opponent. But there's a chance, and we will find it. We will get Cedric and the others back. None of them have come back like Eddie yet. There's still time."

"Unless he's killed them all and dumped their body somewhere!"

"No," Cerys growled. "He hasn't. He can't take that risk, not with all that's happening. He knows every move he makes is being watched. He knows he has to play it cool until all this has blown over."

Barbosa sighed deeply. "It isn't going to blow over. It's going to get so much worse. For all of us."

"I'm okay with that," Tamsin muttered darkly. "As long as it's worst for Nico."

Cerys looked up at a computer screen and sighed. "I've got to go. I have a date."

"Oh, sure. Leave us here to work and slave over these computers while you go out with a really good-looking rich guy," Tamsin muttered.

"Let's not forget," Barbosa said mildly. "That good-looking rich guy also happens to be one of the most evil chanters in the Spectra City."

Tamsin considered. "I'd say it's a wash."

Cerys tossed her handbag over her shoulder. "If you don't hear from me in a few days, call my aunt, Selene. She'll want to know how I went. Just don't mention the chanting bit. She and Uncle Owen are still a bit dodgy about it. Just tell them my rich, handsome boyfriend probably murdered me and tossed my body in the ocean somewhere."

"Hey, when did you start calling Lex your boyfriend?"

"It's for my aunt's sake. She wouldn't mind so much that I was murdered, so long as I had a boyfriend at the time."

CHAPTER 18

Cerys leaned against the door of the penthouse suite. Lex lifted an eyebrow when he stepped off the lift. He laughed. "I suppose I should have been a few minutes earlier. This is the second time you've gotten the better of me today."

She didn't smile. "I was under the impression you preferred a woman who keeps you on your toes."

His eyes narrowed slightly, but his smile did not waver. "Perhaps you're right about that. I do enjoy surprises."

"Do you?"

"Depends on the surprise."

"Ah."

"How about today?"

He smirked. "Are you trying to ask if I'm angry I caught you in my library with Nico and my mother?"

"I'm just wondering why you asked me out tonight."

"I wanted to."

Cerys lifted an eyebrow. "Are you worried about what I was trying to find at your house?"

"No. I'm pretty sure I know what you're about."

She smiled slightly. "Sometimes I'm not sure if you're a hero or a villain."

He looked at her seriously. "Sometimes, neither am I."

She strode towards him abruptly. "Where are we going tonight?"

"Shouldn't you invite me in for coffee or wine or something?"

She considered. "No."

He snorted. "Okay. We'll table that for a later discussion." He offered his arm. She stared at him a long moment. She didn't take it. He sighed. "Is something wrong, Cerys? I promise you, I'm not angry that you didn't tell me you were assigned to the feature. I know you knew with plenty of time to warn me, and I know exactly what you were doing there."

She frowned. "It wouldn't matter if you were angry."

He laughed. "Really?"

She sighed. "Well, it certainly wouldn't help my case, I suppose."

"Is that what this is all about? Helping your case?"

She studied him. "I thought it was."

"It didn't seem that way the last time we were in this hallway."

His eyes were unreadable. Her cheeks pinked as she remembered the heated moment between them, the way his tongue had...and his fingers had...She opened and closed her mouth, but she didn't reply.

He lifted an eyebrow. "How do you feel now?"

"I don't know what to believe about anything anymore. I just want something to make sense."

Lex considered. He stepped forward and took her hand. "Come on. I'll buy you a cheeseburger."

Now she snorted with laughter. "You meant it when you said you were going to take me to the burger joint around the corner?"

I usually mean what I say." He smiled. "Besides, they have the best milkshakes in Spectra."

Cerys eyed him suspiciously. "If you're trying to distract me with ice cream, it's probably only going to work for a little while."

"I accept that."

The burger joint was a small, dimly lit diner called Hambo's within walking distance of the Warren. It was oddly set apart from the other long, wide buildings on the strip. It was situated on a corner and almost flush with the street so that it looked as though it had been placed there by mistake. The outer walls were painted a faded, peeling red that might once have been vibrant. Wide windows revealed the interior, which was black and white like an old-fashioned soda shop.

There weren't many tables in Hambo's. Most of them were empty. A tired-looking blonde waitress in a black and white uniform waved from behind the bar. If she recognized Lex, her dark eyes didn't reveal it. "Sit where you like," she said. The name embroidered on her chest was Sonya. It was the sort of place where no one cared who you were, as long as you didn't bother them.

Cerys looked at Lex. He smirked. He led her to a table beside an old-fashioned jukebox. It was playing a Frank Sinatra song so quietly, the familiar strains might have only been a memory. Lex didn't order wine when Sonja approached them. He ordered a vanilla milkshake. Cerys smiled and asked for chocolate. Sonja didn't lift an eyebrow. She nodded and disappeared through a black, swinging door into the kitchen.

Cerys turned back to Lex. He was studying her with an expression that might have been wary. Then again, she hadn't quite gotten the hang of Lex's expressions yet. She didn't think she ever would. "What happened at the Mobleys?"

She blinked in surprise. "Why would you think anything happened there?"

"Because you've been acting strange since I picked you up. I think I can tell when something's wrong with you."

"Can you?"

"You are not as good at hiding your feelings as you think, Cerys. Not from me, anyway."

She narrowed her eyes. "Something's not right with you and the Mobleys."

Lex sat back in the white plastic seat. He stared at her for a long moment. "It's not so much not right as just...wrong. It's just the way it's always been as long as any of us remember."

She sighed. Her eyes slid away. "What happened to Diana Mobley?"

He blinked. He was silent for a long moment. Sonja brought their milkshakes. They ordered cheeseburgers and fries without looking at their menus. Lex looked pale as a ghost. "Why did you ask about her?" he asked in a low voice when Sonja had gone.

"Colin Mobley told me to."

Lex sighed. "I suppose I should not be surprised. I should never have let you talk to him."

She stiffened uncomfortably in the plastic seat. "I beg your pardon, but you do not have any say in whom I do and do not talk to."

He chuckled wryly. "No. I don't, do I? I don't seem to have a lot of say in anything that you do."

"I'm sorry your family name doesn't hold much power over me."

This did not seem to offend him. "Maybe that's what I like about you. It's something, anyway. I can't put my finger on it."

She looked away. "Are you going to tell me?"

"I'll tell you."

"Will you really?"

"I said I would."

"You'll tell me the truth?"

"Have you ever known me to lie to you?"

"I don't know. I don't really know that much about you. You certainly aren't telling me everything."

"I have told you all you really need to know."

"Now that is a lie."

He considered. "Perhaps it wasn't strictly true. But some things can't be said."

She narrowed her eyes. "To protect your family?"

"Amongst other things. What did Colin Mobley say to you?"

She shook her head. "Not much. He just said to ask you about Diana."

Lex nodded. "He knows how to insinuate just the right thing to create just the right effect. It worked, didn't it?"

She didn't really want to admit it. "I guess it did work."

"You don't trust me anymore."

"I never trusted you."

For the first time since she'd met him, she understood his expression perfectly. He looked hurt. "Is that true?"

She considered. "I suppose it's half true. I want to trust you. In some ways I do. In general, though, no. I don't. I don't know what you want in all this yet."

"I thought I had made myself clear to you."

"I'm not talking about you and me. I'm talking about the rest of it. All of this. You can't keep pretending we're just two normal people without hidden agendas."

"Why can't we be?"

"Because of everything that's going on!" she hissed. "You know what it is as well as me. Probably better. You're going to have to face it eventually."

"I'm facing it, Cerys. Just because I'm not talking about it doesn't mean I'm not facing it."

She opened her mouth to reply. She shut it swiftly. Sonja appeared with two cheeseburgers. The plates were piled high with crisp, curly French fries. Sonja laid them on the table in front of them. She didn't smile. She spun back around and disappeared again. Cerys watched after her. When she turned back to Lex, he was tucking intently into his burger. Cerys sighed.

Lex didn't speak as he ate. He seemed thoughtful. When his cheeseburger was gone, he picked up a fry. He did not place it in his mouth. "Diana was Colin's younger sister."

Cerys looked up at him in surprise. She laid her half-eaten cheeseburger on her plate. "And she died."

"Yes. She died."

"Why did Colin want me to ask you about her? What do you have to do with it?"

"A lot."

Cerys leaned back in her seat. "Okay. I'm listening."

He looked around. "I'll tell you about her. Not here. There's a lot to explain." His glacial pool eyes met hers. "You can trust me, Cerys. I mean you no harm."

She frowned. "I don't think you mean me harm, not exactly."

"Then why don't you trust me?"

"I just...don't know what your agenda really is."

He considered. "I suppose there isn't a lot I can do about that."

"You can tell me the truth about Diana. Maybe it'll be a start."

He nodded. "I'll take it. Finish eating. We can take a walk."

She shook her head. "I'm done."

"That is the best damn burger in Spectra, and you will eat all of it. I didn't bring you here for the ambiance."

She laughed. "All right. I was rather enjoying it."

He seemed content to watch her eat. He didn't speak. He didn't seem at all troubled. When she'd finished eating, he slapped a fifty dollar bill on the table and rose. He offered her his hand. This time, she took it. Lex didn't direct them towards the Warren. Instead, he walked slowly towards Spirit Park.

Spirit Park was in the center of Spectra City. Tall, thick trees formed a dark, shady canopy over the lush, green grass. Rose bushes lined the winding walks and scented the air. In the daytime, it was a popular place for families to gather, couples to meet and children to play. At night, the good people of Spectra knew better than to wander alone into its depths. When darkness fell upon Spirit Park, danger lurked in every corner.

Lex did not seem concerned at all about the ominous reputation of the location. He turned onto a long, winding path towards a short, wooden bridge. They passed over a gentle brook under a pale half-moon. "The Creeds and the Mobleys have been fighting a blood feud for almost a century," he said abruptly.

Cerys glanced at him. "It's true, then."

"Yes. We have tried to hide it all these years, but sometimes one of us gets careless. Someone sees something and draws conclusions."

"What are you fighting about?"

He laughed hollowly. "No one really knows. It started with our grandfathers. They worked together in the mines in California. When they moved here to start new lives, they were still friends. Something happened when they arrived here. No one has ever known what it was. It might have been business. They quarreled about that and eventually broke off to start their own separate ventures. Other people think it was a woman. It might have been that one used their chanting against the other, and they became enemies."

"But you have kept it going, all these years."

"Yes. Our families have been fighting for decades. No one knows why, but there has been so much bad blood and so many casualties and evils done against each other that it doesn't even matter anymore how it started. We have done terrible things to each other."

"Do you fight them?"

"No. When I was younger, Nico and my father would attack Colin and Lochlan or vice versa. It was usually unprovoked. Just a way to let off steam. They liked it, I think. I joined the fight once or twice, but I had no real animosity towards Colin and Lochlan. In fact, I thought Colin was all right. We were in school together, you see. We were kept apart most of the time, but I never had any reason to hate him or want to hurt him."

170

"What about Diana?"

"She was different. Our families grew up side by side, but we weren't allowed to speak to each other or know each other, really. Diana was...I thought she was the most beautiful girl in the world when I was a kid. And she was sweet and vivacious. I saw her sometimes across the garden. I think I loved her even before I knew about the feud. I think I loved her the first time I saw her playing in the gardens behind our houses." He sighed. "I would watch her from my window. One day, she started watching me back. I had hardly even spoken to her before. She was a few years behind me in school. We weren't allowed to talk to each other.

"One day, I did talk to her. She was sixteen, and I was eighteen. We talked about the feud and our families and the fighting. She felt as I did. We didn't agree with it. We wanted it to stop. We met secretly as much as we could after that, at night in the gardens when we thought everyone was asleep. Sometimes we met outside the city so no one would recognize us. Eventually, we fell in love. We wanted to find a way to be together. We planned to convince our families to end the feud."

"It didn't work."

"No. Of course not. It was too old and too bloody on both sides. We were young and stupid. We wanted to be together, so we planned to run away together. To leave them and Spectra and all this behind us."

He was silent a long moment. He paused to peer up at the sky. "Lex, what happened?"

He sighed deeply. There was no expression in his eyes, but there was such a terrible sadness in his bearing, as though something were weighing heavily upon his shoulders. "It was the night we'd planned to do it. She must have been moving along the side of the house to meet me outside the gates. A fight broke out between our brothers and fathers. I don't know who started it. It might have them, but it was probably us. It was usually Nico. He loves it. He loves an excuse to fight. None of them knew Diana was out there. She was caught in the crossfire. She never met me at the gate. I thought she had abandoned our plan, but I found out the truth the next day. She'd been found dead in her own garden."

Cerys exhaled heavily. Lex took a deep, hitching breath. "I never forgave them for what happened to her. Any of them. It doesn't matter who struck the blow, even if it was probably one of us. It was this feud that killed the girl I loved."

She reached out in the darkness and touched his hand. He folded it tightly into his own. "I'm sorry, Lex."

"That's what Colin Mobley wanted you to know. The people I care about get hurt."

"I don't know if that's what he meant for me to know....I don't know what he meant for me to know."

"He meant you to turn on me."

"Well, it's a terrible story, but I don't see why I would."

"Colin never believed that I loved Diana. She tried to talk to him about it, but he wouldn't hear of it. I think...I think he always suspected that I lured her out of her house as a trick. To harm her."

"How could he think that?" Cerys asked, shocked.

"Cerys, I'm a Creed. You of all people should know what that means around here."

"You aren't evil."

"I suppose it depends upon whom you ask. Sometimes it doesn't matter what you really are. It only matters what you do. And what people think you've done."

She considered this in silence a long moment. "Did the Mobleys kill your father?"

He blinked. "Why do you ask?"

"He died the same way Diana did. At least it sounded as though he had."

"He did, actually. Yes. He died in a fight. We covered it up, of course. If anyone found out what we really are...well, I think you know already." He sighed. "It just goes on and on and it never stops."

"Can't you make them stop? Your father is gone. Can't you just talk to them and sort it all out?"

He laughed. "Cerys, a feud like this...it's not something that can be reasoned out. It's just gone too far. It doesn't even matter who killed whom at this point. It won't stop until we are all dead."

"But that can't be all there is. You can't just let it keep going without even trying."

He shook his head. Then he asked, "Have you ever tried to chant against your brother?"

"What?" This change of topic startled her so completely, she paused.

He tugged gently on her hand to start her moving again. "Have you?"

"I...I guess I don't really know. No, I don't think so. Not that I remember."

"I have chanted to heal Nico. And protect him. It works."

"Okay."

"But I can't hurt him."

"What?"

"I can't chant against him. I can chant for him, but not against."

"I don't understand."

"Don't you? It's why I couldn't attack the wraiths. I couldn't do anything to them."

"And they can't do anything to you."

"Right."

"But what does this have to do with anything?"

"It proves one thing. It wasn't the Mobleys that killed Diana that night. It was us."

"And it wasn't you who killed your father. It was them."

"Yes." He was quiet. "Now you know. About that, anyway."

"Yes. I know."

"So what do we do now?"

"I want to find my brother, Lex."

"I want to help you."

She blinked at him in surprise. "Do you really?"

"I've told you I do. I just don't know how."

"I think you do." She paused in the center of the lane and turned to him.

He sighed and looked down. "I really....really don't. I'm trying, Cerys. You say you don't trust me, but you have to believe I am. I'm doing all I can."

"You know exactly who has him, Lex."

He took a step back from her. "I don't know anything!"

"You do know. You just don't want to know."

"I can't talk about this right now."

"Why?"

"I have to protect my family."

"What about mine?" she hissed. She advanced on him angrily. "Cedric is all I have left! And he's gone. Your family may be responsible for what's happened to him."

"We don't know that." Lex's voice was low and strained.

She spun away from him so abruptly, her long, dark hair whipped him in the face. "You know. You know all of it. You're just too afraid to admit it." She started swiftly away.

"Cerys--" Lex stepped forward to catch her arm.

She threw it off. Her eyes flashed in the darkness. "No, Lex. If you aren't with me on this, you're as much a part of what's against me as Nico."

Lex sighed as she strode quickly away from him. He started after her. "Cerys, don't go--"

"Don't follow me, Lex."

He didn't listen. He lurched after her. She stopped on the pathway, but she did not turn to him. "I'm not just going to let you walk away."

"Yes, you are. It's done, Lex. We're done. I never should have thought this would work. This was a mistake."

"It wasn't a mistake! I'm not willing to accept that."

She half-turned her head. "We are not on the same side, Lex. You have your loyalties and I have mine. Nothing is going to stop me from finding my brother. Not Nico, not you. I am going to find him. Even if that means taking your house apart brick by brick."

Lex sighed. Cerys disappeared into the darkness. He didn't stop her.

CHAPTER 19

Nico wasn't at home. Lex was certain of this. He had seen him arrive at Simone's flat in the Cultural District an hour ago. He suspected Nico was aware of his tail. In fact, he was sure Nico had been aware of it from the beginning. It didn't matter. Lex had known he would learn little from following his brother halfway across the city. That wasn't what he'd meant to do. He'd done what he'd meant to do.

Nico had been careful. He was paranoid and anxious. He hadn't stepped out of line in several days. He hadn't done anything in several days. It might be enough to have stopped him. It was, at least, enough to buy Lex some time.

He stole up the stairs to the third floor. He did not duck into the library for a drink. He wanted to. His nerves were ragged. He did not think of Cerys. Thinking of her wouldn't do any good. He wasn't worried about what she thought of him now. She had been wrong. He wasn't her enemy. Right now, it didn't matter. There would be time to sort things out later.

Lex listened for a moment outside Nico's music room door. It was quiet. There was no creak of footsteps. There were no voices. There were no moans inside the walls. He tried the knob. It wasn't locked. The only things in the room were the instruments stacked neatly against the wall. They looked old and desolate and neglected.

The room was too small. He had thought it before. Now he was sure. It was too small. Nico had done something to it. Lex wondered how long he had been blind to what his brother was doing. Perhaps he had never wanted to know.

Lex spun in a slow circle. He saw nothing. There had been something in this room. Nico would not have emptied the room if he hadn't had something to hide. Lex had all night. He'd figure out what it was. If he had to take the room apart brick by brick.

He chuckled humorlessly. Cerys would do it, too. He didn't doubt for a moment she would. He'd save her the trouble. He moved slowly around the room. He couldn't see anything. He was sure there was something to find.

He paused in the center of the room. His lips moved. His eyes rolled back. When he snapped out of the trance, nothing happened. He hadn't expected it to. It was worth the try. He narrowed his eyes. He stared for several moments at the wall. He did not expect it to yield any answers.

It did.

He frowned. Creed Manor was an old house. It had been maintained well since its earliest days. It hadn't been maintained well enough. The white paint on three of the walls had turned the slight yellow of parchment with age. The other was bright, pristine white.

Lex strode forward. He ran his hands along the wall. What had Nico done? He touched every inch of the wall. There was a tiny, hairline seam running down the right side of the wall. He pressed on it. Nothing happened. He dug his fingernails into the paint to pry it apart. It did not budge.

He sighed. He glared at the wall. There was a small, almost imperceptible dent in the plaster to the right of the seam. He pressed on it. It moved beneath his finger.

Then the wall moved. It moved so slowly and silently, he almost didn't notice it. The seam opened. The wall swung forward. Lex stepped back. If he looked at the wall straight on, he almost couldn't see the opening. It was large enough for a man to slip through.

Lex slipped into the crack in the wall. Behind it was the missing space. There was no one inside. There had been something here, though. The space was divided into five separate spaces like small compartments. Or cells. There were no bars or doors to contain the prisoners. Perhaps Nico had used other means.

Lex had not expected to find Cerys' brother alive. He hadn't expected to find any of the missing chanters alive. But they had been alive. Not long ago, they had been here. He remembered the dirty dishes. Nico had been feeding them. Lex cursed. How could he not have known that his brother was keeping prisoners locked up between the walls of the house? He'd heard them. He could have saved them. Now it might be too late.

Lex stared at the partitions. The chanters had to still be alive. Nico needed them for something. He wasn't taking them to murder them. He wouldn't keep them here if he didn't need them alive. It didn't matter what he was doing with them. It only mattered that they were still alive.

Lex spun towards the seam in the wall. He hoped there was still time.

* * *

The panel in the library of Chant headquarters slid open to reveal the hidden laboratory. Tamsin looked up at Cerys in surprise. They always looked at her in surprise. Didn't they expect her by now, or was she still an outsider? X did not glance away from the computer screens. Cerys wondered absently if he ever left the laboratory. She wondered if he ever slept. "I thought you had a date tonight," X said.

Tamsin stared at Cerys shrewdly. "What happened, Cer? Shouldn't you be at Creed Manor having the time of your life right now?"

Cerys spun away. She stared blankly at the aerial map above her head. "No. Not anymore. It's over with Lex."

"What? What happened? Was he upset that you didn't tell him about the interview?"

"No." Cerys sighed. "I am pretty sure it was my fault. I picked a fight with him."

"About what?"

"What do you think?"

"Cerys, I thought you were going to use subtlety. Why do I get the feeling you questioned him directly about Nico?"

"Of course I did."

"How is that going to help us at all?"

"Apparently, it isn't. There's nothing more we can get from him. He's not going to help us. His loyalty is with Nico."

Tamsin frowned. "Why do I get the feeling you aren't telling me everything about it?"

Cerys sighed. "It's not really any of your business, Tam."

The small, blonde woman glared at her. "It is my business. Cedric may be your brother, but you are both part of Chant. This was an assignment from Zar. If you messed it up, you have to answer for it."

"I am not anyone's servant. What I do with Lex Creed is my business."

"You were supposed to find out where Cedric is!"

"Lex doesn't know! He knows Nico has him. He doesn't know where."

"You were supposed to get into the house."

Cerys shook her head. "I don't think that would have done much good. If Lex can't find them in his own house, how am I supposed to?"

Tamsin paused. She sighed. "How do you know for sure he hasn't found them?"

"I don't. Not really, but I believe he wanted to help me find Cedric. I believe he wanted Nico to stop."

"Then I don't understand why you broke up with him!"

"Because he wants all those things, but he refuses to turn against his brother! He won't join us. He will keep us from Nico if he can."

"How do you know?"

"He said he has to protect his family."

"That doesn't mean he won't help us!"

"How can he help us and protect Nico at the same time?"

Tamsin shook her head. "I don't know. Maybe he can't. We don't know what he's protecting Nico from."

Cerys considered this. "From us. From Chant. From Balthazar. He can't protect Nico and be on our side at the same time."

"I think there's more to this than that!"

"You have no idea what went on between Lex and me."

"No. I don't. You're right. But without Lex, we might not have a chance of finding Cedric and the others."

Cerys was silent. She pressed her hand to her forehead. "He might have come over to us. Eventually. But not soon enough. I can't keep wasting time with him when I could be doing something more to find Cedric."

Tamsin looked at her for a moment. Her expression was oddly sympathetic. "Did you totally blow it with him?"

"I don't know. Yes. Probably."

"Are you sure?"

"I don't know him at all. I don't know what he's thinking now."

Tamsin sighed. "So, he was trying to find Cedric and the others."

Cerys hesitated. "I don't know. He said he wanted to help. He didn't say how. I don't know if he looked for them. I just know he didn't find them."

"But he knows what Nico is doing."

"He knows."

"So he probably looked for them." Tamsin looked at her expectantly.

"Yes. All right. He probably looked for them. I believe he wanted to find them."

"Okay, so that means they probably aren't in the house anymore."

"Not necessarily. I told you, that house is a maze. There could have been an army hidden away in there and no one would have found them."

"Lex is smart. And he can chant. If they were in the house, he would have found them."

"Tamsin, you're taking a lot for granted. For one thing, you're taking for granted that anything Lex told me about wanting to find Cedric was the truth. For all I know, he has been doing to me exactly what I was doing to him—using me. He might have been running interference for Nico the entire time."

"You don't really believe that. I see it in your eyes. You don't believe it."

"I don't know what to believe when it comes to Lex."

"I don't believe it."

"You don't even know him."

"No. You're right. I just..." Tamsin took a deep breath. "I really wanted him to be a good guy."

Cerys laughed bitterly. "Yeah. So did I. I really, really did."

"You like him."

"It really doesn't matter. It's over."

"You could go back. You could apologize."

"No. If he is who he seemed to be, it wouldn't be right to use him anymore. If he isn't, he won't be any help to us anyway. He might be more trouble."

"Okay. Did you find out what happened to Diana Mobley?"

"Yes. She was killed. By Nico. Probably. Or Caleb, maybe."

Tamsin was aghast. "They murdered her?"

Cerys considered. "It was probably an accident. He was in a fight with the Mobleys. She was in the wrong place and was caught in the crossfire."

"So there is a feud?"

"Yes. There is really a feud. They're fighting it with chants."

Tamsin lifted her eyebrows. "Well?"

"Well, what?"

"Well, you've dumped Lex. Perhaps the Mobleys can help us figure out what's going on."

"Tamsin..."

"Why not? Colin Mobley told you to call him. You should call him. If nothing else, you might learn something we can use against Nico."

"If there was something, they probably would have used it by now. Lex made it sound as though they would do anything to destroy each other."

"Except expose them as chanters."

"Only because it would expose themselves in turn."

"Call Colin. You never know. You've screwed things up with Lex, but maybe there's another way."

"There is another way."

Cerys and Tamsin spun to Barbosa. He stood in the sliding doorway. His tanned, even features were twisted into a brilliant smile. His dark eyes glinted. He was curiously disheveled, as though he'd spent some time hopping around, mussing up his hair and rumpling his clothes. "What are you talking about?" Cerys asked wearily.

Barbosa's smile stretched into a wide grin. "You might want to wait on calling the Mobleys in. I think I have it."

"What?"

"I have it. The evidence I need to get Nico Creed. And this time it will stick." He smirked. "At least long enough to get us into the house and his private and corporate holdings around the city."

"Zar!" Tamsin flew into his arms. He seemed taken aback. He patted her awkwardly. "This is terrific."

"Are you sure it's enough this time?"

Barbosa help up a slip of paper. "I have the search and arrest warrants signed by one of our judges."

"We have judges?"

"We have everything."

"Well, why the hell haven't they signed off on a warrant before? It would have saved us all a lot of trouble!"

"They couldn't. The D.A. and most of the city's officials are Nico's. They had to be sure it would be enough before they stuck their necks out."

"This time it is?"

"Oh, yes. I wish I could be there to see the look on his face when he's taken away in custody."

"Why won't you be?"

"I don't want him to have any warning. We're executing the search warrants at the same time. I have our people at all the sites. We'll strike at once. He won't even have a chance to call his maid."

Cerys smiled. Tamsin flitted out of the room. She returned moments later with a bottle of champagne. "You have that just lying around?" Cerys asked.

"Well, yeah. We do good work here," Tamsin explained. "You never know when you're going to need to celebrate."

Tamsin popped the cork. Cerys glanced at Barbosa uneasily. "Shouldn't we wait until after we've found them to celebrate?"

"Don't be a stick in the mud, Cerys," he replied. "It took long enough to get it done. Small victories."

"I'll celebrate when my brother is back with us. Alive and well."

Tamsin ignored this. She handed Cerys a glass of the bubbly pink liquid. "We'll celebrate. You can drown your sorrows."

Cerys scowled but she sipped the champagne. She almost felt better.

CHAPTER 20

The news that Nico Creed had been arrested on suspicion of money laundering and fraud shocked the citizens and news agencies of Spectra City. Cerys Knight was the first on the scene. Her photographs of Nico being escorted from Creed Corporation headquarters in handcuffs were splattered across the special edition of the Spectra City Daily. The breaking news coverage ran on the local television stations all day.

She'd had an unfair advantage. She'd known about the arrest before it ever happened. It hadn't taken long for the news agencies to catch on. They'd rushed eagerly to the courthouse to catch sight of the infamous scion before he was led inside. They chattered excitedly around her.

Libby Gore lounged against a great stone pillar beside Cerys. "How did you get those pictures so quickly?" she asked suspiciously. "Were you visiting Lex at the office or something?"

Cerys considered. "Something like that."

"How's it going with you two?"

"It's fine."

"What's he like?"

"Are we here to get the story on Nico, or are we here to talk about my love life?"

"I don't see why we can't do both. This is the most exciting story we've had in about a decade, though. Nico Creed. Arrested. I really never thought I'd see the day. That Barbosa has balls. And he's cute, too. I wonder if he's seeing anyone."

Cerys rolled her eyes. "Libby, you should consider dating a nice guy. Maybe a mechanic or a house painter."

Libby scoffed. "Nice guys are boring. I much prefer guys with enough money and power to know what to do with them."

"Trust me," Cerys muttered darkly. "You're better off without them."

Libby wasn't listening. A black unmarked police car pulled up in front of the courthouse. The reporters were like sharks sensing blood in the water. They rushed towards it in a frenzied flock. They shouted questions at Nico as the officer guided him out of the car. Nico's expression was calm and impassive. He lifted his chin.

Lex was beside him in an instant with another tall, reedy man in a sleek blue suit that looked anxious and determined. A lawyer, probably, Cerys decided. She snapped a photograph. Lex paused before the throng of reporters. "My brother has nothing to say," he told them coolly. "These allegations are baseless and outrageous. I am sure the truth will out in due time."

"Mr. Creed! Mr. Creed!"

He held up his hand. "No more questions."

Cerys snapped his photograph. He looked at her. For a moment, his eyes held hers. Then he turned away and strode into the courthouse beside his brother.

"This is going to be the biggest story of the year," Libby said exultantly.

Cerys stared after Lex. "Yeah. You'd better get it out as soon as you can. I don't think it's going to last long."

"It'll last just long enough."

Cerys sighed. "I hope you're right about that."

* * *

"How can you do this?" Peyton shrieked.

Barbosa ignored her. "Mrs. Creed, if you would please step aside," Detective Abel Dane ordered. "This is an official investigation."

Peyton chased after them. "Do you know what you are doing?"

"We know exactly what we're doing, Mrs. Creed, and if you do not step aside, we will restrain you. Tampering with an investigation is a crime."

She stared at him in shock. "You will regret this."

"Maybe." Dane strode past her.

"Mother, leave it alone. There's nothing you can do. It doesn't matter. They won't find anything." Grace Creed glared coldly at Barbosa and the detectives. "Our family has nothing to hide."

"The disgrace," Peyton moaned. She pressed a hand to her forehead. "Take me to my room, Grace."

Grace rolled her eyes. She caught her mother as her knees buckled. "Mother," she scolded. "I'm sure this is all a misunderstanding. ADA Barbosa will be issuing a full apology before the day is done."

Barbosa smiled wryly. "I would not count on that, Miss Creed. If you would please remove your mother, we would be very grateful."

"I'm not doing it for your gratitude."

"I don't expect you are. Do not get in our way or your brother won't be the only Creed spending the night in lock-up."

Grace and her mother did not seem inclined to try his sincerity. Grace led her mother towards the stairs to their chambers. She glared at Barbosa as she passed. "This isn't over."

"You're right about that, Miss Creed."

Creed Manor was an enormous maze. The army of officers and detectives made slow progress. Barbosa was untiring. He supervised the search, darting from room to room. Some of the detectives knew what to look for. The basement was clear. It was nothing more than a storage chamber for the Creed's old furniture and clothes awaiting donation. Nico's chambers yielded nothing. He didn't even possess a collection of dirty magazines.

"There's nothing here, Zar," Detective Abel Dane muttered softly.

"It's here. They're here. Keep looking."

Barbosa strode into the library on the fourth floor. It was empty, but it had the feeling of a room that was often used. The rest of the rooms in the house had felt like large, magnificent tombs. This one felt almost but not quite warm. He ran his hands along the walls. He stared hard at the bookshelves. If there was a hidden panel, he couldn't find it. He measured the room.

"What are you doing?" Dane demanded.

Barbosa looked up at him. "What do you think? I'm looking for hidden rooms."

"It's probably too much to think they have the same set up as us."

He scowled coldly at the detective. "Be careful what you say, Abel. You don't know who's listening."

Dane looked chagrined. "Sorry, sir."

"Keep looking." He pulled something from his pocket and tossed it at the detective. "Here's a tape measure."

Abel nodded and strode from the room. Barbosa spun in a circle. They had to be here. If they weren't here, it was all for nothing. He strode towards the stained glass window. Rain pelted the glass. The colors ran. He could barely see the Mobley Mansion through the blurred images. It looked bright, as though the sun shone down upon it through the dark clouds. Creed Manor was cloaked in darkness.

"Barbosa!"

He spun. A young rookie officer raced into the library. He was panting in excitement. "Detective Dane found something."

Barbosa lifted his eyebrows. "What is it?"

"Come see."

There was nothing in the room but a stack of old instruments that looked as though they hadn't been touched or regarded in over a decade. At first, Barbosa did not see Detective Dane. Dane's voice issued from inside the wall. "In here."

Barbosa blinked. The crack in the wall widened. The wall swung out. Barbosa sucked in an excited breath. He slipped through the seam. "There's nothing in here!" he growled.

Abel turned to him. He handed him a tiny piece of twisted metal. "No. Not anymore," he said grimly. "But there was."

Barbosa looked down at the metal in his palm. It was gold. It might have been a piece of a ring or pendant. There were two letters engraved into the smooth surface. CK. He looked up at Abel. "Cedric. He was trying to leave us a message."

"Yeah. So he was alive not long ago and had time to do it. But where is he now? And where are the others?"

Barbosa cursed. He kicked violently at the wall. It hardly shuddered. "Damnit! He's moved them. We're too late."

CHAPTER 21

"There's nothing?" Cerys growled. "How can there be nothing?"

Barbosa sighed deeply. "We found his lair. It was empty. He's moved them."

"How did he know you'd come? How did he get to them in time? You timed the arrest perfectly!"

"He didn't know! We were in the house before he was ever even aware we were coming. He moved them before we executed the arrest warrant."

"Someone must have leaked it! How else could he have known?"

"Carlie?" Tamsin put in grimly.

Barbosa shook his head. "She's been kept out of the loop. We know she's on the take. It was kept between our people only. Not even Rutherford knew we were going to strike."

"Something else must have spooked him, then. He moved them before any of this even happened. You pushed him too hard!" Cerys said.

Barbosa sighed. "Cerys…"

"The taps," Tamsin interrupted. "Remember? Nico was opening a new location."

He paused. A look of comprehension dawned on his face. "Oh, my god. Why the hell didn't we consider he was moving the chanters?"

Cerys sighed. "We didn't have enough. Our only hope was Creed Manor. And now it's lost."

"Let's listen to them again," Tamsin suggested in a soothing tone. "Maybe we'll hear something we missed."

"I'll send Dane and the others to look into every warehouse and private building owned by Nico. Especially any new ones," Barbosa said. "We've already had teams looking into them. They haven't discovered anything yet, but Abel will know what to look for."

"Is the evidence you have good enough?" Cerys asked. "Will we have enough time?"

He nodded. "Yeah. It'll stick at least long enough for a grand jury. A good lawyer will get him off, but not before we've had a chance to tear his life apart. He'll be home in a couple days. That's all we need."

"Okay." Cerys took a hitching breath.

Barbosa squeezed her shoulder. "Cerys, Cedric is alive. I can feel it. Nico was keeping them alive." He took her hand. He pressed something into it.

She looked down. Her breath escaped in a sigh. "Cedric's ring. Well, part of Cedric's ring."

"I think he was sending us a message. I think he left this for us to find. He's alive, Cerys. We'll find him."

She nodded. She looked up at him. "I hope we make it before he isn't any longer."

* * *

Lex stared moodily into the deep amber liquid in his glass. On the small table beside him, his cell phone was silent. Cerys hadn't called. He hadn't expected her to. He picked up the phone. He stared at it. He sighed and set it aside. He had more important things to worry about right now.

Marisa was a very good secretary. More specifically, she was better than Nico's secretary. Nico's mail sat in a large stack on Lex's lap. He hadn't told Marisa why he wanted to see Nico's correspondence. She hadn't asked. She was a very good secretary. No one had even noticed that Nico's mail arrived a day late.

There were letters from their clients. There were bills for cell phones and utilities for Nico's warehouses and buildings. Nothing looked suspicious. Nothing looked even marginally interesting. There was an invitation to a client's private event. Lex had received the same one. He'd sent an RSVP earlier that day. He wasn't sure Nico would be out of jail in time to attend.

He would be. The library door swung open abruptly. Lex glanced up in surprise. He stuffed the stack of letters into the briefcase beside his chair. Nico strode directly towards the bar without speaking to him. He poured a glass of scotch. He swallowed it in a single gulp.

"I didn't know you'd gotten out," Lex told him.

Nico turned to him. "Deacon is a very good lawyer, Lex. Did you honestly think Barbosa would be able to keep me in jail?"

Lex snorted humorlessly. "Why didn't you call me?"

"I was well taken care of. Rutherford drove me home."

"I'm glad you're out."

"Are you really?"

"Of course I am." Lex scowled darkly. "We have to talk about what's going on."

Nico was silent a long moment. "You haven't talked to the woman in a few days."

Lex blinked in surprise. "What?"

"The woman. The photographer. You haven't been seeing her."

Lex stared at him, uncomprehending. "What are you worried about her for? We're in the middle of a serious investigation. You've been arrested, for god's sake. We have to prepare for the grand jury."

Nico waved his hand dismissively. "Trifles. It's nothing. They've found nothing."

"It isn't nothing, Nico!" Lex shot to his feet to face his brother. "Barbosa's evidence is solid. I've spoken to Deacon. He is concerned."

Nico scoffed. "He's always concerned, but he'll find a way. He always does. Barbosa doesn't have enough to put me away." He considered. When he spoke next, his voice was thoughtful. "I don't know how he learned what he did. He would have had to own the bank." He smirked. "It doesn't matter. He won't get anywhere with it."

"Nico, it is enough to ruin us!"

"Please, Lex. The entire city knows the truth of what we're about. They always have. They just pretend not to. You know it. They pretend we're not who we really are, but when it comes down to it, it won't matter. We still run this city, and that will never change."

"You're arrogant, Nico. It will be your ruin. It will be the ruin of all of us."

He lifted an eyebrow. "Nothing will ruin me, Lex, because I am powerful. As far as Spectra City is concerned, I am all powerful."

"You're not as powerful as you think!"

"No? And who do you think will stop me? You? Your girlfriend?"

Lex stepped towards him angrily. "This has nothing to do with Cerys!"

"Perhaps it doesn't." Nico bared his teeth in a cold, humorless smile. "Why don't you just let me worry about Barbosa. You worry about yourself."

"Nico, this isn't the end of this."

"Oh, believe me, Lex. I know it isn't."

* * *

Nico paced swiftly across the floor in his bedroom. He reached into his pocket. He snapped open his cell phone. He did not need to thumb through the contacts. He dialed the number from memory. A low, gruff voice answered. "Nico."

"I need your help."

"I'm listening."

"It's my brother."

"I am not sure I can do that, Nico."

"No! He's been acting strange. He's been following me around and making it difficult to work. I just need you to keep an eye on him. I need to know what he is up to."

"Yes, sir."

"Report back to me."

"Yes, sir."

Nico closed the phone. He strode to the door and jabbed the intercom button on the wall. In seconds, Tully's low, calm voice answered, "Yes, sir?"

"Come up."

"Of course, sir."

Tully's room was in the servant's quarters on the bottom floor. It only took him moments to reach Nico's chambers. He knocked once before he strode into the room. He bent in a short bow. Nico spun towards him. His blue eyes glittered. "What is my brother up to?" he demanded.

Tully blinked. "Sir? I'm sorry, sir, but I really have no idea. I have not been able to discover what his intentions are."

"Did you learn anything about the woman?"

Tully inclined his head. "Nothing, sir, but what we already knew. Her credentials seem to be in order."

Nico shoved his hands through his hair. "They can't be!"

"Sir, I was very thorough."

"Someone is leaking information. That is the only way Barbosa could have learned what he has. " Nico moved abruptly to pace the room once more. "Someone close." Tully stiffened. Nico waved his hand at him dismissively. "Not you, John." He sighed. He paused at the window and looked down. "Maybe my brother. Probably him."

"I don't understand, sir."

Nico passed a hand across his face. "What is he playing at?"

"Sir?"

"I don't trust that woman. There's something not right about her. She is up to something. They are up to something. This isn't dating. This is something else."

Tully seemed not to know how to respond to this. "What can it be?"

"I think she works for the ADA."

"What?"

"Maybe she's a cop or a private investigator or something."

"Sir, I spoke to her superiors at the papers in San Francisco. They were quite certain she is who she says she is."

"It's a cover! They're lying!" He spun on Tully. His eyes burned with a mad internal flame. He picked up the lamp on his nightstand. He threw it against the wall.

The glass shattered. Tully did not flinch. "I'm sorry, sir."

"Find out what is going on!"

"Yes, sir."

Nico glared at him. "Are they safe?"

"Yes. They are secured. They will be ready when you have need of them."

"Good. Good. The last thing I need is for someone to begin looking too closely into my helpers."

"Yes, sir, it seems we are in enough trouble."

"I'm fine!"

"Of course. I'm sorry."

"Just do what I said."

190

Tully inclined his head. He spun on his heel and strode swiftly from the room.

* * *

Abel Dane tossed a stack of documents onto the conference room table. "We've been through all of these," he growled. "There's nothing."

"You've searched them all?" Cerys demanded.

"Yes, and we're running out of time," Barbosa said darkly. "Nico's already out on bail and the grand jury is next week. A good lawyer is going to get him off, and we haven't found anything yet!"

"Okay, let's just focus," Abel said. "X has been in the property listings databases. He's pulled up everything that might be useful."

Tamsin sighed. "It could take days to go through all this. Don't we have any leads at all?"

"We have the name John," Cerys said grimly.

Barbosa pushed his hands through his hair. "Yeah, and it would take just as long to look at those listings. We need something better to narrow it down."

Cerys sighed. She passed around stacks of listings. "We'd better get going, then. I'm not giving up until we know we've turned over everything."

Tamsin didn't look at her stack. Her eyes were narrowed thoughtfully. "What have you already searched?"

"We've looked at everything owned by Nico or the Creed Corporation, including the corporate offices," Abel told her.

Tamsin considered. She looked at them all. "Well, what about Lex?"

"What?" Cerys asked.

"He's not being charged," Barbosa replied. "There's no evidence he has anything to do with what's going on."

"That doesn't mean Nico isn't using one of his places for something."

They looked at each other. "I feel a little sheepish we didn't think of that before," Abel admitted in a low voice.

"It wouldn't do any good if we did find something," Barbosa said. "We can't go in. We can't get a warrant."

Cerys sat up. "That doesn't mean we can't take a look at the place. We might be able to see who is coming or going. If we can see Nico or one of his people there, it might be enough."

Barbosa nodded. "I'll get X to look into Lex's properties."

Able sighed wearily when he'd gone. "Lex is not exactly the secret warehouse type," he observed. "You haven't got any ideas, Cerys?"

She considered. "I think...I don't really know anything about him. I don't know what he's really capable of."

Abel frowned. "That is not very reassuring."

"No, it really isn't."

"Have you even talked to him?" Tamsin asked, frowning.

"No, not since the last time you asked."

"I really think you should talk to him."

"What do you care about what goes on between Lex and me?"

"Because it's important. Cerys, we have enough problems fighting Nico. We needed to know Lex won't be an issue."

"He might be. I don't know what he'll do. He says he will protect his family. If that means from us, then he might be a problem."

"That isn't really very good. I don't fancy fighting the two of them," Abel muttered quietly. "If Nico is capable of raising an army of wraiths and kidnapping chanters, their family power is strong. Stronger than any of ours. Even if we do find Cedric and the others, we might not make it out alive."

"We need him on our side, Cerys," Tamsin said. "Even if he doesn't fight with us, he might know where we can look for the others. You need to talk to him. Beg him if you have to. You need to sort out whatever it is that's going on because we are running out of time. Every day that passes, the chances get better and better that Nico will kill our friends or do to them what he did to Eddie. Lex can help. You need to give him a chance to, and I get the feeling it's you who's pushing him away, not the other way around."

Cerys scowled. She didn't want to admit that Tamsin might be right. "Fine. I'll talk to him."

"When?"

"I'll call him tomorrow."

"Why don't you call him now?"

Cerys opened her mouth to reply indignantly. Barbosa saved her the trouble. "Lex has a storage unit downtown. It hasn't been accessed in a couple years," he said as he strode into the room. He looked around at them with dark, glittering eyes. "And a couple weeks ago, he purchased a warehouse in the Industrial District. With cash."

"What?" Abel jumped up and snatched the paper Barbosa held out of his hand. "There's no paper trail. Just the title in his name."

"Right. We could talk to the person who brokered the deal, see if they spoke to Lex directly or how the transaction was completed."

Cerys jumped up. "Or we could go have a look at the place."

"We don't want to go off half-cocked, Cerys," Barbosa cautioned her.

"Half-cocked? This is the first break we've had in weeks, Zar. At least let me go take a look at the place. I'll be careful. If I see Nico or anyone else, I'll come right back here and report like a good little Chanter."

Barbosa snorted humorlessly. "I want you to be careful. We can't afford to lose another Chanter."

"At least you'd know where to find me."

"It's the condition you'll be in when we find you that concerns me."

"There's nothing to worry about, Zar. I'll be careful. No one's even going to know I was there."

* * *

The Industrial District was quiet at night. Most of Spectra City was quiet at night. Lex's warehouse was silent and dark. It was surrounded by other dark and silent warehouses and set slightly apart from the main road. Cerys snapped a few photos of the place. There was nothing to see. No one came and no one went. Rain spattered the corrugated tin roof.

Cerys sighed. The warehouse looked empty. She glanced up and down the street. There was no one here so late at night in this part of town. There would be a stern telling-off if Barbosa found out what she was about to do, but it was her brother in there. She wasn't going to sit in her car and watch a dark, empty building all night. If Cedric was inside, she wasn't going to sit out here and do nothing.

She stepped out of the car. She moved silently across the street. There were no lights in the warehouse. She didn't hear a peep. If the chanters were inside, they were very, very quiet. Of course, if Nico was keeping them in a place like this, it was unlikely he would risk the industrial workers in the nearby warehouses hearing them. Perhaps the place was soundproofed. Nico had built hidden rooms before. Perhaps there was another one inside where Cedric and the others were secreted.

She crept along the side of the square, concrete building. Her boots did not make a noise on the smooth tarmac surrounding it. She lifted herself upon her tiptoes. She peered into a dark window. It wasn't dark. The window was washed with black paint. She could see the faintest pale, yellow glow through the careless strokes of paint. Her breath caught. Someone was inside.

Behind her in the yard, gravel crunched. Her heart leapt. She spun. The figure moved so quickly, he was a blur. He swung his arm at her. Pain exploded in her skull.

She blacked out.

CHAPTER 22

Light filtered through her closed eye lids. Cerys came to slowly. She didn't open her eyes. Her arms and legs were tied to a stiff-backed chair. Two men were murmuring somewhere nearby. "Ah," said a low, smooth voice. Her insides felt like ice. She knew that voice. "She's coming around, I think. Cerys."

She opened her eyes. Nico Creed stared down at her. A small, bald-headed man in a white suit hovered near Nico's elbow. He did not look at Cerys. He did not speak. Cerys looked up at Nico.

"I knew someone would come eventually. I knew someone was spying on me."

"It was a trap," she whispered. She closed her eyes.

"I did not expect it to be you who fell into it." He leaned over her so suddenly, she reared back. His blue eyes flashed. His expression was so cold, he seemed to freeze the air around them. "What are you doing here?"

She lifted her chin. "I don't know what you mean. I've been doing some research on the area for the paper. I didn't realize anyone owned this place. It was abandoned before."

"You're lying! Do you expect me to believe it's just coincidence you ended up here?"

She did not reply. He took a step back from her. He lifted his arms. He muttered softly. His blue eyes rolled back then glowed eerily white. He threw his head back. Cerys gasped as pain shot through her entire body. She bit down on a scream. Then it was over. He glared at her.

"Who are you working for?"

"The Daily," she gasped. "I told you. You know who I work for!"

"I don't believe you. You've been working against me all the time, haven't you? This affair with Lex. It's all been an elaborate deception. Who are you working for? Is it my brother?"

She blinked in genuine astonishment. "What?"

He frowned and leaned down to peer into her eyes. "Is it Barbosa? Are you a cop?"

"A what? I'm not a cop!"

"What then? What are you doing here?" He stepped back as though to study her better. There was an intense, manic glint in his eyes. His mouth twisted. His face illuminated suddenly. "I thought you looked familiar when I first saw you. I knew you would be trouble from the moment I laid eyes on you. I couldn't put my finger on it until now. You're not a cop, are you? My god, how could I be so stupid? All this time. I should have realized. You're a chanter."

She lifted her chin. She did not reply.

"Are you with Barbosa? Is he a chanter, too?"

"I don't know anything about Barbosa."

"Don't lie to me. It all makes sense. I should have seen it before. I should have known this all had something to do with the chanters. He searched everything. He found my hidden room. It's just been a distraction. All along he's been working with Chant, hasn't he? You're both in Chant." Nico leaned over her. "Who's running it? Is it my brother? Is that what you've really been doing when he's supposed to be with you?"

She opened her mouth, then snapped it shut again in confusion. "What? Lex? He has nothing to do with any of this."

Nico's lips moved again. She braced herself. The pain lasted longer this time. When it stopped, a single tear ran down her cheek. She glared at him. "I don't believe that."

"You won't be able to hold me long. I am not the only one who knows about this place."

Nico smirked. "That was the general idea. I think we'll be able to get to the bottom of this in no time." She took a deep, hitching breath. He spun away from her. He held out his hand to the silent man in white. "My phone." He dialed a number from memory. He waited. "Find Balthazar Barbosa. Right away. Tell him to come to the warehouse. He'll know which one. And tell him…I have one of his chanters. If he doesn't come, I'll kill her."

He snapped the phone shut and spun to Cerys. Her stomach roiled. "You're wrong about Barbosa. He won't come. He's got nothing to do with this."

"We'll see. I think we can sort this out. If not, it's all the same to me. I could use another chanter for my menagerie."

* * *

Lex's office at Creed Corporation headquarters was quiet. Everyone had already gone home for the day. Lex narrowed his eyes at the stack of documents the DA's office had delivered earlier that day. He pushed his hands through his pale hair. He sighed. Barbosa's case was good. Nico was in over his head this time. Lex did not know if even Deacon would be able to save him this time. Perhaps it was for the better. Perhaps it was time Nico faced the consequences of his actions. He had been allowed to run wild through Spectra City long enough.

He leaned back in his chair. He pressed the heels of his hands to his eyes. He spun in his chair abruptly and rose to his feet. He paced the large, wood-paneled room. He had already been through Nico's mail. He'd already seen the results of the search warrants. It hadn't been much, but it didn't seem as though Barbosa had needed more. In fact, what evidence of money laundering he thought he would discover in the house or Nico's warehouses...

Lex paused. He blinked. He strode back towards the desk. He shuffled through the stack of papers. It hadn't seemed as though Barbosa had been looking for evidence at all. In fact, he seemed to be looking through the house for hidden chambers and rooms. And he'd found one. There had been nothing there. Lex already knew there was nothing there. What had Barbosa hoped to find?

"He's a chanter," Lex said out loud. Realization dawned on him. Of course he was. Of course. He'd been looking for Cerys' brother and the other missing chanters. He might even be working with Cerys. She had never mentioned him, but she hadn't really told him anything about what she was really up to. He sighed. He should have known.

He stood still in the center of the room. Barbosa hadn't found what he was looking for. Cedric and the other chanters were still secreted somewhere. Nico couldn't risk murdering several people and dumping their bodies while he was the subject of an investigation. They were still alive. And now Lex knew where they weren't.

He yanked the stack of mail out of his briefcase. He'd already looked at everything that day. There hadn't been anything there. There hadn't been anything for days. Nico had spent his entire life deceiving others. He was very, very good at it.

Lex stared at the stack of letters without seeing them. If he was Nico, where would he hide the chanters? He dropped into the leather armchair in front of his desk. He sighed. If he was Nico, he would hide them somewhere that couldn't be linked back to him. Or...somewhere that linked back to someone else. He frowned. Tully? No. He'd already considered that. Tully was Nico's closest man.

Me. If I were Nico, I would implicate me. Why not? His brother had been more resentful than usual even since before Lex had discovered he was behind the attacks. He'd been acting suspicious of Lex for weeks. He'd known Lex was following him. It would be just like his brother to use him to cover his tracks.

He spun around. He strode out of the office. The company mailboxes were on the second floor. Marisa had picked his up that day. Her desk was neat and organized. A stack of mail sat tidily in her inbox. He picked them up. He rifled through them swiftly. Notes from clients, invitations to events, requests for donations, junk mail, a utility bill...

Lex frowned at it. He ripped it open. The address was in the Industrial District. He didn't have a building in the Industrial District. At least, he hadn't until two weeks ago. He slapped the paper excitedly against his palm. He spun and raced out of the building.

* * *

Barbosa looked remarkably calm as a tall, well-built man with long, wavy black hair escorted him inside the warehouse. Nico smiled. "Ah. ADA Barbosa. Welcome to the party. You know everyone, I expect?"

Barbosa said nothing. His eyes flashed towards Cerys for the briefest instant. There was no emotion, no fear or anger in them. She did not speak to him. There was nothing to say. Their situation was really quite clear. Barbosa lifted his chin with so much dignity, he might have been in court giving a righteous statement.

Nico smiled. "Cerys, I don't believe you've met my friend Luca. Luckily, neither has my brother." He glanced at the black-haired man. Luca hovered patiently in the doorway behind Barbosa, as though prepared to stop him if he attempted to flee. "Luca, where is my brother now?"

Luca's voice was unexpectedly soft and almost gentle. "At the office working late. I left him there."

Nico inclined his head. "Fine. Go back and keep an eye on him."

Luca nodded shortly. He spun on his heel and strode out of the warehouse without glancing back. Cerys sighed. She held Barbosa's gaze for a long moment. If he was trying to tell her something with his intense, glittering eyes, she could not read it.

"Are you surprised to see her?" Nico asked in a conversational tone. He laid a hand on Cerys' shoulder. With the other, he reached into his pocket. He withdrew a large, uncut yellow stone on a thick, leather cord. It looked flawed and dirty. He slipped it around her neck. It felt heavy and strange, as though it was slowly sucking out her breath. She jerked. "It suits you, Cerys."

Barbosa's brow furrowed. "What is that? What have you done to her?"

Nico ignored him. "I caught her sneaking around the warehouse. It took me a while to figure it out. I should have known it from the moment I looked at her. I should have known who you really are. You're Chant. Both of you."

Barbosa did not even blink. He reached into his jacket pocket. He drew a long-barreled pistol and aimed it steadily at Nico. His expression was blank. "Let Cerys go. She has nothing to do with this."

Nico laughed. "I think she has everything to do with this. That gun isn't going to do you much good." He lifted his hand towards Barbosa. His chant was almost inaudible. It was over so quickly, Barbosa did not have time to retaliate. The gun flew from his hand. It clattered dismally against the concrete wall. Tully strode neatly over to it and tucked it into his own jacket pocket. "I think you have a better way to fight me than that. You are a chanter, aren't you?"

Barbosa glanced at Cerys. She struggled against the bonds on her wrists. She opened her mouth. Nothing happened. She took a deep breath. There were no words. She was completely aware of her surroundings. She glanced at Barbosa in alarm.

Nico chuckled softly. "Don't bother, Cerys." He leaned over her. "As long as you're wearing that stone, you can't enter a trance."

"What are you hoping to accomplish here, Nico?" Barbosa asked in a reasonable tone of voice.

"I want to know why you're sending chanters to creep around my warehouse! I want to know why you are doing this to me!" Nico growled. His blue eyes burned.

"He didn't send me," Cerys said. "This has nothing to do with him! I was on my own. He's not with Chant. I am."

"Cerys--" Barbosa began warningly.

"I am looking for my brother," Cerys added.

"Ah. Your brother. I might have guessed," Nico said. "Yes. It all makes such perfect sense now. I knew you fit into it. I just didn't realize how."

"Nico, you are in a bad place," Barbosa told him. "You have a woman tied to a chair in front of the ADA about to try your case at the grand jury."

Nico laughed. "I don't think any of that will be a problem. You won't have a chance to present it to anyone."

"Nico, you are in over your head."

"You're the one in over your head! You think I am a fool?"

"I am just an ADA. I don't know what you think I'm trying to do!"

"It doesn't matter. Not really. Not anymore." Nico stepped past Cerys. He lifted his hands.

Barbosa was prepared this time. His dark eyes flashed eerily white. His low, incomprehensible mutter rose in a strange, droning hum. Cerys ducked, but the chant did not strike her. Nico was muttering in front of her. The chants met halfway between the men in a flash of intense, blinding light. They did not dissipate harmlessly into the air. The force of the collision sent them both to their knees. Cerys felt as though a strong, freezing wind had blown past her. Her cheeks felt raw and cold.

The door burst open. Lex was inside the room before Nico and Barbosa had risen to their feet. He paused. He looked around at them all in complete shock. "What the hell?"

"Lex?" Cerys blinked at him in astonishment.

Nico looked between them. He scrambled to his feet. He circled behind Cerys. He laid his hands on her shoulders. He was mumbling softly near her ear.

"What's he doing?" Lex demanded. "Barbosa, stop him!"

"Me? What about you?"

"I can't. Do something."

Cerys could not understand Nico's words.

"It isn't working. He put something around her neck. It must be protecting him from the chant."

Then she could understand him. This is exactly how he planned it. It's been Lex all along. The voice was low and husky and almost seductive. Cerys' eyes felt heavy. Her head fell back. He's the one who sent the wraiths to take your brother and the others. He's evil, Cerys. You know it's true. He's been the head of the family since his father died. Nothing happens in this family that he isn't part of. Did you really believe he was innocent in all this? You know you can't trust him. Did he tell you he didn't know where your brother was? It was a lie. This is his place. It's in his name. He's been playing you all along.

Cerys moaned softly. She tossed her head from side to side.

"Stop him!" Lex growled. He rushed forward. Tully stepped in front of him. His face was expressionless. He held up Barbosa's gun. Lex reared back. He cursed.

It's him you want, not me. He killed your brother.

"No!"

You want vengeance, don't you? Kill him. Destroy him and you will get your brother back.

Cerys' dark eyes spun wildly in their sockets. Nico seized the crystal around her neck. He glanced at Lex. He smirked. He snapped the cord. He took a step back. Cerys' eyes stopped moving. They rolled back to show the whites. Her lips moved. The chant was so soft at first, it was almost incomprehensible. It rose steadily, ominously.

Her bonds snapped. She rose to her feet. "No!" she screamed. She threw out her hands.

Lex and Barbosa glanced at each other. "What's he done to her?" Barbosa demanded.

"I don't know!"

Cerys threw her head back. Her chant rose in a wild, relentless shriek. Her body vibrated with the force of the energy building within her. A window shattered. The chair to which she'd been tied exploded in a shower of sparks. Nico's laughter echoed through the strange tension in the air. "Go ahead, Cerys. Get him."

"Lex, get down!" Barbosa shouted.

"That's right, Cerys." Nico's voice slithered through her consciousness. "It's him you want."

Her hands shot up into the air. Energy crackled around them. It sparked off her fingertips. Then it rushed towards Lex in a deadly wave. He did not duck. He stood perfectly still. He stared at her in shock. The chant did not strike him. He threw his hands up to shield his face. He staggered backwards. Beside him, Barbosa was chanting. The energy ripped across Barbosa's face and arms. It left large slashes. Rivulets of blood dripped down his face and over his collar.

"Cerys!" Lex shouted. "What are you doing?"

Nico scowled. He turned towards Barbosa. He lifted his hands. Lex spun. He dove at Barbosa. They fell together upon the concrete ground. Nico's chant bounced harmlessly off his brother.

Cerys' eyes rolled. She blinked. She shook her head. Nico wasn't speaking to her anymore. The energy around her faded. She gasped. She fell to her knees. She tried to murmur words, to fall back into her trance, but there was nothing left. She pushed laboriously to her feet. She dove at Nico. She knocked him off his feet.

He looked up at her in shock. He scowled, but his trance was broken. He shoved her away from him. "It's all true, Cerys. You know it is. It's all true."

Her eyes were heavy. Her mind swam in confusion. She glanced at Lex. He stared back at her with a strange, haunted expression. He rose to his feet. Beside him, Barbosa sat with his head in his hands. "Cerys, I did not do this," Lex told her in a low voice. She looked up at him. She looked back at Nico.

Nico rose. He dusted off his sleek black suit. He looked at her with cold, glittering eyes. "Can you trust him, Cerys? Can you risk it? He sent the wraiths. He took your brother. He has been in on it all along."

She squeezed her eyes shut. She looked back at Lex. "Nice try, Nico." She did not stand up, but she could still try to chant. She was still too weak. Nico deflected her attack as though it were nothing.

Barbosa stumbled towards Nico. He muttered wearily. Tully was swift. He darted between them. He held a silver wand in his hand. He thrust it into his master's hand. He retreated against the wall and covered his head.

Cerys shot to her feet. She was too late. Nico staggered forward. He met Barbosa halfway. He gripped his shoulder. He raised the wand between them. Light swirled around them. Then it stopped. Nico stepped back. Barbosa collapsed to the floor. He did not stir. He looked small and deflated. His ruddy, tanned skin hung ashen and loose from his bones.

"No!" Cerys screamed.

Lex stared at his brother in shock. Nico advanced upon him. His eyes glowed with a manic, wild intensity. His skin was translucent, as though light was shining from inside him. "You've been spying on me. You've been working with them! You've been trying to ruin me."

"Nico, what you're doing is insane!" Lex hissed. "I have to stop you."

Nico laughed wildly. "You won't have a chance."

Nico didn't chant. He screamed. The sound was so bloodcurdling, Cerys covered her head with her arms and shielded Barbosa. She needn't have. Nico did not attack her. He attacked Lex. It should not have hurt him. It did. Spikes of energy sliced through his skin and drew blood. Lex dropped to his knees. He held up his arms as though it would shield him from the chant.

Nico's body jerked. His voice faded into a soft, desperate whisper. He dropped to his knees. He keeled over onto his face. Cerys jumped to her feet. She prodded him with her shoe. He did not stir. She felt Lex's hands on her shoulders. She spun on him. "Cerys, come on," he growled. "We have to go!"

She recoiled. "No! Cedric is here!"

Lex nodded. He spun around. "Tully! Where--"

Tully was gone.

Lex cursed. "Barbosa?"

Cerys shook his head. "He's alive, but..." She looked at him. Tears streaked down her cheeks. She did not bother to wipe them away. "Lex, help me! If you really want to help me find my brother, help me now."

He did not waste time replying. He spun. They searched. They found nothing. There was no one there. There was no sign that anyone had ever been there. Lex looked at her. "Cerys..."

"Lex, where are they?"

He strode towards her. He gripped her shoulders. "Cerys, we have to go!"

"It was a trap. He said it was a trap. They were never here. He was just trying to lure us...I don't even think he knew what we were after. He just wanted us here."

"Cerys, I promise you, we will find them. But right now we have to get Barbosa out of here, and we have to go."

Cerys wiped the tears from her cheeks. She looked at him. "He is nothing anymore. He's gone. There's no helping him. He might as well be dead."

Lex tugged on her arm. "Then we will have justice for him. Cerys!"

"Okay. Okay, I'm coming."

He bent down and lifted Barbosa into his arms. The ADA by day and leader of Chant by night had been a large, powerful man. He felt as light as a small child now. His skin drooped. His mouth was open. His breath rattled. "God, what happened to him?"

"It's his essence. Nico took it. And then he used it against you. And now, it's gone." She took a deep, hitching breath. Her eyes were suddenly cold and alert. Her jaw set. "Come on. I know where to take him."

CHAPTER 23

Lex stared up at the dark, gloomy house. He glanced at Cerys. "This seems strangely appropriate."

She didn't reply. She strode forward and pressed the door buzzer. She didn't wait for anyone to answer the door. When she opened it, Tamsin and Kate met her in the hall. They looked anxious. Cerys looked at them. The expression in her eyes did not seem to soothe them. "What happened?" Kate demanded.

Lex stepped into the house. "Oh, my god!" Tamsin cried, covering her mouth with her hand. She ran forward to meet him. "What happened? What happened to him?" She spun on Cerys. Her dark eyes glinted. "What did you do?"

Cerys did not step back from her. "It was Nico."

"We have to get him up to the infirmary," Kate said urgently. She moved towards Lex. He looked at her with hollow, emotionless blue eyes. She reared back slightly from him. "Is he safe?"

"What did you do?" Tamsin repeated. "How did this happen?"

"He used some kind of wand. He took his essence." Cerys' voice was low.

"You went into the warehouse!"

Cerys closed her eyes. "They caught me. They took me in."

"He told you not to go! He told you to stay hidden! You didn't listen to him! If you'd just listened to him, he wouldn't have had to come after you!" Tamsin shouted. Cerys held her eyes. She did not back away. "This is your fault!"

"Hey," Lex growled. "This is not Cerys' fault! She was overpowered."

"No." Cerys sighed deeply. She dropped her head to her chest. "It was my fault. I should have listened. I should have been prepared for Nico when he caught me."

"You shouldn't have gone by yourself!" Tamsin growled.

"Leave her alone," Lex said.

"We need to get to the infirmary!" Kate said loudly. "Please. Now is not the time for this!"

Tamsin sighed. She tilted her head at Lex. He followed her up the winding stairs. She did not speak. "What happened?" Cerys asked Kate in a low voice as they mounted the stairs behind Tamsin and Lex. "Why did Barbosa come to the warehouse?"

Kate glanced at her. "He received a call on his phone about an hour and half ago. He didn't say much to us. He just said he had to go."

Cerys sighed. "Nico threatened me. He shouldn't have gone. He should have refused. They wouldn't have been able to find him here."

"Nico would have killed you," Lex said. Cerys hadn't realized he'd been listening.

Tamsin paused on the stairs and spun around. "At least he would be alive now!"

"But Cerys wouldn't," Kate reminded her. "Zar wouldn't have been able to live with that."

"Balthazar isn't dead," Cerys murmured.

"He might as well be," Tamsin said softly. "And now what are we going to do?"

"Tamsin, leave her alone," Kate ordered. "This isn't her fault. Channel your anger towards the right person."

"It is her fault he was in that warehouse."

"Tam, are you telling me you wouldn't have done the same thing? Are you telling me you wouldn't have tried to have a closer look at that place? You would have. Nothing would have stopped you, not even Zar, so don't blame Cerys for Nico's doing," Kate growled. "Fighting amongst ourselves is not going to solve anything!"

Tamsin was silent. When she reached the library, she yanked so hard on the book, it nearly came away from the wall. Lex stared in surprise as the bookshelf slid sideways, revealing X in the systems room. X spun to face them. For the first time since Cerys had met him, he stood. "Jesus, what happened?"

"Nico," Tamsin said darkly.

X cursed. "What the hell is Lex Creed doing here?"

They all looked at Lex. He was standing in the middle of the glass octagon. He seemed to have completely forgotten he held their fallen leader in his arms. "What is this place?" he asked in awe.

They glanced at each other. "Lex, this is Chant," Cerys told him.

He blinked. "So it is real."

"Yeah. It's real."

Lex looked down at Barbosa in his arms. "And Barbosa was the leader."

"Yes. This is his house."

Lex exhaled heavily. "You've been with Chant all along?"

"Yes."

"You might have told me that this has been about Chant all this time, Cerys," he told her sternly.

"It hasn't been about Chant," Tamsin told him sharply. "It's been about your brother."

Lex looked at Cerys. For a moment, he actually looked hurt. "Did you really think I was involved in what he was doing?"

Cerys held his gaze. She considered. "Yes. For a moment, but it was Nico's chant. It wasn't me."

"What are you two talking about?" Tamsin demanded.

"Can we please get my patient into the infirmary?" Kate asked again.

Lex followed her into the infirmary. He laid Barbosa gently upon an empty bed. He watched as she tended to him. "Is this permanent?" he asked.

She looked up at him. Her expression was grim. "Yes. For now. We haven't found the cure."

He sighed. He passed a hand across his forehead. "Goddamnit, Nico."

"Sit down, both of you," Kate ordered sternly. "You look like hell warmed over."

Lex snorted. He waved her away. "I can take care of it."

"I am a doctor."

"I'm a chanter."

She rolled her eyes. "Suit yourself. Cerys?"

Cerys shook her head. "Later." She looked at Tamsin. "I tried to kill Lex back at the warehouse."

"What?"

He looked at Cerys in surprise. "You were trying to kill me?"

"What did you think I was trying to do?"

Tamsin looked slightly impressed. "Why?"

"Nico put me under a chant. He tried to convince me it was Lex who had done all this."

"It worked," Lex said darkly. "If not for Barbosa, I would be dead now."

"So he saved both your asses tonight, and this is what he gets." Tamsin's voice was soft now. She looked up at Cerys. "I'm sorry. I know you wouldn't have let this happen if you could have stopped it."

Cerys closed her eyes. A single tear streaked down her cheek. "I didn't know how he did it. We didn't know what was going to happen. We were fighting, and he just--"

Lex laid a hand on her shoulder. "Don't, Cerys."

"I'm so sorry, Tam," Cerys told her.

Tamsin nodded. "I know. And Kate's right. If it were me...I would have gone right in without even thinking twice if I thought it would get Cedric back." She lifted her eyebrows. "I'm assuming you didn't find him."

"No. They weren't there. It was a trap all along. I think he was waiting to see who was really after him. He didn't even suspect Chant, not at first." Cerys looked at Lex. "He actually asked me if you were part of Chant. He asked me if I was working for you."

Lex nodded. "He's suspected me for a while. I knew he was up to something. After I met Cerys, I realized what it was. I knew he was keeping the chanters somewhere. I've been trying to figure out where."

"Why didn't you tell me?" Cerys demanded.

He sighed. "I didn't want to tell you until I found something. I didn't want to give you false hope."

"If you had, I wouldn't have said those things to you!"

"I know."

"I'm sorry."

Lex nodded.

"What happened in there?" X asked. He was not looking at them. He was

208

leaning over Barbosa. There was no expression in his pale, gaunt face.

"I found the place. It looked empty and dark. When I got close, I realized it was because he'd painted the windows black."

"So it was a trap."

"Yes. Someone hit me from behind. His man, maybe? The one who was there."

Lex inclined his head. "Tully. His man."

"When I woke up, I was tied to a chair. Nico questioned me. He...chanted against me."

"He tortured you?" Tamsin demanded.

Cerys hesitated. "Yes. I didn't tell him anything. He figured it out. I think maybe he knew all along that none of this was about the criminal charges. I didn't tell him about Barbosa. I didn't tell him about you, Lex. He suspected you were leaking information to me, I guess, which I was giving to Barbosa. At least at first."

"I'm not surprised. He kept making remarks that led me to think he suspected I was cooperating with the ADA."

"Anyway, he called someone and told them to bring Balthazar to the warehouse. He was there within half an hour. They argued. Zar pulled a gun on him."

"What the hell did he do that for?" Tamsin asked.

"Maybe he wanted to get out of it without revealing he was Chant."

"He didn't get out of it at all."

"They chanted against each other. Then Lex came in. That's when Nico took over my head."

"How?"

"I don't know. Some kind of chant. It was like his voice became my own thoughts. He convinced me Lex was part of it all. He tried to get me to kill him."

"Which you did."

"I tried. Balthazar protected him."

"Then it was just chaos," Lex muttered. "We were all chanting against each other."

"But you can't hurt your brother."

"No. I tried to protect Barbosa. It was all I could do."

Cerys shook her head. "Then his man--"

"Tully."

"Tully gave him some sort of wand. He pressed it to his forehead and Zar's, and it transferred Zar's energy to him."

"But how?" Kate asked. Her eyes were narrowed in thought.

"I don't know. Some kind of chant. I didn't get a good look. There were crystals on either end. They must do something to direct the flow of energy," Cerys explained.

"Then what?"

"Nico attacked Lex."

"He what?"

"I don't know why he did that. Barbosa was already out, and I was the only one who could chant against him. I don't know why he went for Lex and not me." Cerys looked at Lex as though he might have the answer.

Lex's expression was grim. "It worked. He was able to hurt me."

"But I thought families couldn't chant against each other," Tamsin said.

"They can't. It must have been Barbosa's power that enabled him to do it." They stared at him thoughtfully for a long moment. He glanced away. "I think that's why he's doing it."

"What do you mean?" Cerys asked.

"To kill me."

"But he can't."

"Exactly. Not with his own power. With the other chanters' power, though, maybe he can. Or he thinks he can."

"That makes no sense," Tamsin put in. "If he wants to kill you, why go through all this? Why not just hire someone to do it?"

Lex chuckled humorlessly. "That seems like Nico's typical style, but not with me. This is personal. He would want to do it himself."

"Then why not just shoot you or stab you or something?"

"That's not the way he does things. He loves being a chanter. If he's going to kill someone, that's how he'd do it. And he'd need it to look like an accident or at least the same thing that killed our father. He wouldn't want to have to answer uncomfortable questions."

"I wonder how he figured out he couldn't kill you himself."

"He probably tried," Cerys murmured. Lex furrowed his brow. "Sorry, Lex."

He shrugged. "He's not my brother anymore, not the brother I used to know. Something's happened to him. He's gone crazy."

"Where is Nico now?" X asked.

"I knocked him out," Cerys replied. "We left him in the warehouse."

"Did you take the wand?"

Lex and Cerys looked at each other. They sighed. "No."

"What? What the hell, guys? We have enough problems! Don't you think that might have solved them all?"

"We were a little shaken up!" Cerys replied hotly. "Zar had just--and Cedric and the others weren't there, and I'd just tried to kill Lex--"

Lex laid a hand on Cerys' shoulder. "Calm down, Cerys." He looked at the others. "It was my fault. I should have thought of it. It didn't even occur to me. I was concerned with getting Cerys out of there before Nico woke up."

Tamsin sighed. "So we're pretty much right back where we started except now our enemy knows we're onto him and we have no leader."

"Why didn't you just kill him when you had the chance?" X asked in a low, arctic voice.

Cerys looked at him seriously. "I tried."

"What?" Lex asked, shocked.

"I tried! I knocked him out, but I intended to kill him. He took my brother! He practically killed Balthazar! He tried to get into my head and make me kill you. Now he's got the wand, and he's going to be waiting for us. He might even kill Ced and the others before we manage to figure out where the hell they are. I meant to kill him and make it easier on everyone."

Lex looked at her as though he weren't sure how to receive the information. "Why didn't it work? You're powerful, Cerys. What you did to me--if Barbosa hadn't been there, I would probably be splattered across the warehouse in tiny pieces."

"I don't know. He's powerful. More powerful than me."

"He was amped up on Zar's power, and you were tired," Tamsin said. She frowned.

"No. I mean, yes, but he was drained, too. I should have been able to kill him. I might not be able to kill him with a chant."

They all looked at each other grimly. "So what do we do now?" Kate asked.

"Call Abel," X said. "He will need to know about this. He'll need to figure out what to tell people about Zar."

"This is probably going to negatively affect the grand jury next week," Lex remarked absently.

"I suppose that's a relief to you," Tamsin sniped.

He looked at her coldly. "Actually, it isn't. My brother's gone over the edge. He has to face the consequences of his actions."

Cerys frowned. "I thought you wanted to protect him."

He looked at her. "That was before he started kidnapping chanters to steal their powers in order to kill me."

"That does put things in perspective."

"So, what about it, Lex?" Tamsin asked. "Are you with us or not?"

He inclined his head. "I'll see this through to the end. We have to find the other chanters. And we have to stop Nico for good."

Cerys sighed deeply. "Then we don't have any time to waste. We've already lost too much and too much time. It might already be too late."

"Okay." Lex looked around at them. "What do we do?"

"He's your brother!" Tamsin growled. "Don't you have any ideas?"

He sighed. "Yeah. I did. Go to the warehouse."

"Damnit."

"I don't know how he knew we were coming."

"He didn't. He knew someone was. He was trying to lure us there. Do you think if he really wanted that place to stay hidden, he would have used my name on the title?"

"Yeah, that seems a little obvious in retrospect."

Cerys pushed her hands through her long, disheveled hair. "I can't believe I was so stupid."

"We all were. None of us considered it would be a trap."

"It doesn't matter. It's done now," Kate told them. "The fact is, the others weren't there. We have to figure out where they are."

Tamsin frowned thoughtfully at Lex. "Does your brother have a contact named John?"

"John? Of course. Yes. Tully. His name is John Tully."

Cerys closed her eyes. "And we let him get away, too."

"You guys really screwed the pooch back there," X muttered.

"Shut up, X," Kate ordered. "This isn't helping."

"Tully is usually right where Nico is. He's involved in this," Lex said.

"Then he knows where the chanters are."

"Yeah, he probably does."

"They were alive when they left Creed Manor," Kate said grimly. "We have to believe they still are. Tully will be able to tell us where they are."

Lex frowned. "I don't think he will tell us."

"We'll make him!" Tamsin insisted.

He sighed. "Okay. I'd better get back to the Manor."

"What?" Cerys demanded. "You can't go back there. Nico might be there to finish what he started tonight."

He turned to her. "He can't kill me. Not without another chanter's powers. And I don't know if he can do it even then. He wasn't able to do it with Barbosa's powers." Cerys scowled. "Cerys, I will not hide from my own brother. I will not be kept out of my own house."

Tamsin considered. "If Tully is there, you can question him."

"Lex," Cerys said. "It's too dangerous. What if Nico does something?"

"I am not going to hide from him! I can handle my brother." He strode forward and seized her shoulders. "Cerys, I have to go. I promise you, I will be back in the morning."

"Lex, we have to sort this out before it's too late."

"We will. But right now you have to get some sleep. You're no good to anyone right now."

She scowled. Finally, she sighed. She nodded. "Yeah. Okay."

Lex looked at Kate. "Make her sleep."

Kate glanced at Cerys. Her look was austere. "I'll make sure she does. You can count on that."

"Tomorrow morning," Lex promised. He nodded to them all. He spun on his heel and strode from the room. Moments later, he peered back into the infirmary. "I don't suppose someone could show me the way out?"

Tamsin smirked. "Come on. I'll show you."

"Thanks. Good night, Cerys."

"Night." Her eyes were already drooping. Kate gripped her shoulders and frog marched her towards the door.

"Bed, Cerys," Kate told her firmly.

Abel met them in the library. He jerked a thumb over his shoulder. "Did I just pass Tamsin and Lex Creed on my way up here."

"Yes."

"What the hell is going on?"

Kate looked at him solemnly. "I think you need to see."

Abel glanced at Cerys. "What happened to you?"

"Talk to X. I'll meet you in there. I need to get Cerys to bed. She is about to fall down."

"No, Kate, I need to tell him what happened."

Kate sighed. "Cerys–"

Abel frowned. "It's bad, isn't it?"

"Come on. See for yourself."

"I need to know what happened," he said in a low voice as he peered down at Barbosa's slack face.

Cerys told him. As she did, he paced. His face remained blank, but his eyes flashed. He passed a hand over his face. He sighed heavily. "Abel? What do we

214

do?" Kate asked.

He ignored this. He looked at Cerys. "What the hell were you thinking, Cerys?"

"I was thinking maybe I could see some sign of whether or not my brother and the others were in there!"

"Yeah? And were they?"

She sighed. "No. But we know who knows. And Lex is going to find out."

Abel dropped heavily into a chair. Tamsin rejoined them. "Did you tell him?"

"Yes."

"What do we do, Abel?"

He shook his head. "I don't know, Tam. I don't know. This is bad. We can't report what happened, obviously. If Zar just disappears, everything is going to fall apart with Nico. Rutherford will probably be relieved." He glanced up at them wryly. "They'll probably suspect Nico had something to do with it. They won't have any idea how right that is."

"Zar deserves justice!" Tamsin growled.

"Yes, he goes. And we'll get it for him. I promise you that, Tam."

She scowled. "I hope so. I really do."

"What do we do now?" Cerys asked.

Abel looked up at her. "Get some sleep, like the doctor ordered. You look like hell." He sighed. "This has been about the worst night ever."

"Tell me about it. You're not the one who tried to kill two people."

"And failed," Tamsin reminded her helpfully.

"Yeah. Thanks for reminding me, Tam."

"I'm going to pretend I didn't hear any of that," Abel told her sternly. "We've got enough problems right now."

CHAPTER 24

Creed Manor was as quiet as a tomb. It was always quiet this late at night. Lex felt as though his body was twice as heavy as usual. His head pounded. He didn't have time to waste. He took the stairs to the fifth floor two at a time. There was no sound from Nico's apartments. There was no light glowing under the door.

"Nico?"

There was no response from inside his brother's room. He rapped twice on the door. He tried the knob. The door swung open. The room was dark. Lex exhaled heavily. He braced himself. He groped for the light switch. Soft, white light flooded the room. Nico wasn't there.

Lex sighed. He relaxed. The room was quite and still. It seemed horribly ordinary and pleasant. It felt wrong. A man like Nico should not occupy comfortable, luxurious rooms like these. It gave people the wrong idea. The bed was carefully made. It had not been slept in in several days. The closet was open. Lex peered inside.

There was a large, empty space. Wherever Nico had gone, he intended to stay a while. Lex wasn't prepared to face his brother again tonight, but he needed to find him. He spun and raced down the stairs. The servants' rooms were on the first floor behind the kitchen. There were not many live-in employees in Creed Manor. John Tully and his wife, Lisa, shared a large apartment. Peyton's housekeeper, Margie, lived beside them.

Lex had never seen Tully's room. It had once belonged to their nanny, Fran, when he'd been young. Fran had never allowed the children into her rooms. She'd been a young, pretty woman with long, black hair. When he'd been nine or ten, Lex had adored her. He used to camp outside her room, waiting for her to come out every morning. He knew exactly where it was.

He pounded several times on the door. "Tully! Lisa!" he barked.

No one answered. The door was locked. It didn't matter. There was no sound from within. He had been foolish to think his brother and his man would return to the Manor. He sighed deeply and fell back against the door. He closed his eyes.

"I remember when Frannie used to live here."

Lex blinked. His mother stood before him in her dressing gown. Her face
216

was washed clean of her makeup. She looked like the woman he remembered so long ago, when she had been young and sweet and uncorrupted. She wasn't that woman anymore. Age had etched its lines into her face. Her deep blue eyes were cold and hurt, as though the world she had thought she'd known had proven hostile and cruel. There was grey at the roots of her shining auburn hair.

Lex swiped his hand across his face. "What are you doing here, Mother?"

"Frannie was a sweet girl. She doted on you. She always seemed...afraid of Nico. I think we were all a little afraid of Nico. Something about him has always been wrong. Twisted."

He stared at her. "Mother, are you drunk?"

She snorted. "What is wrong with you? Is that any kind of question to ask your mother? You should be ashamed of yourself."

"Sorry, Mother."

"Tully's gone."

"I can see that."

"Nico came home about an hour ago. He packed a bag."

"Did he say anything to you?"

"Of course he didn't. He just looked at me in that way he has. A few minutes later, Tully came in and took Lisa away."

Lex cursed. "Nico cannot leave town right now. He has to testify at the grand jury next week."

Peyton laughed bitterly. "When has your brother ever played by anyone's rules but his own, Lex? He's always been different from you. Your father knew it, too. Your brother always wanted his approval, but your father couldn't look at him without seeing what was really there, underneath all the charm and cleverness."

Lex blinked at her in surprise. He narrowed his eyes. She seemed different tonight. "Mom, do you know what Nico is up to?"

Peyton sighed. She turned away from him. She did not answer right away.

He frowned. "You've known about it all along, haven't you?"

"It's not my place to interfere."

"You're our mother!"

"Your father was able to keep him in control. It is your job now."

"Mom, what do you know? Why is he doing this?

She shook her head. "Does it matter?"

"Do you know where chanters are?"

She looked up into his eyes. "I failed at controlling your brother. Creed women are not known for being strong-willed." She stepped toward him. "Simone is the perfect Creed woman. She's beautiful, successful, respectable, complaisant."

His brow furrowed. "Mom—"

"She reminds me so much of myself when I was young. When I met your father. I never stood up to him, either, no matter what sort of terrible things he did."

Realization struck him like a blow. He stepped forward and folded her into a bear hug. "Thanks, Mom."

She smiled sadly as he spun away from her. "Lex!"

He paused on the stairs and turned back to her. "Mom?"

"Dear, Nico is still my youngest son. I love him very much. Despite what he's done, I don't want him dead."

"Don't worry, Mom. Neither do I."

* * *

Lex was haggard and disheveled when he arrived on the doorstep at Chant headquarters. He pressed the doorbell and held it. A lilting melody resounded through the house. He didn't try the door. He leaned against it wearily.

It opened. He nearly fell into the house. Tamsin stared at him in shock. "You look like hell, Lex."

He chuckled. "I feel like hell."

"Cerys!" Tamsin shouted over her shoulder. She looked doubtfully at Lex. "You'd better come inside. Everyone's upstairs."

Cerys and Kate met them in the library. Kate lifted her eyebrows at Lex. "Did you sleep at all?"

He waved his hand dismissively. "Been busy."

She frowned at him sternly. "You look awful. What have you been doing?"

"Trying to find my brother."

Cerys sighed. "He wasn't at the house?"

"No. He packed a bag and took off before I got there. Tully was gone, too." Cerys cursed. He strode forward and caught her shoulders. He wobbled slightly on his feet. "Relax, Cerys. I think I know where your brother is."

"What?" Tamsin demanded.

"Lex, you need to get some sleep," Kate said, scowling.

"Not yet."

"Kate, let him talk," Tamsin growled.

"Where is he?" Cerys asked.

"The Cultural District."

"What? How do you know?" Tamsin asked skeptically.

His laugh was slightly hysterical. "My mother."

"Peyton told you where my brother is? She has known about all this?"

"She knows a lot more than I ever gave her credit for."

"She told you Cedric and the others are in the Cultural District?" Tamsin glanced at Kate as though she suspected Lex might require medical attention.

"Not exactly. She told me what I needed to know to figure it out." He laughed wildly. "I should have known all along. I am so stupid! I spent days following him there and never once suspected."

Cerys frowned. She steered him towards the circle of chairs in the meeting room. He did not seem to want to sit down. "What are you talking about, Lex?"

"Simone is keeping them in her apartment. I've been sitting outside her apartment all night."

"Simone Stowe?" Kate asked, shocked.

"She is crazy enough to go out with Nico," Tamsin remarked. "It wouldn't be the first time a woman did something stupid for a man. Did you see anything?"

"No. Everything was quiet. I thought about going in, but I don't think I could have done much good."

"Lex, you need to rest," Cerys told him gently.

"Not yet. We have a lot to do. We have to move quickly. Nico knows what we're doing now. He'll be expecting us. We can't waste any time."

"No," Tamsin said sternly. "We need a plan. We can't just go storming into that neighborhood half-cocked." She glanced at them grimly. "Besides, Cerys wasn't strong enough to kill Nico. He's powerful. We need to think about this."

"If the others are in the apartment, they are probably still alive. Right now, it's a lot safer to keep them than kill and dispose of them." Kate said soothingly. "We have time. You can't go in there like this."

Tamsin considered. She met Cerys' eyes thoughtfully. "Probably Simone is keeping them safe while Nico distracts us."

Cerys sighed. "Okay, so what do we do then?" Lex demanded.

Tamsin stared at them. "We need more firepower if we're going up against Nico again. Zar was the strongest of all of us, and Nico finished him like he was nothing. Lex, you can't even fight him."

Lex scowled. "So?"

Tamsin looked at Cerys grimly. "Cerys, I think you should call Colin Mobley."

Cerys blinked. Lex shot to his feet. "What?" he demanded.

"I thought we had decided against that," Cerys said uncomfortably.

"No. We just put it off because Zar had something else up his sleeve. You saw where that got us."

"Tam's right, Cerys," Kate said. "He could help us."

"What? Colin Mobley?" Lex asked.

Tamsin lifted her eyebrows. "He's been fighting with Nico all his life. He hasn't died yet. He can chant to kill."

Lex scowled. "How do you know he can chant to kill?"

Cerys looked at him warily. "He killed your father, didn't he?"

He hesitated. "Maybe he did. Or Lochlan did."

"Either way, it doesn't matter," Tamsin said sternly. "He knows Nico's style better than anyone."

Lex glanced around at all of them warily. "We are not trying to kill my brother, are we?"

"We'll do what we have to."

Cerys laid a hand on his arm. "We don't want it to come to that, but if it does, we want to be prepared."

Lex shook his head. "I don't like this."

Cerys sighed. "Lex, if I couldn't hurt Nico, and I'm the best we've got right now, we need more firepower."

"We have enough between all of us. We don't need Colin."

"Yes, we do," Kate replied sharply. "We aren't risking more of our people in this fight because you have a grudge against Colin Mobley."

He scowled. Cerys laid a hand on his arm. "We don't even know that Colin would even agree to join us. He doesn't know anything about this. You're taking for granted he would agree to fight just because it's Nico."

"Actually," Lex said darkly, "he probably would."

"Cerys, call him," Tamsin ordered. "Talk to him. It's worth a shot."

"I am thoroughly against this," Lex put in.

"Your objections have been duly noted, but you are not running this operation," Tamsin replied sternly.

Kate smirked. "I guess we know who is now."

"Someone has to."

Cerys sighed. "Okay, I'll call Colin. If he'll agree to meet me, I'll see what I can do."

Lex scowled. "I think he'll probably meet you," he said grumpily. "One thing I know about Colin is he likes brunettes."

"Lex, bed. Now."

* * *

Cerys stared out the window at the dreary streets below the penthouse suite of the Warren Hotel. She sighed deeply. Dark clouds hung over Spectra City. The air was breathless with the anticipation of the coming torrent. Her head ached. Despite her exhaustion, she hadn't slept through the night. Her reflection looked drawn and pale against the glass.

There was a knock on her door. She spun. Her stomach roiled anxiously. She strode forward to answer the knock. Colin Mobley stood in the doorway. There was a smirk on his handsome face. It faded the moment he saw her. "Cerys?" he said. His eyebrows contracted. "You look awful."

She laughed. "Thanks, Colin."

"No, I—I mean. Sorry. I just mean—"

"I know. It's okay. I know I do. Come in."

He stepped into the suite. "I was surprised you wanted to meet me. Especially here."

"I need privacy."

His mouth turned up slightly. "I am assuming you are not coming onto me."

She laughed humorlessly. "Sorry."

"I'm somewhat disappointed."

"No, you aren't."

"Well, I would have been, if you looked more up to it."

"I get it."

"I'm digging myself in deeper, aren't I?"

"Yes." She smiled wryly.

"And I am normally very good with the ladies."

"I'm sure you are. I know the only reason you'd be interested in me is because I was going out with Lex."

He chuckled. "Maybe. But maybe if we knew each other a little better..."

"We're about to."

He lifted his eyebrows. "Really?"

"Not in the way you think. I don't think you'll really like it."

"You might be right about that. Cerys, what is this?" Colin stood in front of the dry erase board with an incredulous expression. He glanced at her. "What is going on?"

She paused beside him. She smiled wryly. "I came to Spectra City to find my brother Cedric. This is the information I have gathered to that purpose."

He studied it silently for a long moment. "Tell me what's going on, Cerys."

"It's a long story."

He glanced at her. "I'm listening."

"Six months ago, my brother Cedric came to Spectra. Six weeks ago, he went missing. I came here to find him."

"What does this have to do with me?"

She gazed sidelong at him. "What makes you think it does?"

"You asked me here. You let me see this. You must need something from me."

"Cedric is a chanter."

He blinked. His expression was guarded. "Okay."

"He came here to find Chant."

"Chant isn't real," Colin growled. "It's just a rumor."

"No, it isn't. It is real. We're investigating the creature attacks in the city."

He frowned. "We? Cerys..."

"You know what goes on in this city, Colin," she said gently. "Don't pretend that you don't."

He sighed. "You're in Chant."

"Yes. I am now."

He spun away from her. He dropped heavily onto the sofa. "I didn't really believe the attacks were happening. I thought someone had made it all up and everyone else was just feeding the hysteria. I didn't want to believe it. I know there are things that go on in the city...dark things."

"Cedric was taken by the creatures."

Colin looked up at her. "How do you know?"

"He let himself be captured. To find out where they were coming from."

He lifted his eyebrows. "Where?" Her expression was so pointed, he sighed. "Let me guess. The Creeds."

"No. Not the Creeds. Just Nico."

He exhaled heavily. "Are you sure?"

"Yes. We're sure. We are very, very sure."

His gaze was suspicious. "What does this have to do with me, Cerys? Why are you telling me all this?"

"We need you, Colin."

"What? For what?"

"We know what you are. We know you've been fighting the Creeds all your life."

He stared at her silently.

"The chanters that were taken by the creatures are still alive. Some of them, anyway."

"They're alive?"

"Nico Creed is holding them prisoner."

"What? That's crazy."

"Really? You've known Nico all your life. Is it really?"

He sighed. "What's he doing with them?"

"He's taking their power."

"How?"

"He has some sort of device. It transfers their power to him."

"How do you know all this, Cerys?"

"I've seen it."

He stared at her. He sighed. "I think you need to tell me everything. And I think I need a drink."

She smiled wanly. She strode to the mini bar in the corner. She tossed him a small, plastic bottle of scotch.

Colin opened it. He didn't bother to pour it into the glass she handed him or mix it with water. He swallowed it in one gulp. "Okay. I'm ready. I think."

She sat down beside him on the sofa. "Cedric told me about the creature attacks in his letters before he disappeared. He told me Chant suspected the Creeds were involved."

"That is what this board is all about?"

"Yes."

He narrowed his eyes at her. "Is that why you've been seeing Lex Creed?"

She hesitated.

"It is, isn't it?"

"It is, but it isn't the only reason. That's not really the issue right now. I tracked Chant and the creatures to an alley in the Art District one night. I met Lex there."

Colin looked startled. "What was he doing there?"

"He was trying to protect the chanters from the creatures."

"Protect them?"

"He's been trying to stop his brother all this time."

Colin shook his head. "Lex is in Chant, too?"

"No, not exactly. We've been trying to discover where Nico was keeping the chanters. Our leader–"

He sat forward. "Who is it?"

She eyed him narrowly for several moments. It didn't seem as though there was any harm in telling him now. "Balthazar Barbosa."

His jaw dropped. "Seriously?"

"Yes."

"That explains a lot. The investigation has been about the creature attacks the whole time?"

"Yes and no. It was a way into Creed Manor. When he was able to execute the search warrants, the chanters were already gone. Balthazar found evidence of where Nico had been keeping them, but they weren't there anymore."

"Have you found them?"

She hesitated. "We tracked Nico to a warehouse in the Industrial District. We thought it was where he was keeping them. I went in alone. I was captured." She sighed deeply. "Nico figured out I was working with Chant and Balthazar."

"He knew Barbosa was with Chant?"

"No. Not at first. He figured it out. He sent for Balthazar, and they fought. While they were fighting, Lex showed up."

"How did he know about it?"

"He'd been looking for the chanters on his own."

"Did he know you were with Chant?"

"No. And I didn't know he was working against Nico."

"Sounds like a fine relationship you have there."

"Don't judge, Colin."

He smirked. "I'm not judging. I'm just urging you to reconsider."

She ignored him. "Nico used some sort of chant against me. He got into my head and convinced me to kill Lex."

Colin blinked. "Is he--"

"No. No, I tried to kill him. Balthazar protected him. Lex is all right. Balthazar...he isn't."

"What happened?"

"We tried to fight. We were all fighting. Nico used the device--the one that takes the chanters' powers--on Balthazar. He is...as good as dead now." She lowered her head. "Nico used his power to attack Lex."

"Why?"

"We think that's what he's been doing. Trying to find a way to kill Lex."

Colin frowned. "But that doesn't make any sense. It's us Nico's been trying to kill."

"Yes, but I don't think this has anything to do with the feud. It's about Lex."

"I suppose I shouldn't be surprised you know about the feud."

"I know a lot of things."

He snorted. "So it seems. What happened after Nico attacked Lex?"

"Nico was drained. He used up all his energy. I was able to knock him out."

"Was Lex hurt?"

"Yes, a little. Not much. Nico was only able to use a short burst of Barbosa's power before it was tapped out and he was weakened."

Colin considered. "I have seen that happen to him before. He's attacked us with more power than he ever had, but he faded out much quicker."

"He was probably practicing on you."

"What a bastard. Did you find your brother?"

"No. They weren't there. We think Nico set up the whole warehouse scene to figure out who was following him. They might never have been there."

"That sounds like him. So what happens now?"

"Lex knows where they are. This time, we're pretty sure."

"So, what are you waiting for?"

She smiled humorlessly. "You."

"What?"

"I went up against him once. I tried to kill him. I failed. We aren't powerful enough to fight him."

Colin frowned at her for a long moment. He rose abruptly. "So you want me to come with you to fight him."

"Yes."

He paced in front of her for several moments. He pushed his hands through his dark hair. He paused and looked at her. He shrugged. "I've been fighting Nico Creed all my life. I suppose this isn't much different except now I have a good reason." He smirked. "Besides, I always wanted to see if Chant was real."

Cerys smiled wanly. "Thank you, Colin."

"What about Lex? What's his part in all this?"

She hesitated. He narrowed his eyes suspiciously. "He's sort of with us now."

"With Chant?"

"Yes."

Colin scowled at her incredulously. "You want me to fight beside a Creed?"

"Colin, Lex isn't like Nico."

He spun toward her. "Did you ask him? About my sister?"

"Yes. I asked him."

He stared at her blankly. "And you're still with him?"

She looked away. "No. Not exactly. I don't know if I was ever with him. It doesn't matter what's going on between Lex and me right now. He is working with us to stop his brother."

"I am not fighting with a Creed."

"Colin, we have a common enemy! This isn't about the feud! It's about stopping Nico and the attacks and getting my brother back!" She stood to face him. "You can do something good with your powers besides warring with your next door neighbors all the time. What is the point of having your abilities if you're just going to waste them?"

Colin scowled at her. "Why doesn't Lex fight him? He's as strong as Nico. Maybe stronger."

"He can't fight him."

"What?"

"He can't. Families can't chant against each other. Their powers don't work that way. They're from the same source."

"But I use my power to heal my father and my cousins all the time."

"Yes. I think you can use good chants on them. You just can't hurt them."

"How the hell do you know?"

"Lex figured it out when he tried to fight the wraiths. He couldn't. Their purpose was to detect chants. They could not see him. They were both immune to each other. He thinks that might be why Nico is taking the other chanters' power. To use against Lex."

"That's a pretty elaborate and insane plan."

She shrugged grimly. "When someone is intent on committing murder, I think they will go to any length."

He sighed. "I know better than to underestimate Nico's obsession." He looked at her sternly. "Cerys, Lex is my enemy."

"Not anymore. Not right now. You both want the same thing. To stop Nico."

He shook his head. "I want to help you, Cerys. I want to help Chant do this, but Lex killed my sister."

She gripped his arms. She shook him gently. "Damnit, Colin, no he didn't."

"He got her killed!"

"No!"

"You don't know anything about it!"

"I do. I trust Lex."

He scowled. "That's the problem. You're under his spell."

"There is no spell. You don't know what he's really like."

"I don't think I care to find out."

"You should. He doesn't want this. He never wanted this. He has nothing against your family. He wants the feud to end."

"Diana—"

"He loved her. They were going to leave together, to be together and escape the feud."

"He tricked her! He led her into the garden, and she was killed."

"No. Colin, I think you know that isn't true. You knew all about them. You know it was an accident. It was terrible. I know what it's like to lose someone you love. Nothing is worse, but it was not Lex's fault."

Colin pushed his hands through his hair. He spun his back to her. "Why that night? Why did he plan to meet her that night? Nico attacked us at that exact moment..."

Cerys considered. "Maybe Nico knew. Maybe he..." She sighed.

"The moment she was in the garden, he attacked."

"It was his chant that killed you sister, Colin. Nico is the only one to blame for what happened to her. Lex wants revenge for her death as much as you. You have the chance to get it."

He strode away from her. He paced silently for several moments. He paused. "You trust Lex?"

"Yes. With this, yes. He wants what we want. I'm sure."

His brow furrowed. "How can I trust you? I don't even know you! You're dating my enemy. How do I know this isn't all just an elaborate ruse to lure me away and kill me?"

She gave him an incredulous look. "Really? Don't be ridiculous."

He sighed. "Okay, yeah. Maybe you're right."

"Colin, please. We need your help. We don't want to lose anyone else. You can fight him. And you can win. Together, we can stop all of this."

He stared at her. He did not say anything.

"Colin?"

He crossed his arms over his chest. "I'll think about it, Cerys."

"We don't have a lot of time, Colin! Every moment—we want to find them alive. Please."

He strode toward her. He caught her shoulders. He nodded. "All right. I'll help you. But on one condition."

She lifted her eyebrows warily. "What?"

"I want to see Chant."

"What is it with boys and lairs?"

"They're cool."

She rolled her eyes. "Fine. Come on. I'll take you there."

CHAPTER 25

"This is so cool!" Colin said. He spun in a slow circle, staring up at the glowing glass screens in the Chant systems room.

"I know, right?" X replied.

"What is all this?"

"Maps of the city. Tracking systems to find chanter activity. Databases, research, other things you probably don't want to know about."

"How come?"

"Plausible deniability."

"This place is so cool," Colin repeated. "I need a lair."

The panel slid open. Tamsin and Abel strode into the room. Abel smirked at Cerys. Tamsin eyed Colin skeptically. She stuck out her hand. "Tamsin Stryker."

He shook it. "Colin Mobley."

"Welcome to Chant. You know Detective Abel Dane?"

"We've met." Colin looked at Abel incredulously. "Detective Dane? You're a chanter?"

Abel snorted. "You say that like it's a dirty word. You're a chanter, too, I might remind you. And you're standing in the headquarters of the largest chanter organization in the state, far as I know."

Colin chuckled. "Yeah. I guess you're right. I suppose it shouldn't surprise me."

"Nothing surprises me anymore," Abel muttered darkly.

"Come on," Tamsin said, tilting her head at Colin. "I'll show you the rest of the place."

"It's not as interesting," X remarked off-handedly.

"No, but it's more important," Tamsin told him gloomily.

Kate greeted them grimly when they entered the infirmary. "Dr. Windsor?" Colin asked. He looked shocked.

She laughed. "Colin. Nice to see you again."

"You two know each other?" Tamsin asked.

"Sure. Colin's family is one of the hospital's main contributors. We've seen each other around."

"You're a chanter, too," Colin said in bemusement.

Abel smiled. "We're everywhere, Colin. You just have to know where to look."

Colin wasn't listening. He stepped past Kate. He stared down at Barbosa in shock. "What's happened to him?" he asked in a hushed voice. "He's just skin and bones. I saw him on the news a couple days ago."

"Nico happened to him," Cerys told him grimly.

"This is what he's doing to them?"

"Yes. This is what happens when he finishes with them. This is what it looks like when you've had your power sucked out."

Colin spun away from the frail, wasted figure in the bed. "How did I not notice this? It was happening right next door to me."

"It happened in my own home, and I didn't know."

Colin glanced up. Lex leaned against the doorframe. His expression was troubled. Colin's lip curled. "Lex. Are you sure about that?"

Lex straightened and strode toward him. "You think I would have let him do this if I knew?"

"I don't know. I think you're capable of a lot of things."

"Colin, Lex, now is not the time for this," Cerys told them sternly. "We have to figure out how we're going to do this. We haven't got a lot of time."

Colin and Lex glared at each other.

Tamsin rolled her eyes. "Can we act like grownups now and figure out how the hell we're going to get our friends back?"

Cerys strode between Colin and Lex and led the way into the conference room. They sat on either side of her. Their tension was palpable. Abel sat across from them. He looked as though he were prepared to break up a fight. His hand hovered instinctively over his hip, though he was not wearing his side arm. Kate leaned against the doorframe.

Tamsin stood peering at them determinedly from the head of the table. "Okay, we know where Nico is keeping our people now. Lex and X have worked up a layout of the flat. It probably won't matter much."

"What flat?" Colin asked, frowning.

They all glanced at him. "The chanters are being held at Simone Stowe's apartment."

He lifted his eyebrows incredulously. "In the Cultural District?"

"Yes," Lex replied.

"How come you know where she lives?" Tamsin asked.

Colin rolled his eyes. "Everyone knows where she lives. She's a regular celebutante these days."

Lex chuckled wryly. "That's what happens when you date a Creed."

Colin's lip curled. "That and you become an accessory to kidnapping and attempted murder."

"That's fair," Abel put in, smirking.

Lex scowled. Tamsin ignored them. "We go in, we get it done, and we try not to make too big of a mess."

Colin looked at Tamsin doubtfully. "So the plan is to just storm the apartment and start chanting?"

They glanced at each other. "Kind of," Cerys replied sheepishly.

"You have a better idea?" Tamsin snapped.

"No, not really."

"Okay, then. We haven't got a lot of time," Tamsin replied coldly. "We need to strike. Now."

"This is a really bad plan."

"You think you could come up with something more elegant?" Lex asked disdainfully.

"Yeah, probably. If I had more time."

"Well, we don't," Tamsin said sharply. "And it's as good as anything else."

"I'll get Simone to open the door," Abel said positively.

"How?" Colin asked.

"I'm a cop."

"Right."

"Colin, you and Cerys will go in first," he continued. "Tamsin and I will follow. Tamsin will take care of Simone. I'll find the chanters."

"Colin, I will cover you while you fight Nico," Cerys told him.

"Why can't Tamsin cover Colin and you take care of Simone?" Lex demanded.

They all looked at him incredulously. "Now is not the time to get protective," Abel told him.

"Is there a better time?"

Tamsin rolled her eyes. "Cerys is more powerful than me. We need her to do the fighting."

"But I can't chant to kill," Cerys added. "It has to be Colin. Someone will have to keep him protected while he fights."

"What about the device?" Colin asked, frowning. "The one that takes the chanter's power?"

"That's me," Lex said. "While you're fighting Nico, I'll get it."

Colin considered. "It sounds simple enough."

"It is," Abel replied. "But we have to be fast. If we don't get the drop on him and he has a chance to use his device before Lex gets to it, we'll be screwed."

"We take him out quick and easy," Tamsin added.

"And before the neighbors notice anything is amiss?" Colin said dryly.

"That would be ideal."

Cerys glanced at Lex. "Is Simone a chanter?"

He shook his head. "No. She just has bad taste in men."

Tamsin shrugged. "Should be easy enough to take her out, then."

"Just don't hurt her," Lex said sternly. "None of this is her fault. She's under Nico's control."

"I think I can manage to take care of a pampered celebutante. No one else needs to get hurt in this. We've had enough losses on both sides."

Cerys shot to her feet. "Okay. Let's go."

Lex blinked. "What? Now?"

"Yes! We're running out of time! What do we need to wait for? I want to find my brother and I want to find him alive! Let's just go. Maybe we'll get lucky and they won't be at home."

Lex stood. "Cerys, calm down. Let's think about this—"

"She's right," Colin said. He rose to face Lex. "What's there to think about? We have the plan. There's no time like right now."

"Stay out of this, Colin. You're just a hired gun because the rest of us don't kill."

Colin stepped past Cerys to face him squarely. "Oh no? Last I checked, you could kill just fine. You just can't do it when it counts. You can't do a damn thing against your brother. You need me. I think that gives me as much say in this as you."

"Maybe we don't need you. We're strong enough without you."

"Yeah? Why don't you ask your girlfriend about that? She's the one who asked me to be here. She seems to think you need me."

Lex opened his mouth to reply. Cerys stepped between them. "Hey! If you two want to have it out, no one's going to stop you, but right now is not the time!" she growled.

"Cerys is right," Tamsin said. "You two can fight over her later."

"This has nothing to do with Cerys," Lex barked.

"No. It has to do with Diana, doesn't it, Lex?" Colin put in coldly.

"You don't know a damn thing about Diana and me!"

"I know if not for you, she'd be alive."

Lex's arm swung back. Cerys was faster. She threw out her hand. Her lips moved frantically. Her eyes glowed incandescently white. The men flew back from each other as though a large, invisible barrier had risen between them. "That is enough!" she snapped. "Save it for Nico! You have a common enemy now. It's time to fight him!"

They glared at each other. Tamsin rolled her eyes. "Come on. Let's channel all that wrath into getting our friends back."

* * *

Cerys vibrated with excitement in the backseat of Abel's black SUV.

Abel peered up at Simone Stowe's apartment building with a calm, resolute expression. Lex looked uneasy. He did not speak. Behind them, the headlights of Colin's silver sedan flicked off. Simone's shades were drawn, but a light burned in the third story window. She was home.

"Let's go in," Cerys said anxiously.

"Just hold on, Cerys," Abel told her in a low, tranquil voice.

A slender figure passed in front of the window. Cerys tensed. Lex sighed. "That's Simone."

Beside her, a tall, broad-shouldered man appeared. Cerys made a strange noise low in her throat. "And that's Nico. Can we go now?"

"Cerys," Abel scolded. Nico's shadow form gestured wildly. "He seems to be yelling at her."

"That doesn't surprise me," Lex replied solemnly. "Nico argues with most people he talks to."

Abel glanced back at Cerys. "Are you ready?"

"Damnit, Abel, can we go?"

"Yes."

Colin and Tamsin met them in the street outside the apartment. They nodded silently to the others. Their expressions were cold and steady. "Let's do this," Colin said in a low voice.

Abel smiled humorlessly. He jerked his head toward the building. His step was confident and assured. He was on familiar ground. The others followed him. Lex fell into step beside Cerys. She felt his hand brush hers. She glanced sidelong at him. He looked grim and troubled. He caught her hand in a cold and slightly trembling grip. He dropped it seconds later.

The apartment building was quiet. There was no guard waiting to greet them. Abel did not hesitate. He marched up the stairs to Simone's apartment. He paused in front of the door. He gestured them. Cerys and Lex moved to the right of him. Tamsin and Colin waited on his left. They all nodded silently to each other.

"This almost feels like a real bust," Abel remarked.

"Do you always waste time talking about it?" Lex demanded in a strained voice.

"Right." Abel smiled. He pounded on the door. "Simone Stowe! Open up! SCPD!"

They waited. For a moment, there was no reply from within. They could hear Simone murmuring urgently. "Get back, Simone!" Nico barked at her from behind the door. "Get to the bedroom!"

Abel glanced at them. His eyes glittered. His body seemed to vibrate with excitement. "Ready?"

He stepped back. Colin and Cerys moved forward in the same movement. They were already chanting when the door flew open. Simone shrieked and backed into the hallway away from them. Abel, Lex and Tamsin darted inside. They ducked as glass vases shattered and furniture splintered around Nico. He stood in the center of the room. His eyes were glowing eerily, intensely white. His lips moved frantically.

Abel slammed the door behind them. The air around Nico crackled and swirled. Colin's dark hair blew back from his face as though he were facing a strong, powerful gale. A shimmering, incandescent barrier of energy surrounded him. Beside him, wide, bloody gashes appeared in Cerys' skin as she absorbed the deadly chants bouncing off the barrier.

Nico jerked as Colin's chant struck him. Rivulets of blood dripped from his nose. He did not seem to be weakening. Energy flowed relentlessly over them. Lex cursed. Cerys could not withstand him long. He threw out his hands toward her. He chanted. Around her, the air glowed.

Tamsin darted toward the hall after Simone. She backed up. Simone strode toward her with her hands out. Her eyes glowed. She was chanting. Tamsin did not have time to retaliate. She collapsed on the floor at Simone's feet.

"Goddamnit, you said she wasn't a chanter!" Abel shouted.

No one answered him.

Cerys fell to her knees. Her trance broke abruptly. She clutched at her throat. "Cerys! Get Cedric and the others!" Abel yelled to her.

He did not wait to see that she had heard him. He spun toward Simone. He lifted his arms. He slipped instantly into a trance.

"Lex!" Cerys yelled. His eyes glowed white. He did not seem to see or hear her. "You have to cover Colin!"

He did not respond, but his body turned as though he'd understood her words. Nico was tireless. His hair stood on end. His face was streaked with blood. Streams of energy flowed from his fingertips and sizzled through the air. The curtains smoked. The paintings on the walls melted and curled. Colin staggered backward. Energy lanced across his face. It bubbled and split. Blood dripped down his chin. Then Lex's chant surrounded him. The slashes on his cheeks shrunk and closed.

Cerys turned and ran past Simone and Abel. They looked battered and gory, as though they'd been beating on each other for several minutes. She did not pause to help Abel. He was a match for Simone. Simone's bedroom door stood open. The room beyond was unoccupied.

Cerys threw her shoulder against the door across the hall. It did not budge. She cursed. She stepped back. She chanted. The door flew against the wall. It hung slightly off its hinges. She lurched inside with a low, desperate cry. Inside the room were four small cots. Upon each cot was a thin, slumbering figure. The men and woman looked still and peaceful. They did not look as though their skin hung loose from their bones or their insides had been sucked out. They looked as though Nico had been keeping them for months under sedation but very well preserved.

Intravenous needles fed them from pouches of clear liquid hanging over each cot. Cedric was thin. His expression was blank and serene. Cerys rushed to him. She knelt beside his cot. His breath was soft and even. She brushed her hand across his cheek.

She tugged the needle gently from the crook of his elbow. She shot to her feet. She could not carry any of the chanters out of there. If they were under sedation, Abel, Lex and Colin would have to remove them. She worked the needles from the other chanters' arms. She leaned down to kiss her brother on the forehead. She could not stay with him. She had to finish the fight.

"Cerys!"

It was Colin who'd called to her. Lex was on his knees. Colin's trance had broken. Nico had not tired or ceased his relentless attack against his brother and enemy. Their bodies jerked. Blood dripped from their noses and from the corners of their mouths. Abel lay face down on the floor in a small pool of blood. Tamsin and Simone dueled violently. Energy slashed across their faces and blew their hair out behind them.

Cerys did not help Tamsin. She could take care of herself. Cerys threw her hands out toward Nico. She chanted. Her voice rose in a wild, intense crescendo. Nico shuddered from head to toe. He seemed to sense her attack from behind. He rotated in a slow, graceful circle, almost as if he were hovering several inches above the ground.

She felt warm, wet blood drip down across her face. Pain lanced through her as though tiny shards of glass were ripping across her body, under her skin and through her insides. Colin's and Lex's protective barriers were weak. Nico's chants tore through them with little resistance. They had underestimated him. Three of them were nearly down. Nico still stood, untiring and inexorable.

Cedric crawled sluggishly into the parlor. He blinked blearily at the scene before him. Chant was falling fast to Nico and Simone, despite their greater number. He could not help them. He could not chant, not yet. Nearby, Tamsin chanted in a wild, angry screech. Her words were incomprehensible, but her fury was powerful and unmistakable. Simone reared backward. Her entire slender body shuddered violently. Her trance broke.

She screamed. The sound was so terrible, so blood-curdling, it seemed to penetrate Nico's trance. His brow furrowed. His eyes turned suddenly from white to startling blue. He blinked. "Simone?" He spun. Simone fell backward as though in slow motion. Nico lurched toward her. "Simone!"

Cedric surged to his feet. He wobbled dangerously. It didn't matter. He fell heavily against Nico as he staggered toward Simone. Cedric lifted the wand between them. He murmured almost inaudibly. A bright, glaring white light flashed between them. The air sparkled around them as though they were surrounded by thousands of tiny, brilliant stars.

Nico collapsed to the ground. His skin hung in flaps on his bones. His eyes rolled backward. His mouth lolled. Cedric straightened. He lifted his hands. "Everyone stop!" he shouted.

Silence fell over the flat. Cedric chanted. His eyes did not turn white. They were shocking, stygian black. His mouth moved, but no sound issued from his lips. Lex and Colin blinked. They rose to their feet. They touched their faces. There was no blood. There was no pain. They looked at each other. "Cerys," Lex said. He started forward.

But she did not need their help. She pushed her hair back from her face. The slashes on her face were gone. She looked at Lex in surprise. Tamsin assisted Abel to his feet. Everyone looked at Cedric, who stood before them like an avenging angel. "Cedric!" Cerys exclaimed. She raced toward him. She could not reach him. It was as though a barrier surrounded him on every side. He was incandescent. Heat radiated off his body.

Then it stopped. Cerys pushed through the barrier. Cedric turned catch her as she vaulted into his arms. "I have to say, I did not expect to see you here, Cer," he told her serenely.

She looked up at him. "Are you all right? What did you do?"

"The device," Lex said grimly. "You used it on Nico."

Cedric's gaze slid to him. He seemed somewhat surprised to find him there. Colin bent down to examine Nico with a morose expression. "I'm sorry, Lex," Cedric told him.

Lex shook his head. "It was the only way."

"It was poetic justice," Tamsin remarked. When Cedric turned to her with a half-smile, she raced toward him. She threw her arms around his neck. She kissed him full on the mouth.

Abel chuckled. He stepped forward to clap his friend on the shoulder. "Good to see you, Cedric."

Cerys' smile faded as she watched Lex kneel beside his brother. His chiseled features revealed no emotion, but his brilliant blue eyes flashed. "Nico," he said softly. He turned his brother onto his back. He brushed his dark hair from his eyes.

"Cerys, where are the others?" Abel barked.

"In the bedroom. They're fine." She laughed almost hysterically. "They are all fine."

Abel nodded grimly. He tilted his head. "Ced, you want to help me?"

Cedric nodded. "They're under sedation. They'll wake up soon enough."

"Cedric, are you all right?" Tamsin asked. Her eyes shone. A single tear streaked down her cheek. She did not bother to wipe it. She practically vibrated with happiness.

He gripped her shoulder. He smiled grimly. "I'm all right. We're all all right now. It's over."

It wasn't, not really. "Lex?" Cerys asked.

He glanced up at her. He nodded. His expression was arctic. "Nico's alive."

"So is Simone," Colin said from beside her. He brushed her long, blonde hair from her face. "She's just knocked out." He glanced warily up at Cedric. "You healed her too?"

Cedric shrugged. "It was sort of an accident."

Colin scowled at Lex. "How did you not know she was a chanter?"

Lex shook his head. "I never even heard her speak the word. I had no idea."

"It would have been nice to know," Abel muttered, scowling. "It would have saved us some trouble."

"It doesn't matter," Tamsin said. She smiled up at Cedric. "It's all over now. We did it."

"What are you going to do with them?" Cerys asked Lex quietly. She crouched down beside him.

He did not look at her. He looked down at his brother. His hand fluttered gently across Nico's brow. "Let me worry about that. You help your brother get everyone else back to headquarters."

"I'll help you, Lex," Colin told him.

Lex looked at him. They stared at each other a long moment. Lex nodded. "Thanks, Colin."

Cerys glanced at her brother. He lifted his shoulders. "Lex, you might need my help."

Lex shook his head. "No, Cerys. This is a family matter. You have your own to deal with. I have to talk to my mother and decide what to do about this."

Cerys sighed. "Lex..."

He rose abruptly to his feet. He strode toward her. He slipped his arm around her waist and drew her up against him. He kissed her soundly on the mouth. "I'll call you."

Cedric lifted his eyebrows. He looked at Tamsin. She smirked. "A lot's happened since you've been gone."

Colin rolled his eyes. "Lex? We'd better go."

Lex nodded. He stepped away from Cerys. He bent down beside his brother. He lifted him as effortlessly as if he were a small child. His expression was grim. Colin lifted Simone into his arms. He glanced at Cerys. She smiled wanly. "Thank you, Colin. For all this. For helping us."

Colin shrugged. "It's not the worst fight I've been in with Nico. I'm almost disappointed it was the last." His lips turned up slightly, as though he would smile. He didn't. He glanced at Lex and jerked his head towards the door.

Lex nodded. He followed Colin out the door. He did not turn back to meet

Cerys' gaze. She sighed. "Come on," Abel said sternly. "What are we waiting for? Let's get everyone out of here before someone calls the cops."

"You are the cops," Cedric remarked.

"Yeah, but I don't think that will get me out of explaining this one. Move it."

CHAPTER 26

It was the first time Cerys had seen the circle of chairs in the library of Barbosa's mansion filled with chanters. They had lost three of their number, but the others had made it out safely and more still flooded the streets now that the wraith attacks had ended for good. There was an air of grim satisfaction in the atmosphere. Nico Creed was finished. He would never hurt anyone ever again. His defeat had come at such a terrible price.

The chanters they had rescued from Simone's flat were thin and worn. They were Mary Ann Gable, Bobby Wilder and Rory Singer. Cerys had never seen Isobel look so cheerful. She sat beside her husband, who was wiry and dark-haired and hardly as good-looking as she. She was almost smiling. She gripped his hand as though she might never let it go.

Spectra City had not noticed that any of them had disappeared. They had not noticed that Isobel had lost her husband. They had not noticed that Cedric Knight had never shown up for his job at Mobley Enterprises. If they had, they had pretended as though nothing at all had changed. Spectra City was very good at pretending as though nothing at all had happened.

Spectra City had barely noticed when Balthazar Barbosa, the rising star of the D.A's office and Nico Creed's infamous persecutor had disappeared. Chant had noticed. Tonight, despite the victory over their enemy and the end of the worst, they thought only of Zar. Cedric Knight sat at the head of them all. He looked strong and healthy. He looked resolute. They all looked at him as though he held the answers to the mysteries of the world.

He held up his bottle of beer as though in tribute. "I wish Zar was here with us," he said in a low voice. "I wish Eddie and Dana could be here to see Nico Creed fall."

The others lifted their drinks. Cerys looked at her brother. He was different than the man who had left her seven months ago in San Francisco to find others like them. He wasn't the man who had chosen to use his power to help others. He was a man who had seen the very worst in other men. He was cold. He was heartbroken.

She stared down into her bottle of beer. It did not possess the solution to her misery. It would not solve anyone's problems. It might help. "Is there a way to help Zar and the others?" Mary Ann asked Kate sadly.

Kate sighed deeply. "No. I don't know. Their essence has been taken. I don't know how to give it back to them."

This did not seem to discourage Cedric in the least. "We will find a way."

"Until Zar is back, someone needs to run things here," Tamsin said. She looked around at them all.

They all looked at Cedric.

Cedric raised his eyebrows. "Me?"

"Cedric, you took down Nico Creed. The big bad wolf," Tamsin told him.

"There will be more Nico Creeds," Abel said solemnly. "Someone had to be ready for them. Cedric?"

Cerys looked at her brother. There was an empty feeling in her belly. Cedric nodded. "Then we will be ready for them," he said firmly.

No one said anything. There was nothing else to say.

Cedric looked at his sister. "What will you do, Cerys?" he asked softly.

She shook her head. "I don't know."

"I can help you there," Tamsin put in. "Zar started something. It isn't finished. We could use you, Cerys. We fight...all the time, but you're good. You're really good. And Maybe with Lex and Colin on our side--"

Cerys stiffened. "Lex isn't on our side. He helped stop Nico, but that doesn't mean he'll suddenly drop everything and join Chant. That doesn't mean he'll stop being a Creed and decide to clean up Spectra City."

Tamsin looked at her shrewdly. "Why don't you give him a chance to decide before you make up your mind for him?"

Cedric glanced at his sister. His dark eyes were gentle. "Have you heard from him?"

"No," Cerys replied coldly. "I talked to Colin. They got back to the manor all right. Colin helped Lex get Simone and Nico inside. Then Colin left. He might have fought beside Lex, but they won't be friends anytime soon."

"What are they going to do about Nico?" Abel asked, frowning.

"I don't know. He didn't know."

"What about Colin?" Kate asked.

Cerys frowned. "What about him?"

"He would be good in Chant," Abel answered. "He's a good fighter."

Cerys considered. "I can talk to him. I think he got a kick out of fighting. Without the feud, without Nico and Caleb Creed, maybe he'll be interested in fighting someone new and for a more constructive cause."

"The first thing we need to do is find a cure for Zar and the others," Cedric said firmly. "We need Zar back."

"There is a way. We'll find a way to save them, and then we'll clean up Spectra City from the top down." He bared his teeth in a humorless grin. "Starting with D.A Rutherford."

Cerys lifted her eyebrows. "You have something on him?"

Abel smirked. "Zar had enough evidence stacked up to take down half the city officials. Pay offs, buried cases, the works. He just didn't use it. He had bigger problems. Once Rutherford sees what we've got, he'll start talking. He'll cut a deal. And when he does, he might be able to stop the corruption in this city."

"It's time we brought in some honest people," Isobel said. The perpetual frown on her pretty face returned as suddenly as it had gone.

Cerys smiled. "It's worth a shot, anyway."

"You could stay, Cerys," Cedric told her.

"Cedric..."

"What? What have you got in San Francisco? You have a chance to live our dream."

She smiled fondly at him. "Cedric, it's not our dream. It's yours. It was always your dream. I wanted to draw comics. You're the one who wanted to live them."

He stiffened. "We were given these powers for a reason, Cerys. Don't waste them. Why go back where you have nothing? Stay with is. With Chant."

Cerys did not reply. She stared down at her hands. "I'll think about it, Cedric."

He smiled as though she had already agreed. He knew her better than anyone in the world. "Good."

* * *

It was a dark and stormy night. The wind howled. Rain pelted the window. The lights of Spectra City were dim and dreary below the penthouse suite. Cerys sighed deeply. It was always raining Spectra City.

She spun away from the window. In the center of the room, faces stared out at her from the dry erase board. They were smiling, happy faces. They were faces that she would never see again, not that way. Nico's charming smile was gone forever. Simone would never stare haughtily into her camera. Peyton's eyes would never gleam. Lex...

She shook her head. She rubbed away the words scrawled across the board. Chant. Zar. Tamsin. The Creeds. She tore Cedric's first letter from the board. It drifted slowly to the ground. Cedric was all right. He was safe. He was healthy. He was home with the people he cared about and who cared about him. She had gotten what she had wanted. She'd done what she'd come here to do. She felt empty inside. There was no triumph in victory.

Cedric's letters fluttered at her feet. The cost had been so high. She wasn't sure it had been worth it. She glanced at her cell phone on the coffee table. It was silent. Lex...she wasn't sure she wanted to hear what had come of Nico after his run-in with her brother. She wasn't sure she was ready to talk to Lex. She didn't pick up the phone.

Nico, Lex, Peyton and Grace smiled out at her from the photograph she'd taken weeks ago at Peyton's birthday party. Cerys snatched it from the board. She peered down at it. It was amazing what could lurk beneath the surface of those brilliant, charming smiles. She clutched the photograph to her chest. She dropped down onto the sofa. She sighed deeply.

A knock sounded on her door. She started. She had not been expecting company. She did not want company. She sighed. She rose to her feet. There was nothing more to fear. She rose. She did not peer through the peephole. It didn't matter who was waiting on the other side of the door.

In the doorway, Lex smirked at her. She blinked in surprise. "Lex."

He did not reply. He strode past her into the room. She sighed. She did not try to stop him. He paused in front of the board. He was silent for several long moments.

"Lex?"

He glanced at her. There was no expression on his face. "So this is why you haven't let me in here."

She shrugged. "Yes."

His face didn't change. "I can see why." A photograph of himself, standing on the court house stairs, frowned back at him. He reached for it. "I might have thought you were some kind of stalker."

Cerys laughed. "I kind of was."

He considered a long moment. "I'm glad you didn't let me in. I might not have taken it so well."

She strode toward him. She paused beside him. "I wouldn't have blamed you. What about now?"

"It's still a little weird."

"Yeah."

"But at least now I know what it's all about." She laughed bitterly. He looked at her. "You were clearing it?"

"Yeah. I found Cedric. Everyone else is all right, for the most part. The attacks have stopped. It's over."

He stared at the board a long moment. "Can I help?"

"Sure."

They didn't speak to each other as they tore the photographs and newspaper clippings from the dry erase board. Lex wiped it clean with the sleeve of his black sweater. Cedric's letters lay in a pile at their feet. Faces stared up at them from the photographs on the floor. When there was nothing left, Lex stepped back. He did not look at her.

"How is your brother?"

She smiled wryly. "He's taking over Chant for Balthazar. He's going to try to find a cure for what was done to him and the others."

Lex considered. "Maybe Colin Mobley can help."

She glanced at him in surprise. "Colin?"

He shrugged. "The Mobleys run a pharmaceutical and medical research company. I know they've been experimenting with chanters."

Cerys frowned. "That sounds bad."

Lex sighed. "Actually, I'm pretty sure it isn't. I don't think Colin or the rest of the Mobleys would hurt anyone. They're trying to help people like us." He looked at her. "He might be able to do something for them."

"You're suggesting I call Colin Mobley?"

He gave her a sidelong glance. His lips quivered slightly. "Perhaps you could give his number to your brother. Let him make the call."

She laughed. "Sure."

Lex backed up. He sat down on the sofa. He patted the cushion beside him. Cerys sat down. She looked at him in silence. His expression was blank. She didn't know how to speak to him anymore. She didn't really know him at all.

"How is Nico?" she asked finally. "And Simone?"

Lex sighed. "Simone came out okay. Whatever your brother did to all of us with Nico's power, he healed her. She's been staying at the Manor."

"You're letting her stay?"

He shrugged. "She's as good as family now. And Mother wants to keep an eye on her." Cerys lifted her eyebrows. Lex chuckled. "It turns out she's a lot more insightful than I gave her credit for."

"How is Nico?"

Lex hesitated. "He's the same. He wakes up now and again and mutters something crazy. Mostly he's comatose. Simone's been taking care of him."

"It's probably not what she envisioned for her future with him."

"No. I'm sure it's not," he replied wryly. "But she made her bed. She helped him do what he was doing. If Colin finds a cure, maybe Nico will be back to himself someday."

Cerys glanced at him. She did not have to say a word.

"Yeah. Colin probably wouldn't go for that, would he?"

She smiled. "No. Probably not. What about the grand jury? What are you going to tell people when Nico doesn't show up?"

Lex looked slightly pained. "Well, neither will the prosecuting attorney. I expect the charges will all just fall apart."

"This is going to look very peculiar."

Lex chuckled wryly. "Yes, but I don't think that will matter. There are a lot of peculiar things that happen in Spectra. No one seems to notice them. Or at least they're good at pretending they don't."

"What will you say?"

He sighed. "We expect Nico won't be himself for a very long time. Even if Colin does find a cure, he's in bad shape. He's as good as gone. The family lawyer suggested we hide him and allow the authorities to believe he's left town."

"That will look very bad for your family."

He shrugged. "It will reflect poorly, but there are worse things."

"Like the truth?"

"Yes. Exactly like the truth. Without Barbosa in the D.A.'s office, the charges will be dropped. It will be a public relations nightmare for a while, and then everyone will forget all about it, the way they always do. None of it will have mattered."

Cerys scowled. "Balthazar was the only one standing up to anyone in this town," she said in a low voice. "Now he's gone and it's just a free-for-all again."

"It doesn't have to be, you know." He looked at her.

She was silent a moment. "Have you heard anything about Tully?"

Lex sighed. "No. As far as I can tell, he's disappeared. He might be half way across the country by now."

"He did terrible things. He should be brought to justice."

"I agree. I will do what I can to try to find him."

"How?"

"I have people who can find people."

"Ah. Of course you do."

He chuckled wryly. He glanced at her. "What are you going to do now, Cerys?"

She shrugged. "I found my brother. I did what I came here to do."

"So, what? It's back to San Francisco?" His expression was wry. "To your job and your work friends and people you can't connect with?"

She didn't take offense to this. She considered. She sighed. "Cedric wants me to stay and join Chant. They're going to try to clean up Spectra City. Get out all the dirty cops and politicians and judges out there."

"That's a big job."

"Yeah."

"They could use your help."

"Not just mine."

He did not respond to this. "It will be easier with Nico out of the game." She chuckled humorlessly. He looked at her seriously. "It would be even easier if you had someone on top that could help. Someone who can get you where you need to go and who has some clout with these people."

She looked at him. She lifted her eyebrows. "You?"

He shrugged. "Bruce Wayne did it. He was CEO of Wayne Enterprises by day, crime fighter by night."

"Bruce Wayne isn't real."

He laughed. "No, but I've spent enough of my life doing what was expected of me. It didn't turn out well. Don't you think I deserve to live my dream for once?"

She smiled. "Actually, yes. I do."

"So?"

"So what?"

"How about it?"

"How about what?"

"This. Chant. You. Me."

She lifted her eyebrows. "Are you asking me to fight crime with you?"

He smiled. "Yes."

"Well..."

"Come on. What else have you got to do?"

She sighed. She considered a long moment. She shrugged. "Yeah. Okay."

Lex was silent a long moment. He looked at her earnestly. "Hey, could we try not to focus on my family this time?"

"Are any of them planning on kidnapping my family again?"

He thought about this. "No. Not that they've told me."

She smiled. "Okay."

"Although, Nico didn't tell me that he was planning on doing that, either."

* * *

Lex lifted his head as the bathroom door swung open. Cerys padded out in her bare feet, swaddled in his fluffy blue bathroom. He lifted a languid eyebrow. She squeezed her long, wet hair in a matching blue towel. "When are you going to get a place?"

250

Cerys paused. She looked at him archly. "Are you getting tired of me already?"

"No. I was just wondering if you were going to keep staying at the Warren indefinitely or if you were going to finally decide to stay in Spectra City."

She considered. "I like the Warren. It has a nice view."

"You aren't even there most of the time. You should stop paying for it."

"I'm not. It's still on the Daily's expense account."

He frowned. "Have you even applied for a position there?"

She hesitated. "Not exactly."

"Are you playing hard to get?"

"Maybe."

"Are you suddenly going to change your mind about all this and go back to San Francisco?"

She sighed. "You sound like my brother."

"I just want some kind of sign you're actually going to stick around."

"I told you I am."

He caught her arm. He tugged her down onto the bed beside him. "It isn't good enough."

"What do you want from me?"

He leaned over her. His mouth hovered inches above hers. She felt his breath on her lips. She lifted her head to meet him halfway. He didn't kiss her. He leaned away from her. He reached above her head and fumbled in the nightstand table. She sighed and fell back against the pillows. He smirked. He held a shiny, colorful pamphlet in front of her face. She groaned

"Lex. What are those?"

"Apartment listings."

She laughed. "Okay, okay. I get it."

"Yeah?"

"Yes. I will look for a place."

He considered. "On second thought, I like having you around. You could have your own room. This place is so big, we wouldn't even run into each other for days if we didn't want to."

She rolled her eyes. "Yeah, right. I think we'll all be better off if I find a place in town. Besides, there's no way your mother would agree to me moving in here."

He thought about it. "She might, if she thought you would be willing to take up the housekeeping duties."

"You must be joking."

"Yes, I am. I've seen your hotel room."

She laughed. "All right. Let me see them."

He held the glossy pamphlets out of her reach. "Later."

"But you want--"

"We can look at them later."

She smirked. She wrapped her arms around his neck to pull him down to her mouth. His lips moved against hers. She opened her mouth to stroke her tongue suggestively against his. Lex reached between them to loosen the knot holding the bathrobe together at her waist. She opened her legs to him as it fell open. His hand skimmed up her thigh and across her belly. She sighed. Her head dropped back as he pressed hot kisses on her throat.

On the nightstand beside them, Lex's cell phone trilled.

Lex groaned into her neck. "Ignore it," she ordered. She tightened her arms around his neck. She flicked her tongue against his earlobe.

"It might be important."

"Lex! It's date night."

"I know. I know." He reached for the phone. He glanced at it. He looked down at her. "It's Cedric."

"Ignore him."

"But--" She reached down between them. Her hand skimmed across the front of his trousers. He groaned. "Cerys..."

She sighed. "It's not healthy for us both to have brother issues."

He laughed. "That's low, Cer." He snapped open the phone. "Yeah?"

"Lex, X is showing chanter activity in the Waterfront District. It looks big. I need you to go take a look."

Lex glanced at Cerys. "Now?"

Cerys scowled. "What does he want now?"

"Is my sister with you?" Cedric demanded.

"Yes."

Cedric laughed wickedly.

"This is becoming a trend, Cedric. I am beginning to think you're doing this on purpose."

"Don't be ridiculous. I have no interest in your love life."

"You sure seem determined to ruin it."

"Quit complaining about your failing courtship with my little sister."

Lex smirked. "I assure you. It's far from failing."

Cedric paused. "I like you, Lex. It's best that I don't think about you with Cerys, or I might do something I'll regret."

Lex chuckled. Cerys looked at him. He shook his head regretfully. "Your brother has ruined date night."

Cerys sighed. "Damnit, Ced. You did this last week."

"Oh, I wouldn't want to interrupt date night," Cedric said. "I'm a reasonable guy. Bring her along. Someone needs to keep an eye on you, anyway."

"What? I'm perfectly well-behaved." He sighed in disappointment as Cerys climbed out of bed to pull on her clothes.

"Colin is already on his way there," Cedric said warningly.

Lex perked up. "I thought he was working late at the office with Kate."

"He was. They finished up for the night and came by to check on Zar and Eddie. I think he's feeling a little bored cooped up in the lab all the time. He wanted some field time. I told him he could go check out the Waterfront."

Lex grinned.

As though he sensed it over the line, Cedric sighed. "Just don't do what you did last time. Abel has enough problems with Rutherford's grand jury coming up and trying to keep the PD from investigating Zar's disappearance. He doesn't need to have to clean up after you and Colin."

"Yeah. Yeah. We'll behave."

"Sure you will. I swear, the world would be better off if you two were still trying to kill each other. At least then you only screwed with each other."

Lex laughed. Cerys sat down beside him and held out her hand for the phone. He held it away from her. "You're in trouble now, Cedric," Lex told him. Cerys tugged the phone out of his hand.

"Cedric, are you doing this on purpose?"

"You two are conceited. Not everything in the world revolves around your love life, Cerys."

She scoffed.

"Would you mind getting to work? I don't have time to banter with you all night. People need our help. That's what we do, remember?"

Cerys rolled her eyes. "Yeah. Yeah. We're on our way."

She snapped the phone shut and glanced up at Lex. He wrapped an arm around her waist. "Ready?"

She curled her lip sullenly. "Yeah."

He smirked. He kissed her soundly on the mouth. "We'll have enough time to finish what we started when we're done fighting crime and saving people."

She laughed. He was already chanting. The air around him crackled. Brilliant white light burst from his eyes. She pressed her face against his neck. When he stopped muttering, she lifted her head. A cool breeze lifted her hair. She stepped away from Lex to glance around the dark, moonlit boardwalk along the waterfront.

Stars glittered overhead. The storefront windows in the shops behind them were shattered. Glass shards sparkled on the beaten wooden boardwalk. Cerys sighed. "Where's Colin?"

"Over there." Lex sounded untroubled. "It's them we should worry about. I think Colin's doing just fine."

Two men lay several feet away. One of them sprawled across a pile of blood-streaked glass shards. The other was pitched over the railing, as though he'd been interrupted leaping over into the bay. Cerys rolled her eyes.

Beneath a streetlight to their left, Colin Mobley dueled with a short, thin man in a long, grey trench coat. Energy sizzled in the air around them. Lex strode forward as though to assist his friend, but the chanter in the trench coat fell to his knees. Blood dripped from his nose and out of the corner of his mouth. His eyes darkened. He pitched forward onto his face.

A tremor passed abruptly through Colin as though he were shaking himself. He tilted his head to the side. His eyes rolled down. He seemed surprised to see them. "Man, you could have saved some for the rest of us," Lex complained, striding toward Colin to clap him on the shoulder.

Colin smirked. "Not that I'm not happy to see you guys, but I told Ced I could handle this one on my own. I thought it was date night."

Cerys looked at Lex incredulously. "Do you tell everyone when we plan to have sex?"

"No. I tell them it's date night. You told him just now about the sex."

Colin lifted an eyebrow. "I thought you were a lady, Cerys."

She scoffed. Lex scowled. "I knew Cedric was doing this on purpose."

Colin smirked. "He didn't like the sex part, either, I take it?"

"Don't talk about sex with my girlfriend," Lex said.

"She talked about sex with me first."

"Okay, let's move on from the sex."

"Now that I've taken care of things here, I assume you will be moving onto the sex."

"Okay, that's enough about the sex," Cerys said. She rolled her eyes. "With you two carrying on like this all the time, it's no wonder my brother keeps interrupting date nights with pointless chanter chases."

Colin smirked. "Our fearless leader likes to remind us who's in charge."

Lex scowled. "That's true. If I'd known he'd be such an autocrat, I might have thought twice about joining up with you people."

"We people?" Colin demanded incredulously.

"I seem to remember this was all your idea, Lex," Cerys reminded him with a frown.

He smirked and wrapped an arm around her waist. He pressed his lips to hers.

Colin rolled his eyes. He turned toward the chanters scattered around him. "You guys want to help me clear up here? You might as well do something since you came all this way."

There was no reply.

"Guys?" Colin spun.

Lex and Cerys were gone.

The night was still and quiet. Waves lapped serenely against the pier. Colin sighed. "Guess not." He knelt down beside the thin man in the grey trench coat. "I don't suppose you want to wake up and chant yourself to HQ? No? I didn't think so." He exhaled noisily. "I don't care what Cedric says. Being a superhero really is not as glamorous as comic books would have you believe."

THE END

About the Author

Stella Drexler is the author of Hex Breaker available from SynergeBooks, CHANT and Angel of the Abyss from DC Dreams, and the upcoming Nightmare Island Series from Writers-Exchange, as well as several other novels, comics, short stories, essays and shopping lists. She lives in the moment with Mr. Drexler and their Helper Monkey, Casanova. In between working on new books or spending time tamping out the occasional fire, Stella can often be found exploring, adventuring, eating, drinking, dancing, singing, shopping, laughing, sighing, smiling, and otherwise having fun.

Read Stella's Blog at:

www.stelladrexler.wordpress.com

For more titles by Stella visit:

www.diogenesclubpress.com

www.ingramcontent.com/pod-product-compliance
Lightning Source LLC
Chambersburg PA
CBHW071602180626

46819CB00002B/102